THE
LAST
GIFT
OF THE
MASTER
ARTISTS

BEN OKRI was born in Minna, Nigeria.
His childhood was divided between Nigeria,
where he saw first-hand the consequences of war,
and London. He has won many awards over the
years, including the Booker Prize for Fiction, and
is also an acclaimed essayist, playwright, and poet.
In 2019 *Astonishing the Gods* was named as one of
the BBC's '100 Novels That Shaped Our World'.

ALSO BY BEN OKRI

FICTION

Flowers and Shadows
The Landscapes Within
Incidents at the Shrine
Stars of the New Curfew
The Famished Road
Songs of Enchantment
Astonishing the Gods
Dangerous Love
Infinite Riches
In Arcadia
Starbook
The Comic Destiny
(previously *Tales of Freedom*)
The Age of Magic
The Magic Lamp
The Freedom Artist
Prayer for the Living
Every Leaf a Hallelujah

ESSAYS

Birds of Heaven
A Way of Being Free
The Mystery Feast
A Time for New Dreams

POETRY

An African Elegy
Mental Fight
Wild
Rise Like Lions (Anthology)
A Fire in My Head

PLAYS

The Outsider
Changing Destiny

THE
LAST
GIFT
OF THE
MASTER
ARTISTS

BEN OKRI

An Apollo Book

First published in the UK as *Starbook* in 2007 by Rider, an imprint of
Ebury Publishing, a Penguin Random House division

This rewritten edition first published in the UK in 2022 by Head of Zeus Ltd,
part of Bloomsbury Publishing Plc

975312468

A catalogue record for this book is available from the British Library.

ISBN (HB): 9781803285672
ISBN (XTPB): 9781803285689
ISBN (E): 9781838935887

Typeset by Ed Pickford
Cover design: Leah Jacobs-Gordon

Printed and bound in Great Britain by
CPI Group (UK) Ltd, Croydon CR0 4YY

Head of Zeus Ltd
First Floor East
5–8 Hardwick Street
London EC1R 4RG
WWW.HEADOFZEUS.COM

For those who endured
For those who endure

Introduction

THIS IS A story of a people on the eve of catastrophe. Others can tell of the catastrophe itself. I want to see the people in the last days of their innocence.

In human consciousness, where time has unimaginable contours, who can tell when events begin, and how they come to be?

My main intention in the writing of the novel was to imagine the time before the lives of Africans changed forever, just before the Atlantic slave trade. I wanted to recover a certain state of mind, to interrogate the spirit of a people and discover what made them susceptible to the catastrophe that was to befall them. I see parallels with the current environmental crisis, as we hasten towards an end that we refuse to see.

I felt I had to effect in the novel a mythical and poetic recovery of a civilisation. I had to be open to the ordinary and the magical, for the magical is nothing more than an expansion of consciousness.

In this novel, first published as *Starbook* in 2007, I wanted to find a new way to write about the tragedy that diminished the life of a people. It was a tragedy they didn't know they were going through. Families suddenly lost sons and daughters and there was no explanation for their loss. It must have seemed a fearsome mystery.

The conjunction of tragedy and mystery is at the heart of the way the story is told. There had to be a tone of unknowing, for the people were still steeped in the rhythms of their lives while something terrible was happening to them.

The vantage point from which the story is told is both human and cosmic. The tale comes from somewhere beyond history, from somewhere in the consciousness of the land and the people, where all things, all traumas, all wonders, are remembered.

When I came to rewrite the novel, it was the tone I concentrated on most of all. What was needed was a new clarity. In the original I wanted to do too much. When I rewrote, I made things simpler. Then the political dimensions of the novel could rise again from the fabular depths of the tale. For me, the political, aesthetic, and intimate should each have an equal place in a work of art, part of the unseen tapestry of reality.

What I was aiming for was a style at once poetic and lucid, rich and clear. The novel had to hover between the glimpsed, the remembered and the lived.

The world is made of a stuff lighter than tears.

Our gifts should be
A giving without end.

Otah of Agborland
2007–1959 BCE

africa is a reality not seen
a dream not understood...

countless cycles of civilisation
and destruction are lost in its memory
but not in its myths.

A Fire in My Head
Ben Okri

Art is the highest task
And the proper metaphysical
Activity of this life.

Nietzsche

Read slowly

BOOK ONE

The Prince

1

THIS IS A story my mother began to tell me when I was a child, and never finished. The rest was gleaned from the book of life among the stars, where all things are known.

IN THE HEART of the kingdom there was a place where the earth was black and sweet to taste. Everything planted there grew profusely. The village was built in the shape of a circle. In the centre of the circle stood the palace of the king.

There was a thick forest around the village. Four rivers met in the forest. The shrinehouse was at the rim of the village, and a path ran past it from the outside world. Those who dwelt in the heart of the kingdom lived in a magic dream, an oasis of huts and good harvests, in the midst of an enveloping world of trees.

There is a saying from the village that my mother used to tell me.

'It's not who you are that makes the world respect you, but the power that stands behind you. It is not you that the world sees, but that power.'

The village was small, but behind it, around it, stood the majesty of the forest.

At night it was rich with enchantments. In the day it was sunlit green. A barely audible music rose from the earth. Gifted children could hear the trees singing.

On certain nights, when the moon was white and full like the perfect egg at the beginning of creation, the wise people said that the trees whisper stories into the abundant darkness. Those stories, they said, take form and wander the world.

The people of the village rarely went into the forest. It was powerful and unpredictable, like the mythology of a strange god.

3

IN A TIME when imagination ruled the world, there was a prince who grew up in the serenity of all things. He was my mother's ancestor. Of all the people in the village he was the only one who loved playing in the forest. He was handsome and bright. The elders suspected that he was a child of heaven, one of those children not destined to live long.

The prince was never so happy as when he played alone in the forest or by the river. He was a favourite of the mermaids and the forest nymphs. He took them flowers and gifts he'd made himself, and he played music for them. Because he was a child of heaven he could do what he wanted, so long as he did not express a wish to die.

The soothsayers at his birth predicted an unusual life. He would be a king and a slave. He would be sold like a goat, would fight in a war, would suffer like a great sinner, and live like a god. He would be the freest of men. The most baffling prediction of all was that he would die young in his old age or die old in his youth.

The elders expected him to be sickly, but he wasn't. He showed no interest in kingship. Politics bored him. He preferred working with the farm labourers, harvesting corn, splitting firewood, teasing maidens, building huts for frail old women of the village, piping music around the edges of the kingdom, haunted by the beauty that fringed the world.

It touched their hearts to see his fragile body bent to the difficult tasks he set himself, or to watch his presence dissipate in the music he teased out in the myth-infested forest that was his second home.

What were they going to do with this royal vagabond, this

noble tramp, who swayed the hearts of women, and moved the soul of the kingdom?

No one offered him their daughters, for fear he would desert them early for the land of death. Yet all the maidens loved him mutely, dreamily, from a distance. When he spoke to them with his soft voice, they became petrified. When he touched them, on the shoulder or arm, they said it was like being beautifully scalded. Many of them suffered love-fevers.

One girl he played with in the river fell ill, and died unexpectedly, in a kind of happiness.

With malice, some people hinted that a curse hovered over the young man, and that one day...

4

HE GREW UP in harmony and, following the traditions of the royal family, was initiated into the mysteries of the tribe. He went through seven initiation ceremonies. Their purpose was to show him his place in the firmament. They would reveal to him the grave responsibilities of kingship and the greatness of heart he must cultivate for such a strong destiny. The most impressive initiations took place in the forest. He witnessed the raising of the ancestral spirits in their fearful splendour. He spent seven nights in the company of the dead, so that the thoughts and deeds of human beings would never bewilder him.

After the initiations he became silent, yet more open. His utterances, though clear, became opaque. His voice changed, becoming both deep and gentle. Sometimes he seemed remote, but more often was full of the spirit of wonder. He became an enigma to everyone. He was an enigma to himself. He didn't know who he was anymore.

He spent more time in the forest, along the river, listening to the birds, searching for answers to the questions that the initiations had awoken in him like thunder.

The elders began to fear that instead of making him a greater man, the initiations had made the prince more vulnerable. They feared he was going mad. They feared he might attempt a return to the ancestors.

They decided that what he needed was a wife.

HE DIDN'T NEED a wife. He needed time.

No one thought to leave him alone, so that he could find his own way. They fretted over him with their fears and projections. They made him the concern of the whole kingdom. He had no space to grow into his own man. They interfered with every aspect of his life, spying on him everywhere he went. They suspected his quietness, misunderstood his gestures and saw sinister aspects in his innocence.

The prince began to roam the forest to escape their prying eyes. If they had not worried over him so much, what happened would never have happened, and mysteriously the world would have been the poorer.

Destiny conceals strange illuminations in the suffering that life visits on us. The tale of fate is entangled with mystery. Dare one say such and such shouldn't have happened? History is replete with things that shouldn't have happened. But they did happen, and we are what we are because of them.

History has not yet yielded all of its harvest. Who knows what events will mean when time has done its ambiguous work? The prince ran from one prison into something worse. Who is to say why? In the presence of things glimpsed in the book of life one can only be humble. The ultimate purpose of history is beyond the mortal mind. All one can say is that such and such a thing happened. Make of it what you will. The prince went searching for meaning in the hills, and one day came upon a maiden by the river, with a bucket of water on her head.

He took her for a sign.

6

SHE WAS NOT beautiful then. At that time she was quite plain. Her face was odd, verging on ugly, like an evolving work of art. But there was something about her that was rare and that was waiting. It was something fine, like a cloudy uncertain dawn, with hints of an especially brilliant day.

The prince did not fall in love with her immediately. She was clumsy and out of colour. Often beauty seems awkward in its early stages. Often excellence is unpromising in its youth. Who can guess that a butterfly will emerge from the mess of matter that is a caterpillar?

That's how she was then, at odds with the unique spirit growing in her. The young all have clear eyes, but hers had a touch of paradise. But he didn't notice any of that.

He saw her as a sign.

7

FROM THE CAREFUL way she fetched water, and the silent words she addressed to the river, the prince knew that she believed in the spirits of the place. He decided to play a game with her.

As she was getting ready to leave, he called out to her in a nasal voice from his hiding place behind the bushes. She started in surprise, dropped the bucket, and looked around her.

'Who is it?' she cried.

'Your time has come,' the prince said, in the nasal tone associated with spirits.

'But I have not lived yet,' she pleaded.

'Answer my three questions and you can live,' he said.

She fell to her knees.

'I'm ready.'

He laughed to himself among the wild flowers.

'First,' he said, 'where does the river end?'

'In the wisdom of God,' she replied.

This startled him. The wind blew enchantments over the two of them. Spirits gathered at the water's edge.

'Where does our suffering end?' he asked, a little sternly.

'In the happiness that lies beyond all things,' she replied.

He caught his breath. The river glimmered with gold and silver. He breathed in wonder, and the air he breathed changed his initiations into something settled, the way an angel crystallises into a child. Time converged there.

'And last,' he said, 'what are we all seeking?'

'The kingdom,' she replied, 'which we are in already, which we have got, and which is our home.'

Again the answer astonished him. He fell into a deep silence in which he was borne by the wind and the fragrance of wild frangipani into a dim realm where, for a moment, he glimpsed a white horse with a golden horn in the middle of its forehead.

When his mind cleared, he saw that the girl was rising from her position of prayer. He felt he had to say something while the picture held. Then he saw a white mist rising from the river, like a shroud, and it drifted towards the girl, momentarily obscuring her. Seized with a sense of immensity he had never felt before, and having the presence of mind to break through it, he said:

'Come back tomorrow. Come alone.'

The mist briefly cleared, and he saw her nod. Then before he could think what else to say, she got up, lifted the bucket to her head, and disappeared.

8

HE LEFT HIS hiding place and wandered the forest in this new mood of joy that bordered on madness. What had come over him? He sang love songs to the birds and the trees, and wrestled with spirits in the air. Everything made sense. Everything seemed simple. He saw all the people in the world as one.

He wandered in this exalted state, dreaming of the girl he had just seen. She was so clear to him that she seemed to be accompanying him. He spoke to her and imagined what she would say to him now. He remained spellbound by her luminous eyes and her awkward face.

The elders found him in this state and, fearing he was unhinged, they grappled with him. They were surprised when he offered no resistance. They bore him on their shoulders to the royal palace.

He re-entered the village a different person. He saw it all anew, as if he were waking from a sleep that had lasted all his life.

9

IN THE PALACE the first thing he noticed was the slaves. He stared at the many servants and his father's numerous wives. Then he saw his father. It was all strange. He thought: who are all these people?

'Are you well, my son?' the king asked.

He stared at the fleshy, powerful face of his father. He stared into the sensuous eyes. The king did not smile. He never remembered his father smiling. He often laughed, but never smiled.

The prince smiled at his father. The elders nodded sagely. But when the prince then threw his arms round his father's neck, they were alarmed.

'I only asked if you were well, my son,' the king said, embarrassed. 'There's no need for all this. Remember who you are. Control yourself.'

The prince didn't control himself. He went on hugging his father, breathing in his smell. It was potent with the personality of the king. He was suffused with the king's power and the herbal fragrance of his spiritual fortification. He held on to his father as to a great tree. He held on even when the king threw up his arms in exasperation and began to laugh. It was a wonderful laugh that rocked the kingdom.

All the elders began laughing too. They linked hands and sang praise-songs to the prince and the king, dancing in a circle around them. But still the son held on to his father's neck. He felt the king's great laughter shake his frame, filling him with energies, healing him. The spiritual strength of kingship poured out of the father, along with the love he could not express to his son, which was there in the embarrassment of laughter.

Suddenly, the son drew away.

'Father,' he said, 'I'm not well. I saw a maiden today who touched my heart. I don't know who she is or where she comes from. Because of her I'm not well. But I've never felt better in my life.'

Then abruptly he left. The elders looked at one another. The king was taken aback.

'My son has been bewitched,' he said to the elders. 'Keep your eyes on him. Find out who this maiden is that has clouded his mind.'

The elders genuflected. Instructions were given and put into motion. The forest became the home of spies.

THE NEXT DAY the prince went back to his hiding place in the thicket. An intuition made him take a convoluted route that confused the spies who were watching behind every tree. He arrived long before the time, and waited for the maiden to appear. He hadn't slept all night, or thought he hadn't.

He hadn't slept because he had spent all night wandering the world looking for the woman who bore his love in her womb. His love grew in her like a child. She was pregnant with his love for a long time, for a generation. His heart grew bigger and bigger in her and she grew bigger and bigger to accommodate his heart. Then he lost her and began searching the world for her and couldn't find her.

'The world you are searching is your heart,' his father said.

'But who is the woman?'

'She is the mother of the world.'

'Will I ever find her?'

'Your search was over when it began,' his father replied, 'but you didn't know it.'

The prince wasn't consoled. He was still searching when he woke.

THE FUTURE HOVERED over the waiting prince. The sun overtook the shadows it cast at the appointed hour, but the maiden didn't appear.

The prince watched as women came to the river to fetch water. They laughed and played and went away, balancing buckets on their heads. Their voices lingered long after they had gone. The sky was clear. Insects trilled in the forest. He waited till the noonday sun changed colour and flashing swords pierced earth and water. The odour of wild flowers drifted on the hot air. While he waited, he slept. And while he slept voices spoke around him. Sorcerers chanted over his sleeping form. When he woke, it was evening, and she still hadn't appeared.

He went home with a heavy heart. He didn't notice the trees in the forest or the cats that eyed him or the spies that watched him. When he got to the village he saw a group of men and women he had never seen before. They were fetching wood, carrying loads, digging latrines. The men looked downcast and the women unhappy. He asked who they were. A burly man with a warrior's face replied:

'We are men and women captured in war. We are slaves of your kingdom. We do your dirty work till our ransom is paid.'

'What are slaves?' the young prince asked.

'The lowest of the low,' the man replied.

'What does that mean?'

'It means we are nothing. We do whatever you tell us. Our people don't know where we are. We don't want to be here. We want to be in our own villages with our families.'

'So why don't you just go?' the prince asked.

'Because they'll kill us if we try. We're slaves, sir. Captured people.'

'What are you doing?'

'Digging latrines.'

'How long have you been here?'

'Not long for you, too long for us.'

The prince was about to ask another question when the elders found him and hustled him away.

'Your highness, you can't talk to these people.'

'Why not?'

'They're animals!'

'Animals? They're not animals. They're human beings,' the prince said.

'They are slaves, your highness, and a prince can't talk with slaves.'

'Why not?'

'Because it's forbidden.'

'Who forbids it?'

'The laws of the kingdom.'

'The laws? Who made the laws?'

'The wise ones.'

'What wise ones?'

'From long ago.'

'Then they must have been fools.'

'Your highness, they were your ancestors.'

'Then I'm ashamed to have such ancestors.'

The elders were shocked, but said nothing more. They took his words as further proof that he was deranged, or bewitched as the king had said.

12

THE PRINCE WENT straight to the palace. His father was on the throne, fanned by two servants. He was hearing a deposition from the inner council when the prince approached him. The king listened to his son without blinking. When he had finished speaking, the king stared at him for a long time, then he laughed. A troubled laugh.

The king summoned the elders. When they were gathered, he asked the prince to repeat his request. Innocent and calm, the young man spoke.

'If I am to be the king one day,' he said, 'I need to know what good and what evil we have done as a people.'

A deep silence followed. Then the elders began to murmur. Their murmurs turned into debate and then into dispute. They argued among themselves about what was evil and what good. Sometimes the things that were thought evil turned out to have excellent consequences, and some of the good things disastrous ones. They argued furiously. One elder said it was too soon to say what was good and what was evil. Another asked how you defined those terms anyway. The prince listened in amazement. He heard them speak of tortures, murders, wars, rapes, floggings, outcasts, banishments, burning of villages. He thought he hadn't heard right. One elder said these things were not evils but necessities, acts of defence needed to protect the kingdom in justified war.

The king became impatient.

'Are you going to answer my son or not?' he bellowed.

The elders stared at the prince. The prince stared back at them. Then, quite suddenly, the king began laughing again, and the elders, relieved, laughed as well.

The laughter of the elders, threaded with sinister energies, was disturbing to the prince. He had never heard laughter like that before. It almost made him sick. The king, seeing him turn pale, stopped laughing. The elders fell silent.

'You have not answered me,' the young prince said.

The most important of the elders, the senior custodian, stepped forward.

'As a people, we have only done good. We have done no evil. The bad things we appear to have done were for good reasons. We are a good people with a clean conscience. You should be assured, your highness, that as a future king your hands, like the hands of your ancestors, will be clean.'

'What about the slaves?'

'Dear prince,' the senior custodian said, 'there are no slaves in the kingdom.'

'What?' said the prince in disbelief.

'It's our job to worry about these things, your highness.' The custodian went on. 'Your job, in time, is to rule with clean hands.'

'How can my hands be clean if there is wickedness done in my name?'

'No wickedness, dear prince. Whatever is done is done in the name of the kingdom and for the good of the people. Your hands will always be clean.'

The custodian smiled benignly.

'So there are no slaves in the kingdom?' the prince asked.

'Yes.'

'Yes there are or yes there are no slaves?'

'No.'

The prince was exasperated. He turned to his father who remained grim and mute.

Suddenly the prince bolted from the chamber and was gone before the elders could do anything. Shortly after, a commotion was heard outside. There was shouting and the clash of weapons. Someone cried out. Then the prince reappeared in the hall, with seven of the slaves he had seen earlier.

'You can't bring them in here!' the elders shouted.

'These are slaves,' the prince said. 'These are people captured in war.'

'Not slaves,' the senior custodian replied. 'They're criminals, sold by their own people. Murderers, running away from justice. Dogs in disguise, beasts to their own kind. We make them work. We don't hurt them. They eat, they can marry, they can earn their freedom. They're not slaves.'

'I want them freed!' cried the prince.

'Your highness, don't get involved in these matters. Keep your hands clean. Don't enquire too much into these affairs. Things are more complicated than they seem. These people have no ropes around their necks. They are practically free. There is an ancient understanding between villages and kingdoms. These threads are too entangled to unravel in a day.'

The prince was silent. The custodian made a sign for the slaves to be removed. Soldiers came in and led them away.

'What else must I not know?'

'Many things.'

'Like what?'

The chief custodian paused and looked at the king. The king nodded. In a dry voice, the custodian spoke.

'Like outcasts. Like kings buried with their servants. Like low castes who work in the dark, never seen, never allowed to marry above...'

The custodian went on, in an even voice, pouring out a list of the good and evil practices of the land from time immemorial. He spoke of days when no living things were killed, days of laughter and nights of storytelling, days celebrating children who were forbidden to cut their hair, spirit days. He spoke of nights when the ancestors were honoured, festivities when the villages bring gifts and stage dances for outcasts. He spoke of the practice of lepers left out to die in the hills, the abandonment of deformed children, the flogging of thieves and adulterers, the banishment of cowards and murderers, the drowning of witches... The laws were rigorous and reasoned. The list went on and on, for what seemed like hours, till the prince began to hallucinate. Then he fell down in exhaustion.

'He's overwrought!' the custodian said, as they bore him to his quarters.

That night the king went to the bedroom of the prince and watched him sleeping. At dawn the king left. He was silent most of the next day. Silent and thoughtful.

13

NOT LONG AFTER the king left, the prince woke up. His first thought was of the maiden. He had a swift bath, drank some water, took an orange and a guava, and hurried off to the river.

The prince waited by the river feeling quite ill, trembling in a mild hallucination. He dozed and thought he saw his father staring down at him.

Then seven women, in splendid white robes, appeared out of the river. Three of them had musical instruments he had never seen before, gleaming like polished silver in the sun. Laughing and singing, the women linked hands and danced in a circle on the surface of the river. As they danced, they rose in the air, like a circle of angels, and then they came back down again and landed on the shore.

There was one among them of such outstanding beauty he thought she must be their princess. Her eyes shone like moonlight. Her face, clear in its beauty, had a happy sadness. Her skin was smooth as rare stones at the bottom of a river.

The other women clustered round her. They made a lovely bed for her with flowers they picked from the bushes along the shores of the river. She lay down languidly. Then one of the women struck up her instrument and they all began playing a delightful, unearthly music. The princess sang:

Who can know why we wait?
For love comes like a gentle fate.
To love is to suffer, is what they say;
To suffer sweetly is better than to decay.
Life is not a river under the sky,
And many things must happen, who knows why?

When she came to the end of her song the woman began to hum. The other women hummed as well and giggled. Silence fell over them as the lights made their beauty shine more brightly. They stared into the air. Then the woman said:

'O we are so happy today. All is well in the kingdom. So let us prophesy a little under this gentle breeze.'

'O yes,' they cried. 'Let's prophesy a little!'

'Who shall begin?'

'The princess shall begin!' the women said in chorus.

'All right,' she replied.

Then she picked up a white flower, spun its stalk between her palms, and sent it whirling into the air. It turned, spinning, and sailed away down the river in the light breeze.

'I speak backwards and sideways, but always speak the truth,' she said. 'There will be a meeting between a prince and a dream, and a magical line will be conceived. The prince will become a slave before his son is born.'

She paused and looked round the glowing faces of the women.

'Freedom will be in chains for a thousand moons. Stones will give more love than the hearts of human beings. Sweetness will be made from the suffering of a whole people. Music will come from their bones. Then light will return.'

The women spoke in a chorus, with the princess leading:

'Out of fire comes purest gold.'

'The spirit never grows old.'

'Songs of fishes that taste the flesh of men.'

'Songs of chains that eat the flesh of women.'

'Joy in the head, and wonder in the heart.'

'From this kingdom magic will never depart.'

The women danced in a rising circle. The world glowed with the brilliance of their white robes. Far away the king measured the good and evil in the land with his strides in the dark. Someone wept in the forest as if the sorrows in the world were too much for the earth to bear.

A single flower spun in the breeze, and it fell on the face of the prince.

He was woken not by the flower, but by the awareness that the day had darkened. He felt as if he had been waiting by the river all his life. The maiden he was waiting for did not appear. Without hearing the great weeping in the forest, without noticing the eyes that followed him in the dark, he stole back home.

14

WHEN HE RE-ENTERED the village the light was different. Everything seemed to be touched with a rich blue colour. He wandered to the fields and saw the women at work, children tied to their backs with broad strips of cloth. They were harvesting the crops. He watched them in the cornfields, yam fields, and cassava fields. With machetes they expertly cut the pineapple fruits from their thick green stalks. He saw all the women as his mother. His own mother had died early, when he was still a child. He knew her only by her stories and sighs.

As he watched the women, he saw for the first time how hard they worked. He spoke to them. He learnt that they woke before dawn, prepared food for the family, swept their yards, cleaned the house, and went to the river to wash clothes. When they returned home, they prepared the afternoon meal, washed the utensils, and made for the distant farms. In the evening, they went to the market to trade, often coming back with heavy bundles on their heads. They made several journeys, on foot, and fetched water from the well or the river. Then they attended the women's meeting, prepared dinner, and discussed family matters with their husbands and relations. They took turns in looking after the sick. They went to bed very late. They were always the last to sleep and the first to rise. They bore children, raised them, told them stories, taught them the legends of the tribe, and instilled into them the ancient traditions. They supported their husbands in everything they did. They were the pillars on which the kingdom was balanced.

'But you must be slaves!' the prince cried, when he grasped all this.

The women were offended.

'We're not slaves! We're freeborn women. We're the mothers of the kingdom, upholders of tradition. Without us nothing would work in the land. We're half the kingdom. Do you not think we are proud of it? The men depend on us. The children need us. This is a great thing. We have talked enough. Can we go back to our work now?'

The prince left them and went to the palace. He called for the custodians and the elders. When they had gathered, under the watchful eye of the king, he spoke.

'If I am to be the king, I want to know about the lives of our women. How do we treat them? They work from dawn to dusk. Why do they work so hard? What do we do for them in return?'

The king laughed. The elders, taking his cue, laughed too, but not as enthusiastically as before. They were becoming troubled by the young prince. Never had any royal asked so many questions.

'Answer the prince!' bellowed the king.

'We treat our women very well,' replied the chief custodian. 'They have no complaints.'

The prince was amazed. Before they knew it, he was gone again. There was shouting and commotion outside. The prince returned not long after leading a group of young and old women into the secret chamber. One of the elders cried:

'You can't bring women into the Hall of Custodians!'

It was too late; the prince had brought them into the presence of the king. Under the prince's questioning the life of the women emerged. It seemed so burdensome to him that he kept looking round in consternation. He gazed about him in surprise that everyone thought these lives normal, even the women. They appeared to make light of what seemed to him intolerable.

He heard a catalogue of duties and functions. He heard of marriage at an early age, circumcision, bearing children while still almost children themselves. He heard of endless chores, in illness or in health; of impossible tasks fulfilled every day. Yet, the women had no representation on the council of elders. They bore the deaths of children and husbands and carried on. They lived through wars and famines and carried on. They aged quickly, seemed insufficiently loved, had no holidays, but worked and worked at one thing or another, and then died. Then they were replaced with another wife. There seemed no end to the catalogue.

Did he live in the same space as other people? Had he been in a dream?

The king watched tears form in the prince's eyes as he listened to the women. These women were his mothers, his sisters, his companions. The elders made fun of the women as they spoke. They teased them about how much they exaggerated, how much they really enjoyed their responsibilities, the power it gave them to have the world dependent on them. The women laughed and admitted that they had a lot of power. The chief custodian said:

'Your royal highness, the women have not told you the whole truth. They are the secret movers of the kingdom. Men rule by day, women rule by night. Night is more magical. Men perform deeds in public, women undo them in private. Men make history, women make legend. Legend lasts longer. Men conquer bodies, women conquer hearts. The heart guides the world. Men think, women dream. Dreams create the future. Men think they rule the world, but find the world has turned into water. Women understand that water. Men make laws, women make ways. Men know death, but women know life.'

The chief custodian paused. The king watched the prince, who had his head tilted, as though he were listening to music. The custodian, lowering his voice, continued.

'If men make mistakes thousands die; if women make mistakes, a whole tribe perishes. Men can be stupid and the world will not fall down, but if women are stupid the world comes to an end. It is important that women are wise. The greatness of a people is a tribute to the greatness of its women.'

Pausing, the chief custodian looked at the women. None of them had changed their expressions. The prince still had his head tilted, a faint smile on his lips. The chief custodian went on, more quietly, so that everyone had to strain to hear him.

'God help us if they should fall into lazy ways, for then the kingdom will turn to dust and be scattered to the four winds. A kingdom cannot afford its women to lose their vision.'

The chief custodian shook his head violently and raised his voice, startling the young prince.

'I see visions of a world gone mad because women have lost the wisdom. It is a world without sense, a world of despair and madness. Such a world is already cursed by the departure of the gods. An empty world. As you can see, your royal highness, there are two sides to this matter. On the one hand, much labour; on the other, great blessings. It is women who bring happiness to the world, through their mysteries.'

THERE WAS SILENCE when the custodian finished. The king made a sign, and the prince spoke.

'I want to be initiated into the mysteries of women,' he said in a gentle voice.

The king roared with laughter. The elders and custodians joined in. All the way down the labyrinthine corridors, throughout the palace, the servants, cooks, and handmaidens laughed.

Soon the forest and the river and the whole kingdom was laughing. Only the prince stayed serious. He said it again. He wanted to share in the condition of women, their suffering, their beauty, their majesty, their grace.

The king stopped laughing, and stared calmly at his son. The women, conferring swiftly among themselves, withdrew from the presence of the king, genuflecting till they were out of the door.

That evening at the convention of the women of the village, a unanimous decision was reached. The prince would be the first and only man in the kingdom to be initiated into the mysteries of women.

The initiation took place that night, in the place where women do their greatest work, in the secret consciousness of the world. They initiated the prince with the help of his mother's spirit, who was influential in the highest court of women. From beyond she went on looking after her son.

16

THAT NIGHT THE prince asked his father about his mother. The king told him stories about her till he fell asleep.

Then, in his sleep, a goddess came to him. She took him to the realm of the dead. His mother was not there. The land of the dead had no depth and no time. He met many of the new dead. The dead were in a dream they could not wake up from. Then the goddess showed him the book of life. In it he saw his mother's life and she came alive. He spoke to her and listened to her for a long time. She told him about many things to come. She also told him that he would forget them when he woke up. It was the most blissful experience of his life.

Then he fell into a deeper sleep and his mother disappeared. This was when the women initiated his spirit into their mysteries. He walked in his sleep to a shrine near the river. Figures in white robes buried him in the earth, leaving a hole for him to breathe. They performed rituals over his buried body. Then disinterred, newly born, newly bathed in the river, they anointed him with potent oils and blood and the juices of nocturnal herbs. Then they made him recite certain oaths and permitted him to dwell in the presence of the great radiant mother of all things.

Still asleep, the prince returned to his bed.

THE PRINCE WAS different when he woke up the next day. But he didn't know how.

He seemed to have developed an extra faculty, another head. His eyes saw things they had never seen before, as if they were on loan from the spirits. The world was new to him, yet it was ancient and familiar. He understood more things than he had lived.

He felt he carried within him the wisdom of multitudes, a thousand forms of dying, a million ways of living, an understanding of the simplicity of all things. He had the lucid feeling that the many ways led to the one. The many forms were one formless harmony. The thousand histories were all one moment, one breath. All suffering and living was just one astonishing tale of illusion.

He felt as light as a bird, and free as a dream. But he was troubled by a knowledge which burned in him, like a tragedy about to be revealed by lightning flash.

He told no one what he felt. But all the women looked at him with love. There was a glint in their eyes, a secret knowledge, as if they would make love to him there and then, in public, if only decorum would allow it.

He had become seductive to the women in an inexplicable way. It made their eyes linger on him.

He had the same effect on spirits. Even objects seemed to fall in love with him.

18

On the third morning of his awakening he went to his hiding place on the riverbank and waited for the maiden to appear.

In that dawn the river that never sleeps seemed to quiver with a beautiful light he had not seen before. The river was golden and brown and vast. Cranes and sunbirds played on its shore. The prince watched a solitary heron stride along the water's edge like an actor talking to himself.

The prince was fond of herons. They were royal birds. He loved their ability to be majestic as well as small. Sometimes they looked like ragged creatures not worthy of notice. To survive they must not be brilliant. If they were showy they would not catch fish. They were wise birds, concealing their beauty for a higher purpose.

The heron walked lightly on long thin legs. It seemed to tread just above the ground. Each tread was tender, almost tentative. Appearing to have no interest in anything at all, it struck the water swiftly, and casually swallowed down a fish. It did this with great economy.

He stared at the bird in dreamy contemplation. Feeling it was being watched, the heron made itself boring. The prince knew the trick and wasn't fooled.

It was difficult keeping his focus on a bird that made itself bedraggled and devoid of interest. The prince kept his eyes on it with a great effort.

19

HE KEPT HIS eyes fixed on the heron even when he saw, out of the corner of his eye, something extraordinary emerging from the earth. The more boring the heron became, the harder was his concentration, and the stranger was the thing forming out of the corner of his eye.

Then he heard guttural voices. He heard drums, bells, and cow-horns. Voices were hollering, as if a whole world was coming into being. While all this was going on, the prince tried to keep his gaze on the white heron.

But a tremendous event was blooming on the riverbank. It was a masquerade, blazing with reds and yellows. It had purple legs, white feet, black toes. Its raffia skirt was of orange and gold. Black smoke billowed from its seven heads. The more the prince noticed it, the more the heron was erased from the world.

The shadow of the masquerade danced on the river. Its heads blocked out the sun. There were odd things on its body. When the prince looked closer he saw the writhing forms of dead babies. He saw disembodied heads, with eyes wide open, tongues sticking out, hanging from golden ropes. There were dangling limbs that twitched, feet that kicked, toes that wriggled, fingers that writhed, eyes that stared every which way, lips that jabbered, and hearts that pumped out blood.

The masquerade began dancing as if set free from long slavery. It waved its trunk-like arms in the air. Every step it took made the kingdom tremble. Every time it jumped the land quaked and the riverbed cracked, as if creation itself were being broken down and split asunder.

All this while, the prince struggled to keep his attention on the heron.

33

20

Eat eat eat the world
Conquer conquer conquer the world
Rule rule rule the world
I am the king, the king of the world.

Blood blood blood in the world
Death death death in the world
Enslave enslave enslave the world
I am the king, the king of the world.

Ha ha ha ha ha ha ha ha ha ha ha

AS THE MASQUERADE laughed, its dance shook the king-dom's foundation. The land split open and people fell into the chasms. Huts and houses collapsed, trees crashed down and the forest shrieked. The prince heard the falling screams.

Then he saw, as if in a dream, the heron standing upright in a place populated with bronze sculptures. And among the bronzes was the maiden he was waiting for.

He understood then that she came from the secret tribe of artists.

He knew that he was fortunate to have seen her when he did and that he would have to persevere if he was ever going to see her again. He would be very lucky to inspire her love.

He had dreamt her, but she had not seen him. She didn't even know he existed.

ALL THE WHILE, the masquerade was consuming the trees, eating the shore, drinking up the river, and leaving behind a dry bed of skeletons. It ate the bushes, breathed in all the air, broke off the sun and began to devour it, bringing on night. Only when the masquerade was about to set upon the prince, because he had paid it too much attention, did he remember the royal bird.

The heron made the subtlest movement, enough for its magnificence to be revealed, and the prince saw it as a radiant thing in a dying world.

The masquerade thundered and leaked blood. Liverish fluids filled the hollow world and the river became a river of blood. The swallowed sun shone from all parts of the masquerade.

Then the heron stretched out its wings and flew over the blood-red river. As it flew it changed all things and restored a new attention to the world.

The masquerade tried to swat down the heron with its many hands, but it got all mixed up and began to fight itself. It got tangled up as the heron nonchalantly sailed on.

The heron didn't notice the masquerade. But the masquerade, in its attempts to slay the heron, cut off its own heads, blinded itself with its own spears, and pierced its own heart.

The clash of mighty armies never wreaked more havoc than the battle of the masquerade against itself. Then with a sigh that released all the air back into the world, it fell into the blood-red river and drowned. And the sun, freed from its body, purified the waters. It rose, and its light transfigured the world.

The heron sailed on into the sky. The prince bade it farewell with tears in his eyes.

And still the maiden did not appear.

THE PRINCE MADE his way home through a forest alive with spying eyes. As soon as he got back to the village he became aware of the silence in the air. He had not heard that silence before. Shadows hung over the huts and houses. Between things, between the trees, the huts, the walls and the gates, invisible beings invested the air with wavy shapes. He had not noticed them before. All this troubled him.

Then he was struck by something new in the faces of the men and women and children who greeted him as he went to the palace. It was something like the shadow of doom.

He hurried on.

In the palace, he summoned the elders before the king. He wanted to know the disposition of the gods and the origin of monsters and shadow forms. He wanted to find out about the sinister forces that warred against the welfare of the kingdom. He wanted to know the origin of evil in the world.

The king frowned as he listened to his son.

The elders protested. The young prince was interfering with the running of the kingdom. He was wasting their time. They should be deliberating on important matters of state.

'Like what?' asked the king.

'Collecting levies...'

'And what else?'

The elders listed things of significant state concern.

'But you never discuss these things at all,' the king said, sternly. 'You squabble endlessly. You constantly postpone coming to a decision about anything. You are always waiting to see which way the wind blows, always protecting your interests. You spend time doing profitable business with one another, advancing your privileges, acquiring wives, furthering the interests of your children, family, and tribes... Can you remember the last time you came to a collective decision about anything?'

'Many times, your majesty,' cried one elder.

'Name one time,' replied the king.

There was silence. The elders consulted among themselves. They soon began to squabble in low voices. The king gave his characteristic laughter.

'You see! The decisions that are taken happen by themselves in the very teeth of the crisis. Don't complain about the prince's requests. He is my heir and future king. Do what he asks!'

The elders stared at the prince. There were signs on their faces that he could not read. They asked for more time in which to prepare themselves.

'I want answers now. There is no time to waste,' said the prince.

The elders nodded. They took him to the council room and told him, one by one, as in a ritual chorus, the genealogy of monsters, the origins of evil beings, and the permutations of dark forms.

They took him out of the palace to the shrines where he consulted the oracles.

'Strange people will come in silence, with fire, bearing new words that will destroy old worlds. Gods will be in flames. There will be an earthquake in which the earth does not tremble, but in which the people will be silent for one hundred and forty years. A new sun will rise. The people will be made new with the dance of the gods. Made new and blessed. But only after the lamentation of flowers, the rebirth of rivers, and the reuniting of brothers and sisters across the great sea.'

These things the oracle uttered.

At the shrine he consulted the priestess of the father god. The disposition of the gods was more oblique. The priestess, in the dark, gave him this message which she uttered as if in a trance.

'Lost is the way handed down to you by your ancestors who came from elsewhere bringing wisdom and guidance. Find the hidden masters.'

Then he went to the guardians, who communicate with the ancestors through divination and dreams. The mood of the ancestors was obscure.

They spoke, but in a language the diviners could not understand. They sang, but the interpreters could not hear the words, nor the music.

23

THE PRINCE FELL asleep amid all the contradiction and was borne lightly to his bed. That night the invisible beings in between things paid him a visit in his sleep. Briefly, he was shown the origin of evil in the world.

An angel had disobeyed the supreme being. The angel worked on man and woman, and they disobeyed too. Then they fell into the unreality of the world.

The prince saw that evil was ignorance. Evil was darkness. It exists where unreality reigns.

He saw that evil served a strange function, which is to provide the opposition needed for the soul to grow. The destination of the soul is beyond good and evil. But evil is the one thing that human beings must transcend, to find a new place in heaven.

The prince was shown all this. He understood much more besides. Then the gods appeared to him. The ancestors spoke to him in songs. What the ancestors said to him he absorbed but forgot. He would remember them later when terrible events sprang them out as his own thoughts, his own deeds.

That night the evil forms he had attracted paid him a visit. To see them is to be seen by them. They troubled the prince's dreams.

These dark forms entered the prince because he was an open soul who gave all things habitation. He was not yet strong enough to resist them, though.

This possession was part of what would make him strong. His ancestors believed that the soul must be attacked by what it must learn to resist. If the soul survives the attack, it becomes impregnable. If it doesn't, a good soul perishes and has to begin again where it left off its journey.

That's how it was with the prince.

24

THE EVIL FORMS that visited him were so terrible that a great unease entered his spirit. The dreams he had were awful. Monsters began to eat his flesh, till only his heart remained. Liverish spirits slid into him and wriggled in his being. Vile-looking critters took up occupation in his brain and held meetings about how to conquer the kingdom of his soul.

Then he saw unspeakable acts. He saw women who poisoned their husbands and married their husband's brothers, men who murdered their wives and buried them in farmlands, warriors who beheaded the conquered and danced at night with their skulls under a luminous moon.

All the hidden evils in the kingdom that he saw in his dreams affected him so powerfully that he slid into a profound sickness which lasted a long time.

Everyone thought he was going to die. He wouldn't eat. He couldn't speak. He barely stirred from his bed. He was unconscious for long stretches and when he was awake he stared at the ceiling for hours without seeing. They said his soul had fled his body and his eyes longed for somewhere beyond the sky. For a long time he refused to see anyone, even the king.

They brought friends, relations, comedians, beautiful young princesses whom he had been thought to favour. He looked through his friends, was deaf to the entreaties of beauty, and did not register the jokes of the comedians.

They brought in musicians to play rousing tunes, with syncopated drumbeats that seduced the feet into dancing. But he did not betray the slightest pulse of delight. The musicians played tender and bewitching melodies, laced with sorrow, music so moving that palace officials reported seeing dogs weep. But not one tear reddened his eyes.

25

THE KING DIDN'T laugh anymore. He wandered gloomily through the corridors of the palace. He had never been affected by anything under the sun, not defeat in battles, nor the deaths of children, triumphs in statecraft, prosperity in the land, periods of unexpected happiness, or sudden invasions. He would laugh at crises or victories, setbacks or accomplishments.

But the king was subdued by his son's illness. He had never really expected the prince to last long in the world. He had reconciled himself to the omens that said the boy was doomed to die early.

He had expected him to die in childhood. But the prince had survived fevers and reached adolescence. Then the king had feared that one evening, without warning, death would claim him. But the prince had thrived, and grown strong. He took on challenging tasks and worked in the fields like the ordinary people of the land.

Through all this the king had laughed. When the prince had expressed an interest in the deeper matters of life, the king had been delighted.

Laughter was the king's way of breathing. It was his way of thinking and not thinking. He had been laughing since he was young. Behind his laughter lay a profound soul that saw deeply into the mystery of things.

26

THE KING THOUGHT much about the strange sickness of his son. He ruled the kingdom with an abstracted air. His wives found him unusually preoccupied and his advisers were disconcerted by his long silences and vacant stares.

He would sit for hours in the prince's chamber, watching him sleep. He remembered that at his son's birth the diviners were confused. They had said that the alignment of the stars was auspicious and enigmatic. A white horse with a golden horn in the middle of its forehead had appeared fleetingly in the village square. Then a message was brought to the king from the oracle.

'That which is best will be lost so that that which is greatest can be found.'

The shrines swarmed with white birds. A rare animal caught in a net was seen staring out with calm eyes near the palace. The king ordered it to be freed.

Meteors were seen at dusk. A golden light shone in the sky in the middle of the night, alarming the wise ones of the kingdom.

The king remembered how favoured his son had been at birth by the people. The women, especially, loved him, even before his arrival. His coming had been whispered to them in dreams.

Listening to musicians playing outside the chamber, the king thought about his own youth. He thought about the prince's mother, who he still loved above all others in the world. Thoughts of her filled him with a sweet sorrow. He laughed tenderly to himself. When she was dying the queen had said to him:

'This son of ours will need great support if he is going to fulfil his destiny. I will give him all the strength he needs from the other side. Tell him to think of me when he is in trouble and I will move heaven to help him.'

She had paused and looked up at him with a smile.

'As for you, my love, I am always in your heart. I am your happiness. I want you to always laugh and never dwell in sorrow about anything. We have been great companions on the path together. We know the glories of the mountaintop. Be a great king and an even greater man. Be joyful. We will be together in dreams.'

She seemed to be fading, but she looked up and brightened.

'My dear, the day's harvest has been done. Maybe I'll cook you something special. You'd like that, wouldn't you?' she whispered, and then she was gone.

The king didn't like thinking about the death of his wife, not because of the sadness but because he didn't believe she was gone. He laughed often because she was there with him in the palace.

But the king was worried about his son. Many prophecies hung on his son's life. If he dies before a certain age, the kingdom will perish. If he does not bear the evil in the land, the kingdom will collapse. If the white spirits do not purge the world of the evils they have unleashed, the world will be broken asunder. If the king stops laughing, hope will fly from the kingdom, and the people will be finished. Many prophecies. Many responsibilities.

THE KING OFTEN wandered the kingdom at night, watching over his sleeping subjects. He derived great strength from protecting those who slept, defenceless, in his realm. The good and bad slept the same way, under the mercy of immense forces.

He sent his spiritual protection to all who slept in his kingdom.

Sleeping farmers and traders, witches and wizards, thieves and magicians. Sleeping servants and palm-wine tappers. Sleeping hunters and fishermen, storytellers and musicians. Sleeping babies drawing in the vital air of the world. Sleeping men on the verge of infinity, exhaling the last miracles of life. Sleeping women on the edge of eternity, dreaming of their children's futures. Sleeping herbalists. Sleeping dogs in the village square. Sleeping horses flicking their tails. Sleeping flies and busy insects. Forests sleeping at night, breathing out pure energies, balancing the earth. Sleeping flowers soft in the dark. Sleeping clouds drifting above.

The king loved them all. But he loved none more than his sleeping son, who lay dying beneath his helpless gaze.

AT DAWN THE king sent for the greatest herbalists. They arrived in large number, pouring in within a few days of each other. They treated the prince with many potions, subjected him to incantations, baths, massages, and midnight exposures to spirits summoned in the sacred forest. Nothing they did made him better.

They changed his diet, altered his sleeping position, and drew out with their teeth sinister objects from his body – a long thin bone, the black tooth of an ageing dog, the claw of a vulture, a gleaming cowrie shell. These objects, they claimed, had been projected into the body of the prince by people with evil in their hearts.

They bent and knotted him to force out the evil spirits lodged in his flesh. They prescribed a course of spirit-flogging, which was roundly rejected by the king.

They had him carried backwards, in precisely delineated circles, to perplex the evil occupants in him. They bared him to the harsh rays of the noonday sun and the dim rays of a yellow moon. They entered his dreams and commenced battle with the shadows that lurked in his mind. But all the herbalists succeeded in doing was make his nightmares worse.

29

THE PRINCE HOVERED between life and death for a long time. When the people heard, they descended on the palace. Mothers swarmed there in their hundreds, babies tied to their backs. They left their farms, their marketplaces, their homes, and came and sat in silence outside the palace, keeping vigil. Their lamps were alight day and night.

The women made aromatic dishes of great delicacy and had them sent in to the prince. All night they prayed to the gods for his life. Their prayers lightly scented the kingdom.

Men also came to pay homage and show their support in the dark hours of the prince's illness. Famous warriors set aside their swords for a season, calling a temporary truce in their wars so they could join the vigil. Their rough, brooding aspects were softened by the women murmuring in prayer.

Dancers, wrestlers, criminals, magicians, priests of obscure religions, and wandering griots travelled great distances to the palace. Those that could brought their work with them.

Hunters brought game, priests offered sacrifices, and drummers re-tuned the nerves of the kingdom with the rhythms of their sacred instruments. The drums summoned the ancestors from the invisible realms, where they dwell behind a veil thinner than the morning mist.

30

WRESTLING MATCHES WERE staged in the fields outside the village gates. People assembled in silence to watch the ritual contest between the champion of the prince's life and the champion of death. Battle rocked back and forth. Sometimes the champion of death seemed to be winning. Then the champion of the prince's life would recover and the audience would sigh loudly in relief.

This went on day after day, with no clear victor in sight. It followed the course of the prince's illness. It ebbed and flowed as news dribbled out about the prince's condition. Their spirits were kept high by the electrifying rhythms of the talking drum.

During the lulls in the match, acrobats performed feats of tumbling and juggling. They walked on ropes in the air. Gymnasts amazed with turns and twists of their bodies. They performed their feats with a ritual mood. It was all meant to empower the spirit of the prince as he fought for life.

After the acrobats came the wandering griots.

In the darkness that fell over the village, these traditional storytellers held the attention of the crowds and took them on fabulous journeys through forests and through time, with songs and dances, incantations and impersonations. The audiences gasped as the griots turned into cheetahs before their eyes, into monsters, into giant falcons, spreading panic, or spoke with seven voices echoing from deep resonating chests.

They performed tales of warriors who fought demons, tales of heroes who travelled to the realm of the gods to bring back the secret of immortality.

They kept the crowds in a state of terror and enchantment.

ROBBERS PROWLED AMONG the audience with their acolytes. For once they used their skills to make sure no crimes were committed and no thefts took place during the vigil.

It seemed the mere presence of these famous figures of crime was enough to deter wrongdoing. More so than the presence of soldiers and protectors of the realm.

Anyone who sought the opinion of the people might have learnt that there was a special role for criminals in the land. It had to do with the prevention of crime, as like understands like.

The reputation of the criminals gave the vigil an air of safety and authenticity, such as the king's guards alone could not have commanded.

32

MAGICIANS ENTERTAINED THE crowds as they made calabashes disappear, swallowed swords to the hilt, and caused water to spout out of dry stones. They made dead birds spring to life, turned blocks of wood into cats, transformed spears into stalks crowned with roses.

Priests led the crowds in strange prayers and stranger rites.

Spirits appeared at night among the yellow lanterns and conversed in odd languages with people who understood them perfectly. They told the children stories so vivid that they remembered them all their lives. The stories were passed on to their children, and are told to this day, in many villages, under moonlit skies.

Spirits wandered through the palace, listening to rumours, conspiracies, plots, lies, confessions, and secrets. Knowing what was to come, they listened and said nothing. They listened, and passed through, like spies for the future.

All manner of people and spirits and ancestors and insects converged, from many realms, outside the palace. They had all been drawn there by the gentle personality of the prince, who they had heard about in the rumours of the world.

They kept on converging. They chanted and sang and prayed and dwelt in long silences, holding up their lanterns for the prince, encouraging him to get better, so that the land would be whole again.

33

THE ELDERS WERE frightened by the effect the prince's illness had on the people. In all their combined memories they had never heard of a more extraordinary display of affection for a prince. A king can command such adoration, if he is a good and wise king. But a prince is another matter. Besides, they were perplexed at how the prince had managed to become so famous.

The elders thought that they were the controllers of reputation, the sole guardians of the gate through which a person's name and deeds were trumpeted to the world. They had not done any such trumpeting for the prince because they were looking forward to reducing his powers when he became king.

He seemed a weak figure, an excellent candidate for royal demotion. He was perfect for control and intimidation. The elders intended to make themselves more powerful. Then they would get rid of the future king altogether, and the land would forever be ruled by them, the council of elders.

All these were whispered hopes. They were hinted at so indirectly, in such convoluted proverbs, that only the subtlest inner circle of elders knew of this intangible current of thinking. Ostensibly these elders were the very model of loyalty. They were the loudest and most passionate defenders of the existing order. It would be treasonous to think them otherwise.

Now, the elders were confounded by the great love the people bore the prince – people who had never known him, never seen him, and perhaps never would.

There is a kind of love which it is easy to subvert. When a person is loved for their deeds, their conquests, their heroism, their goodness or their affection for the people, these are easy enough to destroy. Rumours and lies and distortions can undo such reputations.

But love which is felt for apparently no reason, felt because of an ineffable affinity, because a people can't do otherwise, is a love inspired by the gods. It is therefore impossible to destroy, distort or weaken. Attempts to thwart such a love only strengthen it. Doing nothing allows the love to grow at its natural pace, inexorably, till it becomes a vast and silent adoration.

The elders were undone by this magical love. It rendered them powerless. They were marginalised by it. Suddenly they felt how useless they were. They found themselves spectators in a grand love story between the people and the prince. They realised how unknown and unloved they were, and they resented it.

This was new to them. This was a sign that their ancient institution, their place in the scheme of things, was insecure. They felt a new age dawning, and they were not in that age. The prince's illness was killing them off. They were dying of the love the people bore him.

It did not take the elders long to realise that something had to be done.

34

THE KING WAS moved by the tenderness of the people. He watched from the palace window the heaving crowds that gathered from all over the known world to show their support. Fishermen, market women, boxers, mendicants, albinos, runaways, merchants, visionaries, adventurers, quarrelsome bar-owners, warriors from the distant lands, the crippled, the blind, the anxious, the lonely, the dying, the young, the strife-ridden, all manner of people converged, and kept on converging, as if the illness of the prince were the illness of the world.

THE KING, WHO had a great heart and wise innocence, embraced in his spirit the crowds that had overrun the palace. He was no stranger to wonders.

He had helped to bring about all that he saw around him. All things made him laugh, because of the wonder hidden in them. He knew the hearts of men and women at a glance. He could read their intentions. He knew the destiny of their thoughts. He knew the disasters to come and the great adventures. He knew what the stars foretold in their misalignments. And in all things he found laughter.

He found laughter in good as much as in evil. He found laughter in all those who thought they could escape the effects of what they set into motion by their hidden deeds and dreams. He laughed at the harvest of good and bad intentions. He laughed with love in his heart.

THE KING HAD initiated the new spiritual practices in the kingdom. He had guarded the secret rites brought to the land long ago by magi. He had been initiated as a child into the wonders of the sages from the land of the magic river where stones had been raised into perfect structures for the adoration of the sun. His people originally came from that land.

Long ago he had entered the chambers of death and had gone beyond them. He had dwelt among higher beings who whispered the secret ways in silence. They whispered them through timeless moments of an eternal life that shone above the African sands.

He glimpsed all things inwardly. The world as he saw it, obscure yet clear, was a place where the drama of spiritual evolution is staged.

The king saw the people as the children of his love, as a gardener loves the seeds that will become the fruits and flowers of the earth, for the nourishment of the people and the enrichment of the stars.

IT WAS WITH such simplicity of spirit that the king saw the crowds gathered outside the palace. He laughed tenderly at the spectacle of their piety and their love.

He sent food and blankets out to the people who had gathered. He sent his medicine men to make sure that the ill among them were treated, that the pregnant women were looked after, and that the women who gave birth were helped.

He sent his bards among them to bear witness to their dreams, and historians to register their deeds. At night, while they slept, he went among them in simple disguise and watched over their sleeping forms and partook of their dreams and shared their distress. It was good education for him. It enhanced his laughter.

38

THE PRINCE WAS still ill. On his favourite bed of hardened clay, softened with down, he tossed in dreams. He woke while asleep and lived in a separate realm, as if freed from his body. He got lost in a labyrinth of narratives and images.

His sickness was very deep. It snatched him away from his home and dragged him through the forests, past the elders, who were men of teak and thunder. They blocked his path and always he had to find a way through them so he could continue his quest.

The sickness dragged him through mud, through valleys, across rivers, over mountain ranges, and down into the dark earth. He journeyed with the sickness in a darkened world where there was no moon, only voices. The voices echoed in the dark, as in a giant room. He recognised them as the voices of the elders.

His sickness took him deep into the earth and at last he emerged in a grey world, where everything was made of ash. A pale light that was no light spread evenly over everything. There was no one in this world. No spirits, no shadows, no ancestors, no voices, no laughter. It was a world of ash and a pale light that was no light.

The prince sat and waited patiently for time to turn him into nothing or into everything.

BOOK TWO

The Master Artists

I

Prelude

MANY ARE THE things to be read in the inscriptions of the world. Many are the truths, facts, dates, times, and events. Many also are the signs and omens, the symbols and resonances, the secret messages and hints, the enigmas and mysteries, and the tantalising flashes of meaning to be sensed in the inscriptions of the world.

Many are the faces to be seen in stains on walls, in shapes on the ground, or on water in buckets glimpsed at odd angles in a certain frame of mind. Many are the people noticed standing still in a forest that turn into a cluster of bushes, when a moment before they were women conniving or a group of men plotting evil. Many are the marches of battalions that sail past in cloud formations, massed towards war. Many are the evenings when the sun seems to bleed light, as if leaking out all the blood spilt in wars and pogroms and genocides, bleeding light into our world for all the wicked deeds that we send up to heaven.

Many are the times when the moon quivers in its halluci-natory power, as if it were an oracle bloated with too many prophecies, or a transparent gourd of palm-wine intoxicated with its own potency. Many are the moments when the moon speaks a cryptic tongue to the eye, when it is half-eaten by the sun or the dark, when it is red, or blue, or stippled with inscru-table images, or chewed at the edges, or pitted with signs, or when faces old and intimate, the face of one's grandfather, or of a stranger seen in a crowd, appear on it, above our superstitious gaze.

Many are the empires that reveal themselves in decay on blotches on stone walls. Many are the nations that appear on patches of mud long after the rains have gone. Many are the shapes of divination that show up in tea stains on white pages or on tablecloths.

Myriad are the things seen on the surfaces of the meaning-transparent, meaning-infested world.

MANY ARE THE well-studied forms of augury: the disposition of leaves at the bottom of a teacup; the configuration of cowries thrown on a mat and deciphered by a master's spirit; the scattered petals of flowers at dawn; the teasing of bells by a tinkling breeze; the formation of birds sent by the gods to speak to lands that will not listen.

Many are the ways the gods speak to us: through dreams, which we remember dimly, which we forget, which we misread, creating more chaos instead of clarity; dreams that we act on too directly, as if they spoke a literal language; dreams that we fear; dreams that bewilder, which we get others to explain, when the key is with us alone.

Many are the ways of seeing the future, glimpsing the remote past. Some stare into crystal balls, into clear waters. Some read the fall of kola nut lobes in enamel bowls. Some interpret the footprints of herons. Some scan the past in momentary visions outside time. Some use the Bible or Virgil or the Koran or other sacred texts. Some resort to sorcerers and consult wizards that may or may not know the complexity of the stars. Some travel in the minds of tortoises to the beginnings of the race. Some fly to the moon on the back of beams of light. Some wander deaf among angels. Some consult the ancient oracles and ponder enigmatic messages from the gods, delivered in broken verse from the Sibyls. Some hear prophecies in the mouth of babbling children, or the language of crows, or the accidental words that reach them in the marketplace, or words uttered by strangers or the insane.

Such are the perplexities of man and woman in a world where the past and future do not speak, and where the present has not fully revealed itself to our partially seeing eyes. We live our days between knowing and unknowing, blind in a vast panorama of revelations, a perpetual theatre of timeless events, where real history is as much the future as the past, an infinite living book in which all things are present. We live in wonders and do not see.

Many are the wonders to be glimpsed in the book of life: the beginnings of the universe, the death of stars, the obscure life of a thief, the rich hidden life of a maiden, the abstracted life of a queen, the last days of a musician leaning against a column, a biblical flood, the lives of the ancient philosophers, an evening in Atlantis, an afternoon on a normal day in a desert town in Africa, the sight of a baby lost in a city of groundnut pyramids, the glorious dream of Alexander, the happy exiled days in the life of my mother, the magical adolescence of my father, and all the stories known and unknown, lived and unlived, in the endless chain of universal life.

Many wonders are to be glimpsed in this eternal book, and I have chosen this story and don't know why.

WHEN SHE HEARD the questions in the wind, that day by the river, the maiden's life changed forever. Before that day she lived deep in a dream.

Everything was strange to her. She felt as if she had come from another constellation and found herself marooned on this planet, completely lost. Her good fortune was that she was born into the tribe of artists, into a family of gold-shapers and bronze-workers.

Her tribe lived in villages surrounded by forest. Their lives were dedicated to listening to the oracles of the spirit. They made art from their listening.

They created sculptures in secret and displayed them at night in the village centre or near the shrines. The art they made was often a warning of disturbances to come, in the family, the tribe, the land, the world, or in the spirit of one man or woman. The tribe might wake up one morning to find the wooden sculpture of a man chained to another man, and wonder what it meant.

These images led to great discussions and there were interpretations and misinterpretations. Often many years would pass before a famous image revealed its social purpose or spiritual value. Then the familiar image would become strange again.

These images needed master interpreters to decode them, else their continued inscrutability bothered the tribe. They would send a long way for wise men or women to come and decipher the images that haunted them. An uninterpreted image was intolerable.

Many famines, plagues, wars, earthquakes, abductions, and outrages had been averted or minimised, because an artist had created an image, displayed it near the shrine, and it was properly interpreted for the larger benefit of the land.

The tribe had become legendary for such artistic services. With this status they had won the freedom to live as they wished, to best serve their vision and the goddess of artistic revelation.

4

THEY WERE A unique people. To some tribes they were a rumour, a legend. Most people did not believe that they existed.

This suited the tribe of artists immensely. It cloaked them with invisibility. It freed them from external constraints. It allowed them to be dreamers, listeners, makers, guides, and dealers in mystery. It made them messengers of the gods, travellers between realms, image-bearers, creators of supreme beauty in the land.

They were free. Their art was not only about divination, revelation, omens, and warnings. They also created works of lamentation and jubilation. Their bronze-castings celebrated life in all its aspects, with images of lovers, of a mother and child, a young man hunting, athletes, good harvests. They created works of art that were simply beautiful in themselves, works that gave pleasure and health to those who gazed on them, works that were like sunlight, or rainbows, or the light on the face of the river, the sparkling eyes of a happy child. These works were often made in secret and appeared in the mornings in the most surprising places in the village.

They also made works that were dark and intimidating, works fraught with nails and blood rituals, incarnating evil and therefore earthing it.

Sometimes an artist might place their work beside a frequently visited well. Sometimes it was hidden in the forest to be stumbled upon by hunters, travellers or children playing. Sometimes the artist would plant the work in the centre of the path leading out of the village. They might have it dangling from a tree. They might even arrange for children to bear it up and down the village square, while singing the line of a song.

The artists were always anonymous. No one ever knew who had created which work of art. This way the dreamer was free to reveal their deepest hopes, fears, and visions. Depending on their power and relevance, the works were interpreted and acted upon.

Some works were not found for many years. They might be discovered decades after they were left somewhere. But whenever they were found was when their meaning was deemed necessary for the land.

Sometimes a work is discovered at the exact moment when what they prophesy is about to cause havoc to the people. The work helps them see what they wouldn't have seen.

As much as their creation or interpretation, the finding of such works was of great significance to the tribe.

Many works have still not been found. The things they warn of lie sleeping and unseen.

5

THIS WAS THE tribe that the maiden came from. Her father was an enigma. He appeared to do nothing. No one knew what he did in the community, and yet he prospered.

Some said he was a great sorcerer and could create gold just by thinking it into being or by living long enough with a stone under his pillow.

Some said he traded with spirits.

Some said he was the secret guide of an unknown king.

He was often away from home for long periods. No one knew where he went. Yet he was aware of everything happening in the tribe and the land.

He spoke little, seldom laughed, and had the piercing eyes of a hooded eagle. He was rumoured to be one of the greatest artists in the tribe and a key guardian of its esoteric traditions. No one knew this for sure.

The maiden's mother was also an important figure in the tribe, and a great artist. She came from a long line of makers. She would sometimes look at her daughter and say:

'She is not from here. She will not stay long. When she has found what she is looking for she will return. We must slow down her discovery.'

Delaying her discovery: that was the bass-note of the maiden's life.

6

BEFORE SHE HEARD the questions by the river, the maiden had been shy, awkward, plain, and hard-working. No one remarked her. She was not beautiful. None of the men had singled her out for marriage. She had not inflamed any loins. She was a bit of a worry to her mother. She spoke little and ran away when anyone spoke to her. She was uncomfortable in the company of others.

She was always wandering off by herself into the forest. She would find a quiet place by the river and gaze into nothingness, yearning for the peace that only death or a great love can bring. Hidden in her desolate spot, she sang sad songs to herself, absent-mindedly, in a low voice.

Sometimes a wonderful mood came over her. Then she would skitter along the shore, performing cartwheels and sudden dances. She might play at being a crab or a bird. She would talk to the wind, to spirits, to immortal and imaginary friends, confiding her deep yearnings to the air. She would be overcome with an inexplicable joy that made her want to jump out of her skin. In times like this she made up songs and the music to go with them. Or she might rush back to her father's workshop and begin a wood-carving, in secret.

7

IN ONE SUCH mood, under the inspiration of an indigo happiness, she began a new work. The carving she made turned into a mould. Using her father's authority with the men of the foundry, she had the casting made. She was amazed at the beauty that had sprung from her hands.

She had created the bust of a queen in a fine-patterned regal head-dress, with sensuous in-turned contemplative eyes. It was a face she had never seen before, the face of her youthful and dangerous happiness.

She kept the bronze among her possessions, till she could figure out what to do with it. Every morning at dawn she brought it out and mooned over it. In the night she cradled it.

At that time she seemed even more alien to her mother.

'What am I going to do with you?' her mother would say. 'No man will marry you. You have no beauty. You don't talk. You're not lucky. You don't have the art of women, the art of sweetening life. You're too unfriendly. Your eyes see too much. They're big and a bit frightening. You'll grow old, lonely and unloved the way you are. What shall I do with you?'

'Nothing, mama,' the maiden would reply.

Then she would do some work about the house. She might fetch water from the well or wash clothes by the river. She might wander about in the immemorial hum of the forest, or go to the square to gaze at the sculpture the whole village was talking about.

FOR ONE SO young, she was wise in the ways of art, though she didn't know it. As an only child she had spent much time watching her father in his secret workshop as he shaped magic symbols in gold or bronze. He worked like a sorcerer in wood and iron, with flint and fire and molten things.

He worked with spells and incantations, as if with the greatest secrets of life. He did inexplicable things. She watched in silence as he worked with sparks in the air, with plants and oils. She watched as he made a red rose appear on a white table, just by concentrating on the space.

Sometimes when he heard people coming towards the workshop, he would hurry out with his daughter through a concealed passage, into the forest, to spy on those who were trespassing on his terrain. Then the workshop would become invisible. A white mist, scented with roses, would envelop the surrounding spaces.

Once when the horsemen of a big chief had come to take him away, she saw her father vanish from their midst and turn into pure white air, leaving a falcon standing in his place.

The soldiers seized the bird, but her father's amused laughter echoed in the forest as they rode away.

SHE WAS WISE in the ways of art and gold because she had grown up in her father's workshop. He explained nothing to her. But when he wanted her to learn something he would cough, look at her in a certain way, and perform the operation slowly. She learnt in silence, by his example. She learnt also from the mood he created around him.

She learnt that all the great mysteries, and the art of making things happen, are simple if you know the laws involved. Her father embodied the laws. Everything he did was steeped in the arcane way. Yet he was light, simple, and unassuming. He could be taken for someone ordinary. When asked what he was doing, if he happened to be with friends, or having a drink, he might smile and say:

'I'm listening to the oracle.'

This was a favourite phrase of his, often used to deflect curiosity, and it became an expression of the tribe. They became known as people who listened to the oracle. Whenever someone was asked what they were doing, they invariably gave that reply, whether they were doing something trivial or not. Many of his expressions entered the language of the tribe that way.

He was mostly silent. His silence drew attention to what he said. His words resonated in the land and altered the thought-patterns of the age. The works of art that provoked the greatest reactions were suspected to be by his hand. Some claimed they could detect the tone of his spirit in certain works. He was considered the master artist and magus of the tribe.

The fact that he was the only one who never commented on works found in caves or forests, that he never took part in discussions caused by such finds, made him vaguely complicit in their creation.

Surrounded by mystery, radiant in health, luminous in aura, gifted with an awkward ability to appear normal, shining with integrity, respected by the mighty, feared by the ambitious, and regarded with awe by many, it is not surprising that many bizarre deeds in the land were attributed to him.

No one could stare long into his eyes. His mild and gentle face resisted inspection. People felt the unaccountable charge of his presence.

The maiden grew up in the protection of his legend. This helped to save her from complete isolation in the world.

10

WHEN HER FATHER was absent, her world returned to its particular strangeness. Often she sensed that trees, birds, flowers, and forms in the air were trying to tell her something. She felt the urge to learn their secret languages.

It seemed that the world had messages for her which she wasn't getting. This made her attentive to animals. She heard hidden meanings in what people said and sensed the presence of angels in unlikely places.

Often she had a feeling, while daydreaming between chores, that she had returned to her real home on a distant planet and was living a full life among forgotten loved ones there. This perplexed her.

Sometimes at night, when she slept, she found that she was the father of a whole tribe, its wise patriarch, with innumerable children. They could all fly and they built with their minds and they loved across time and space. They were masters of galaxies and they were bigger than giants, larger than the earth. Their heads grazed the outposts of heaven and their dreams took them to the realm of angels, in whose presence they were small.

And when she awoke it was always with a shock, as she realised that she could not fly, that her body had weight and that her thoughts were so unfree. She felt like a prisoner in her body. She felt like an exile, banished from a home she never knew.

And she wept often at dawn, at the humiliation of being human. She wept without knowing why. It was as if she suspected that she ought to be an angel, a being at ease among the stars.

THAT'S PERHAPS WHY she was silent. She was silent when the whole tribe was troubled by the latest work in the square, the big wooden sculpture of three men and a woman bound together at the ankles by chains. They gave the impression of stoic dignity, as if gods had been made the slaves of fools.

Everyone was stumped by it. No one had any idea what it meant. The sculpture was so powerful that it appeared in the midst of those who talked about it. Suddenly the sculpture was everywhere, in people's minds, their dreams, their work, their play. It haunted their every activity, like a spirit trying to draw attention to itself, or a nightmare that couldn't be shaken off, an illness that never arrives and never leaves.

The sculpture paralysed those who gazed on it. For after being seen, its horror grows, like an infection in the body. It was more terrible in the mind than in reality. Such was its impact that those who saw it did not know what to do with their heads afterwards. They wandered around obsessed and bad-tempered. Some felt the need to do something awful or undertake a spiritual pilgrimage. Many felt driven to find out as much as they could about the sculpture, how it came into being, what it was saying, and to do something about it.

But the sculpture was mute, and the elders began to whisper the unthinkable. They suggested that the work, in its ominous power, was sapping the soul of the tribe and that it should be hidden away as a dangerous object, or be destroyed before it ruined the spiritual cohesion of the people.

No work of art had ever had such a profound effect on the tribe. The sages suspected that sorcery was involved in the creation of the work. It bewildered the interpreters. The more they discussed it the more meanings and hints it revealed. Things got so bad that two men fought over their interpretations, and one of them was killed. It was the first time a man had died because a work of art could not be understood.

ONE MORNING, NOT long afterwards, a woman woke with a cry. She understood what the work meant. She said that it was an anathema that would come upon the land. Screaming that it was better to die than to suffer what was to come, she drank poison and died where the sculpture stood.

Soon everyone heard about this mysterious work that wreaked havoc on the mind. They came in their multitudes to see it. High-pitched wailing was heard at noon. Young girls fainted in its presence. One man went mad when he beheld it. A sage tied himself to it, making himself the fifth figure of the image. He refused to eat till he understood the work. He died on the fourteenth day, still bound to the sculpture.

The sage had declared that he should not be buried till someone had pierced the mystery of the work. His body rotted beside the sculpture for a month, spreading disease. Then the elders decreed that he must be buried far from the work, far from the shrine, to stop further contamination.

The sculpture continued to have its strange effect. People camped in front of it and refused to leave. The sculpture spoke of a tragedy of unimaginable proportions, a tragedy so great that it threatened the world. It seemed the world would never be the same again because of the intolerable suffering the work breathed out in its jagged forms and agonised shapes. Yet it spoke of divine resolution beyond human understanding.

13

THEN ONE EVENING a white bird with a yellow flower in its mouth alighted on the sculpture and all the people around began to weep spontaneously. It seemed that something about the sculpture, caused by the presence of the bird, precipitated a mass change in feeling.

The weeping went on all night. The women wept, and the children cried, and the men broke down into loud sobs too and couldn't be stopped. It seemed some deep unaccountable sorrow had awoken in them.

The weeping shook the tribe. Someone covered the work with a white cloth so it couldn't be seen. But its power multiplied in the minds of those who had seen it. The wise ones declared that it was better for the work to be seen than for people to be haunted by its power in the mind. They said that seeing the sculpture might soothe the madness it caused.

One night a group of elders arranged for the work to be stolen away. But in its place its absence shone. Its absence made more crowds gather; the space where it used to be became more magnetic than ever. It seemed to retain, in a cloud-like form, the very image they had removed.

People who had never seen the work before saw its form in the empty space. It was more majestic than ever. The empty space became more fascinating than any of the other shrines of the tribe. Multitudes gathered to witness the marvel of the sculpture that wasn't there. It shone in the dark like a living spirit.

THIS APPARITION OVERWHELMED the tribe. Every night the space of the invisible sculpture shone brighter than a full moon. Hallucinations descended on the people. And soon the sculpture appeared everywhere.

People saw it by the river; they saw it sailing past in the sky. Farmers saw it in their fields among the cornstalks. Hunters saw it disappearing behind baobab trees in the forest. Women saw it at the bottom of wells when they went to fetch water. There would be a sudden cry. Someone would rush out of their hut shouting that the absent sculpture stood near their bed. It became a plague of the mind.

The apparition roamed the countryside. It was glimpsed in the hills. A rumour ran wild in the land, and became real in the dark, as people reported that the image was multiplying. It was no longer four figures chained to one another; it was ten, then twenty, then a hundred. Then it was a whole tribe. Then it was a long chain of people stretching across the forests and savannahs, into the sea, swallowed by the waves of the nameless ocean.

After a month, the people didn't see the sculpture anymore, neither with their eyes, nor with their minds. It vanished completely. The space where it had been became truly empty.

A strange peace returned to the tribe.

THE MAIDEN HAD gone to see the work just before the elders had it removed. She was so oppressed by it that she couldn't sleep for weeks.

There are works of art, poisonous to the soul, that the eyes shouldn't see. There are works of art so terrible that they should only be seen as a reflection, in a mirror, like the head of the Medusa. There are works only meant for initiates and strong-souled masters. Such works should be hidden away, for generations, their power changed by time into the gold of their highest fruition.

There are works of art that should be described to the young, hinted at, till the young are fortified enough to know such terrible truths. The work that had caused upheaval in the tribe was as troubling and mysterious as any of these.

She saw the work in the flush of her youth, in her awkward, dreaming years. She intuited that the work was the beginning of the end of a great cycle. She did not know what cycle that was, but she did know that in some way the work signalled the end. It hinted at the end of her world, and the playtime of the tribe. The end of the easy spaces between the living and the dead. The end of healing art and a storytelling life. The end of songs and incantatory cymbals and dances that speaks of everything. The end of the sun and its power to renew the spiritual journey of the tribe. The end of the gods. The end of meaning in life and purpose in living. The sculpture filled her with all these terminal intuitions.

16

WAS THIS WORK a sign that the gods had abandoned the people? What else could it be?

It showed three men and a woman, chained together, all of them huge like giants, their heads bowed, their faces broken. The greatest humiliation had been heaped on their bodies. And yet they shone, like gods, unconquerable even in the vilest suffering. Something about the towering nature of the work suggested that only the great can bear such suffering. They bore evils and still their light shone through. They bore it as a sacrifice, a purification, for the human race.

The injustice and the nobility of the sculpture was what broke the spirit of the maiden. She saw the work and was never the same again. It was as if she had been poisoned by a glimpse into her own destiny.

SHE WAS UNABLE to sleep after the encounter. At night she stared at the moon and the stars, and sang tribal laments and wept. She muttered disconnected phrases about evil. In her dreams she drowned at sea to a chorus of songs she didn't understand. She was haunted by the notion that she was surrounded by the children of a fat servile wife with white hair.

Her mind was troubled by visions. Obsession chased her eyes inwards. The sculpture tormented and accused her. In waking dreams one of the figures was her father. Leaning over her, he spoke.

'My daughter, if God cracks the sacred vessel, God leaks into it. What God breaks, God fills. We break that we may be blessed. We have to make a choice about who we are going to be, but we have not made it. We suffer because we have not chosen. We could be powerful on this earth. Instead we scratch the soil, like animals. But time will flow back to the kingdom. Our suffering will be changed into the gold of the soul. And history will be a strange dream read in an invisible book among the stars.'

But she didn't understand these words. She babbled at dawn and cried out about the horror of the work. Her father, playing a flute, administering potions, tried to soothe her spirit. But she was hard to soothe. She was proof that a work of art can succeed too well and cause evil.

Her father considered this. He considered the responsibility of master makers. If what they create unleashes disturbances on the people, mustn't they also be healers? But how do you heal that which, to grow, must be ruptured? Mustn't the gourd of the human be broken for the higher spirit to leak in? How do you heal that which, in the fullness of time, must be for the greater glory of all things?

18

'WHAT AILS YOU, my child?'

'All the evils in the world.'

'How do you know about them?'

'I saw them in that sculpture.'

'That work is just a dream.'

'It has woken us to horrors, but not shown us how to live with them. It's better to die than to know such things.'

'You blame the work?'

'Everyone curses the work and its maker,' cried the daughter.

Her father was shaken by her reply. He stared into the amber of things. He stared into the dust and red gold. He thought about the light that enters through the wounds, bleeding history on an invisible sea. He stayed silent.

Far away, in the forest, he heard life and death in the wind, like twins. Trees called out the names of the fallen and the taken. No one heard the trees. No one heard the names.

'The maker too was in a dream,' the father said at last, wearily.

'Then curse the dream if we must wake from it and see. We cannot bear to see, father. It makes us mad to see.'

The father didn't say anything more. The maiden slept. He breathed incantations over her. He spoke to her future and strengthened her soul, preparing her for her destiny.

EVERYONE IN THE tribe was an artist. Into art they were born. Art conceived them, gave birth to them, nourished them, and helped them grow. Art sustained their lives and guided them.

Art devoured them. They grew old and died of it. They were buried in art. In art they were immortalised.

Art was their god and their devil, their destruction and regeneration. All things came from it and fed back into it. Art was their religion, their science, their seduction, and their recreation. It was their hell and their heaven.

Every crisis came out of art and was redeemed by it. Plagues were seen as a failure of their art, a failure to see, to listen, to interpret, to prophesy. A failure to have vision. Famines were perceived as a curse, because of their failure to create, to anticipate, to adapt, to move on to fruitful places, to be free. Diseases, illnesses, bad fortune, were all perceived as failures of art, the art of living.

At the shrines of creativity and truth, they were humble. To them the god of art ensured balance and harmony in the universe.

GOOD FORTUNE, THE beauty of their children, festivities, wonderful harvests, and happiness were signs of success in their art. This meant that the doors between heaven and earth, between the spirits and the living, between past and future, nature and humans, man and woman, were open. And because those doors were open no bad things festered. For the bad things emerged, were seen, and transcended.

Their laws were laws of art. Known laws and unknown ones, esoteric and exoteric, superficial and deep. There were important laws of disharmony and imbalance. To them chaos and asymmetry were profound laws.

They no longer favoured such simple things as harmony and balance. These had been fully explored for generations. They had advanced to the higher beauty of broken cadences, the lightning flash of forms that cracks the soul asunder, till a new vision is glimpsed.

They favoured tactical rawness and strategic indirection. They liked eyes where the navel should be. For the navel is a kind of eye, and the eye is a navel linking humans to the unknown world. They liked fusions and metaphors.

They had their aphorisms of art. The greater the chaos, the greater the art needed to create the highest beauty and, paradoxically, the greatest simplicity. The most complex works ought to appear as lucid as a child's song. The work of the greatest masters should speak to a child or the village idiot.

THEY BELIEVED THAT art was the bridge to the creator. Art was their prayer and confession, their work and play, their meditation and striving, their illness and healing.

To other people, wealth, status, beauty, and lineage were desirable in marriage. But to this tribe, it was art. Men wooed women with art. Works that showed intelligence, courage, steadfastness, strength of spirit, tenderness, imagination, love, and humour influenced a woman's choice of husband. If you weren't a good artist, you didn't stand a chance of getting an excellent wife. Men also chose wives by their art. The works of women that showed wisdom, subtlety, delicacy, patience, beauty, resilience, capacity for reconciliation, good-heartedness, and the inspiring of good dreams influenced a man's choice of wife. If you weren't a subtle artist, you didn't stand a chance of getting a fine husband.

When families wanted to bring couples together, they first exchanged works of art. These works were lived with, slept with, thought about. The inner characters of the individuals were thereby allowed to emerge. Interpreters were hired to read the spirit of the couples through their works.

The tribe believed that nothing revealed a person more than their art. As individuals they could deceive or conceal. But in their art the truth about them is naked. Beauty in art was not enough, for beauty sometimes revealed a troubled personality, or an unstable mind. What is concealed reveals what is absent. Coolness may mask excessive passion, or deadness of heart. Too much passion may mask an absence of feeling. It may also reveal frivolity, sentimentality, lack of perspective.

Size counts for nothing. The small may reveal huge ambition. The large may reveal laziness, or the inability to concentrate. The small may also hint at a mania to control, and the large may show generosity of spirit, if combined with care and focus.

Reading the character behind the art was intrinsic to the tribe. All were born interpreters. But some were specialists. If they were great artists, they sat on the highest councils of the tribe.

22

EVERYTHING WAS AN aspect of art. Farming was based on aesthetics.

Maximum effect from minimum effort was the artistic principle on which war was conducted. They believed in winning without fighting.

The tribe was rare in having perfected the art of war. They rarely fought. When they had to fight, they fought spiritually. They fought artistically. Their victories were never public. There was no bloodshed. No one felt conquered. Often it seemed as if they had lost. In this way, they thrived. Warfare was anathema to them, because it reduced the number of artists in the world.

Another tenet of the tribe was that all men and women were artists. To be alive was to be a co-creator. At least you created a destiny.

As all people were artists, humanity was considered the greatest work of art. All are contributing to the greatest vision that will ever be, the vision of above and below, on earth and in heaven.

The tribe was therefore fundamentally serene about all things. They lived in the freedom of a knowledge that was more than knowledge.

23

FROM BIRTH CHILDREN were encouraged to create, to dream things. There was no word for art in the language. Art was not God. It was one of God's ways of creating the universe. The universe was the ultimate work of art.

To the tribe, vision was primal. But it must be the vision of creators, their ideal, their hopes, their purpose, even when purpose is denied.

To have no purpose was considered highest. It implied that the artist had submitted themselves to a vision greater than themselves. They were only the channels by which mysteries came to be. The tribe believed that only a poor artist knows what they have created.

The greatest masters say nothing about their work because there is nothing to say. There is nothing to say save that it was done. It was seen, rendered, and remembered. It was carried across, brought here, imperfectly.

They believed that the less one makes, the more one makes.

24

IMPERFECTION WAS A great law of the tribe. They were always unlearning. They begin as masters and end as children. They end innocent and not quite here. Rooted on earth and in heaven at the same time.

Sophistication, brilliance, allusion, richness, metaphor, politics, and beauty in a work were considered signs of youth and its greatness. The great masters, however, had nothing. Their works were empty. But the world read everything into this emptiness. They read their own fears, desires, intuitions, and communal prophecies.

Sometimes an incomparable work of art is a charged empty space at which multitudes converge.

A space in which mass revelations occur. Like the space that now obsessed the maiden.

IN THAT TRIBE everything that happened to the individual became art, if it did not become illness. When they were ill, when they had troubles of the mind, they had to create the art that would heal them.

Other tribes came to them for art that could heal sicknesses in the land. But one of their central beliefs was that if an individual in the tribe was ill they had to make the work of art that would lead to their healing. It could be a carving, a culinary combination, a design of cloth, a game, a meditation on a leaf, a song with a magic refrain, a dance, measured breathing, a good conversation, an intelligent argument, excellent cursing or love.

The invention of riddles, parables, word-play, puns, sounds without meaning but with hidden power, an insight, an intuition, an invented symbol, a blending of herbs, were all considered works of art. Initiation into the mysteries was deemed spirit art.

When the maiden fell ill because of her obsession with the vanished sculpture, it became clear that she had to create the art of her own healing.

THE TRIBE LOOKED forward to an individual creating the art of their own healing. Everyone paid attention to the art created. It revealed the secret cause of the problem. Often it might reveal something about the tribe. Often it might be personal. If it was personal, it enriched the gossip of the tribe.

As with all people who work with the spirit, gossip was also revealing. It was a kind of art too. Rumours hinted at what would become true in an unknown form.

It was soon rumoured that the maiden was preparing to go into seclusion, to receive the vision for her own healing. That she was the daughter of an enigmatic master made the rumours that much more interesting. Some said she had chosen a cave. There was excitement about what she might create. Many wondered if she had inherited her father's touch. She would be the test of his powers. If she proved average, this would diminish the myth that surrounded him.

That was the nature of gossip. One becomes significant or diminished, in absentia, for the amusement of the tribe.

THE MAIDEN OFTEN followed the trail of ants, just to see where they led. She spent hours learning the destination of snails. Her mother fed her fried unripe plantains, fresh spinach, and watercress from faraway markets. She bathed her daughter like a little child, and prayed over her, and tempted her with lovely bales of newly dyed cloth. She nourished her, sang to her, beautified her. She watched her daughter wander off to the river and watched her return with a gourd of water on her head, or a basin of washed clothes, singing a sad song to the wind. These moments both warmed and saddened her mother's heart.

'What will we do with you, my strange child?' her mother would sigh.

From birth an unusual destiny had been foretold for her daughter. An ambiguous star had hovered over the moment of her conception. This is not a child from here. She is from a distant star. Her people are not human. They have faces like the gods. They travel from one end of the world to another on moonbeams. They are sent to other worlds to live out a story that has one meaning to that world and another meaning to their own people. What seems like suffering to us is to them a dream. They suffer only when they forget that they are free. For most of her life it will seem as if she is lost. Then one day she will wake up and she will be comfortable in her body. Then her real life will begin, beyond the sea. She will bring the music of a distant star into the narrow spaces of this earth, and reconcile the people to their forgotten origins.

But who says these things, who whispers them? Fortune-tellers of the tribe catch stories from faraway stars, as they sleep by the shrine, when it is the hour of prophecy. There are voices that whisper from the universe into the hearts of mothers. There are things that speak from the invisible future. Messages appear from the book of life. The past is untold, the present unclear. The future has been and gone: it whispers in dreams, in signs, in song.

Her mother listened to it all as she fed, coaxed, and nourished her. Meanwhile the maiden prepared to create the art of her own healing.

The mother watched the maiden grow odder, plainer, slighter, as if she were a bird puzzled by the sorcery of flight. And yet she could taste the clouds already.

The mother nourished her daughter and gazed on her as one lost to destiny.

ENIGMAS GREW IN the maiden's heart and made her simple life complicated. The rituals of the tribe became distant to her. She felt herself becoming an outsider to her land, to her body, to her life. She didn't know why.

Often at night she would wake in the stifling heat of the clay hut and would bring out a doll she had fashioned long ago. She would whisper stories into its ears of fragrant wood. Sometimes she would bring out the bronze bust of the young queen she had made. She would speak to it as if it were her. She felt on those nights that she could be a young queen, lost to her kingdom, or a servant girl. She liked the idea of being either. Sometimes she played the role of the servant girl to the bust of the young queen.

'Is there anything you want?' she would whisper, and then, in the dark, she would bathe or dress the queen.

As she slept, she lived out many adventures which she never remembered, with people who were familiar but whom she had not seen before. Then she would wake up a little confused to find herself on a raised clay bed, in a warm clay abode, in a room that was unfamiliar to her. Then the illness brought on by her obsession with the sculpture would take hold of her again, like a sickness of the mind.

Half in a dream, she would set about her chores. She fetched water, washed clothes, helped her mother prepare breakfast, brought in firewood from the forest, and cleaned the house with broom and wet cloth. When her morning's work was accomplished she would hurry to her father's workshop.

What she saw depended on what her father allowed her to see.

She would sit quietly on the floor and watch him work, or pace, or stare at the wall. Then suddenly he would pounce on an unfinished work. With swift sure motions he would carve from the block of wood a living form that a moment ago didn't want to live.

29

HER FATHER'S WORKSHOP teemed with dreams and indigo moods. She was convinced spirits were there and that her father created his astonishing works with their help.

She had often heard him speak to them in a strong voice. She had seen him give orders to this or that portion of air. He spoke with great clarity, as if they were hard-working attendants that needed things spelled out.

Her father's workshop was alive with these invisible attendants. Often while she dozed, in that atmosphere of teak and smoky presences, she saw them. They would be planing, glazing, polishing, varnishing, casting, carrying, and shaping the creations in wood that populated the workshop. She saw them as rather intelligent and humorous-looking beings.

The spirits did exactly what they were told to do, no more and no less. They followed instructions to the letter and to the limit. Nothing altered their mood. They were always cheerful. Though they were made of light and air, they seemed indestructible. They worked without rest. Even when her father had shut up the workshop for the day, they seemed to go on working. They banged and hammered, as if always at the endless artistic tasks which the master had set them.

When the maiden woke, she never saw the spirits. They seemed to vanish in an instant. All she saw were the brooding sculptures that jostled for space in the crammed workshop.

The sculptures were everywhere. They were fiendishly, mischievously, alive. They breathed out of their wooden nostrils. They stared, pitilessly, at their surroundings. They listened to everything, rather intensely. They seemed, more than anything else, to be thinking. Their definite opinions and judgements were tangible, like dark wooded mist, in the shadow-filled spaces of the workshop. There were many thoughts, moods, and notions in that air.

There were demons with wild eyes and tranquil brows, children with intelligent eyes and antelope ears. There were crocodiles and monsters and severe warriors and sages who gazed with sublime indifference upon all things. Kings who were lascivious and cruel and lazy-eyed, like lions after a huge dinner, stood beside half-human creatures of unimaginable beauty. Loveable fools, lonely old women, girls in love, law-makers, and the mad jostled next to one another. Twins, facing different directions, stared from huge panels. In shadowed corners gods and goddesses reigned in the light of their own radiance. All permutations of the real and imagined lived there, in wood and stone and bronze. They all breathed and dwelled in the dark spaces of the workshop.

One of her favourite works was a tortoise so real that it seemed to move, ever so slowly…

She could never disprove the mystery of its motion.

HER FATHER WAS at his trestle table, in his work-clothes. He worked as if he had seven arms, as if there were three of him. Sometimes she counted her father in four places at once. He would be planing here, hammering there, stretching the skin of an animal over wood to fool the eye, or rooting in the shadows in his shrine. He was always working with spells and incantations that charged the atmosphere of the workshop and sent her off into dreaming.

She had the oddest dreams in her father's workshop. She dreamt that she was on a ship tossing on the waves. She was in its bowels, lying upside down, with a chain on her ankles. She was facing the feet of another who was also chained. There was blood on the chains. She was like one dead. She floated above the chained people who were lying head to foot, and foot to head, in the vile-smelling hold of the ship. There was wailing everywhere in the crushed space. Women were dying and calling out the names of their ancestors in many languages. Death and doom was thick in the dream. She saw hundreds of bodies drowning in the white waves. She howled in the dream and drifted away among the stars. Then forms in mists of gold led her back down to a land where dead humans were planted and long sweet canes grew from the earth of their bodies. Then at last she saw the sea differently and returned to her home of giants.

What dreams she had, in her father's workshop, as she listened to his incantations...

And while still in the dream she would see spirits appear in the workshop, as if conjured out of the smoky atmosphere.

32

THE FIRST TO appear was the spirit of fire. He was a mighty figure and he shone like polished bronze. His face was impassive and severe. His eyes were made of flames. The air crackled and fizzled when he appeared. He was silent and awaited his instructions.

'Spirit of power, spirit of fire,

Obey my command, and make things higher.'

With this, her father sent him to the forge at the back of the workshop. Immediately the blazing copper glowed in the moulds. They would become life-like busts of kings and queens and the father god who created all things from the great word.

The second spirit to appear had a smiling face. He was the spirit of making. He had seven hands and three heads and many eyes. He was tough and lithe. His eyes shone like moonlight.

'Spirit of making, secret of the ages,

Obey my command, work in stages.'

He received his instruction with big smiles and a happy mood, and was soon busy with wood and basalt stone. He began carving, from their raw shapes, the forms that the master had outlined.

The third, light as air, was the spirit of inspiration. She was luminous and beautiful. Constantly changing form, she radiated pure delight. Her aura shone clearly all around.

'Spirit of inspiration, awaiting a simple instruction,

Obey my command, reveal our civilisation.'

And with her face turned inward, her gem-like eyes transfigured the clutter of the workshop into a paradise of art, a promised land.

The maiden was happy as a child at the appearance of the third spirit. She marvelled at how, upon receiving instructions from her father, it vanished into air and became the magic that shone from all things, as if the mother goddess was revealing herself in all that was.

Her father worked on in his splendour. His taut skin shone through the sweat of his brow. His three eyes were brilliant in the dark light of the workshop.

33

THE MAIDEN SAW the glow of the forge in the distance and the brightness of gold flowing into future forms. She heard the steady sound of a head taking shape from the trunk of a dead tree. And she listened to her father murmuring at his work bench, invoking new forms into being, teasing a living face out of stone.

All over the workshop the spirits were busy. Their hands were everywhere. They went past in silence and never spoke. They never ruined anything. When their task was finished, they went to the master for further instructions.

They ended a task with the same tranquillity with which they began it. They were never tired, never elated. They began and ended in the same mood, engaged in an infinite work in which beginnings and endings were merely illusions.

The spirits were alive during the enchanted hours of work, the unforgettable hours of her youth. The rumours might be true. Her father might be the unknown master of the sculpture that brought on her illness. Clearly he worked with spirits. What else could explain the genius of the man? Where else did his towering productivity come from, if not from the spirits?

She always meant to ask him about this.

One day, she remembered to do so. She woke gently, stirring on the bench. She noticed the spirits vanish into the dark spaces with her awakening. In the face of vanishing evidence, risking the wrath of interrupting his concentration, she decided to broach her question.

'Father, is it true that you use spirits to do your work?'

There was a long silence. Then the silence spoke. What did it say? It said: Child, questions do not ask the questions you

106

really want to ask. They disturb the order of things. They bring forth answers that might trouble you forever, answers you might wish had not been brought forth. Do you know what you are doing asking questions, child? Terrors hide in questions. Prolong your happiness, in these years of enchantment, when all is well in the dark groves of childhood, where dreams are as real as rivers.

34

THAT WAS WHAT the silence said, as she listened to cobwebs growing in the dark and lizards scuttling among the thinking forms of stone heads.

Many years and many dreams passed before the silence was over. In that time she had been raped by a slave-master across the seas. She endured it repeatedly, at noon, when the house slept. Three children to two slave-masters had been borne. One night she had run away and walked six hundred and twelve miles to join a colony of freed slaves. She had grown old telling stories of her magical childhood to incredulous children. And then by candlelight she was dying. She was with the ancestors, and at peace. She had just grasped the deep meaning of her life's suffering and the forgotten beauty, when the long silence ended. Then she heard her father, in his gentle sonorous voice, answer the question she thought she had asked.

'Do you see spirits?' he said.

She was awake now. She heard time's gentle flight in the silence. Its wings brushed her face, ageing her tenderly, beginning her long silent bloom. She could not see the spirits. But she was sure they were there.

'I see them when I sleep,' she replied.

'In your dreams?'

Was there a mocking smile in her father's interrogation? Not mocking. Amused. An amused smile in his voice. Are you ready for revelation, child? the silence seemed to say after he had spoken.

'Yes, I think in my dreams.'

'You dream of spirits?'

'Yes, I think so. But they are real, and they are usually here, working for you.'

'But in your dreams.'

'Yes, father, in my dreams. But they are real.'

'But you are dreaming them.'

'Yes, father.'

'So you are responsible for them.'

'No, father.'

'Why not?'

'Because in the dreams it is you who commands them. It is you they obey.'

'Do I create your dreams?'

The father was smiling broadly now. Are you ready to be enlightened, child? the silence seemed to say.

'I don't know.'

'You mean you suspect I can do it if I want?'

'It seems to me, father, that you can do anything.'

A silence, like a calming mantle, descended on her. A cooling sensation. Did the world change a little? She felt it had, but did not know how. It was as if an inaudible vowel sound had altered the spaces. Her father seemed transfigured, on the verge of being invisible. He was a work of art himself, whose meaning always eludes.

'All the questions you will ever ask were answered before you were born, my daughter. All you have to do is remember, or return.'

'How? You confuse me.'

'In our tribe we create out of dreams but we create in broad daylight. Our works have more meaning and more truth than we realise at the time. But it is not meaning or truth that we seek.'

'What do we seek?'

'We seek the source. That's why we are detached about what we create. It serves a higher purpose than we understand. The artist who creates is not important. Only what they create is important. Servants of the higher powers are helped to do their work. That is why some have the power of ten while others have the power of dust. Through our works must shine not the power of the person, but the power of the source. True fame should belong to the force that guides us in the dark.'

THE FATHER STOPPED. She had been listening to another lesson which she heard while her father had been speaking. Her father's voice was a bridge to another realm, where the real learning is done. When her father stopped, her secret lesson was over.

A bizarre joy filled her heart. Had she heard a word of what her father said? Only much later, in another land, in the fragrance of honeysuckle, on one of the few days of her adult life when she knew true happiness, did she hear what her father said. But she heard it only because she repeated it, to her child, who would one day change the world through the power of art.

Her father breathed deeply. The maiden listened. She was now back in the workshop, in the shadows, among the iroko heads and wall geckos and cobwebs and eyes that look but do not see and faces that carry into the future the only traces of a tribe vanished from the earth forever.

She was back now and listening. Her father did not speak for a moment. When he did it was in disconnected fragments, as though repeating words that were being whispered to him.

As if in a dream, he said:

'We are listeners to the oracle. Some listen, but do not hear. Some hear, but do not listen. Those who hear are touched and changed.'

Then he said:

'Free to be truthful to their dreams.'

A little later:

'But they live, invisibly.'

And with a pause:

'After the suffering, gold.'
A short silence. Then:
'When they don't notice, best work is done.'
With a soft inflection:
'Obscure life of a master.'
And with a sigh:
'When they see you, hide again.'

36

HE SPOKE AS if he were somewhere else.

His words seemed to join, dance, and separate in her mind. They seemed spoken not just by her father, but by the spirits she could not see, and by the stone heads and the bronze busts and the figures brooding and breeding in the nocturnal spaces of the workshop.

The fragments became words from beyond. She listened as her life changed.

'We do not see what we judge.'

'Conditions change.'

'Now is not now.'

'The winners have lost.'

'Life is a masquerade.'

'What we are seeing is not what is happening.'

'There is a shadow over all victories.'

'It is not here that life is lived. Only where it is felt.'

'All are dreams.'

'It rises and it falls.'

'Only in light can truth be found.'

'The real condition of things does not show.'

'To die is not all.'

'Plant there, reap here.'

'Seek the light that comes from the rose and the cross and the vanished kingdom under the sea.'

'Prosperity and poverty are not what they seem.'

'Beyond is where it really begins.'

'Slaves are masters in heaven.'

'Whatever happens, it is getting better.'

'Then all will be one.'

THE FRAGMENTS BECAME whispers. Then there was a long silence. They say sorcerers can transport your spirit to distant lands, while leaving your body behind. These fragments from her father transported her to many places. Now, in the silence, she was unsure of the world in which she found herself. She was uncertain even of her father's existence.

She was nonplussed. Questions she hadn't asked were being answered. Fathers have their way of initiating their children into the unknown journey ahead.

There was a sigh and a smile from her father in the dark. Was he there? Had he gone? Had he left the sigh and smile behind?

The maiden, seeing nothing in the dark, waited for it to become clearer. But the silence said: Child, nothing gets clearer here, only there. The clearer, the more unclear. Nothing is completed here, only there. Here is incompleteness. Unfinished things. Fragments.

What else was being said?

She listened. Then, from out of the dark, with no one there to have uttered them, came the words:

'And still they are haunted by the work.'

And nothing more.

38

SHE FOUND HERSELF alone in the workshop, with only her father's complex mood lingering in the air. Maybe he had never been there. She got up from the chair and made her way home. As she walked down the forest path she breathed in the fragrance of asphodels.

There was something in her that was still unwell. Whatever it was had been deepened, not altered. Yes, she was still haunted by the sculpture of chained figures. Enigmas grew about her heart and made strange her simple life.

Time felt precious and new, as if it were over. And all she had was the fragrance of a life vanished forever in a fading dream.

II

1

THE TRIBE WAS still expecting her to create a work that would heal the sickness of her spirit. Their expectation weighed her down. They asked her many questions about the work. It became the subject of rumours and gossip. It was not unusual for two people to meet and have a conversation like this:

'Is there any news yet of the work she is supposed to be doing?'

'She broods, but does not breed.'

'An illness that does not produce art is a bad illness indeed.'

'Her father is strange.'

'Was he not seen on the moon some time ago, dancing with spirits?'

'Some say he made the sculpture that nearly drove us all mad.'

'The one that has poisoned the mind of his daughter?'

'Maybe his art is a curse.'

'One word from him and we might have to change our location again, like cattle in the hills.'

'I'm not surprised that his daughter behaves the way she does.'

'Lions with blood in their eyes don't give birth to roosters.'

The forest would echo their laughter.

'It is not good when there are illnesses but no art.'

'When there are sicknesses that are not fruitful.'

'It means that the wells become poisoned.'

'The crops give bad harvest.'

'Sickness without song makes the whole tribe sick.'

'Her failure to heal herself will be catching.'

'Children will get new diseases because of her.'

'The daughter of our powerful master will become an abomination unto us.'

'Problems of the powerful destroy the land.'

'They have to clear up their troubles.'

'And give us art to make the air good again to breathe.'

'She must create something, before we all die.'

'Or we will have to banish her.'

'Send her into the hills.'

'To join those infertile in art.'

'We will not perish because one person is unable to dream.'

'We must protect us all.'

'That sick girl will not create our fall.'

The speakers would separate and spread their unease through the tribe. Others did the same. Slowly the unease and the expectations worked on the maiden and made her illness worse.

2

ABOUT THIS TIME she had the feeling that some significant event should be happening to her, but wasn't. Her body was full of a ripe rich expectation. Her heart would burst into bizarre palpitations, as if any moment someone she longed for all her life would suddenly appear and take her away to a land of dream.

She became jumpy. She peered into every stranger's face, and waited for a voice.

She fell into a condition akin to stupidity, and wandered about in a state of pitiful innocence.

In an odd way the same thing was happening to the tribe. Everyone lived in a state of wide-eyed waiting, expecting something momentous to happen without warning. Ennui and restlessness descended on them like a fatal ailment. Resignation crept over everything. Artisans worked listlessly at their masks, women drowsily wended their way to the river, and children dully played. Dense breezes brought heat, forgetfulness, and a sleepwalking quality by day.

The tribe seemed to empty out, to become hollowed and diminished. Masks and masquerades, awaiting their spirit possession, hung about the village square devoid of significance.

Some fearful thing was devouring the spirit of the tribe. Some dreaded thing was devouring the soul of the land.

For the tribe was the secret heart of the land.

3

THIS NEW DEADLY air was never more visible than at the secret council meetings of the hidden masters of the tribe. Their meetings took place once every three moons. They convened always in the dead of night.

They came without candles or lamps; and wore masks so as not to be recognised by other members, either by their voices or faces. Only certain passwords, signs, and handshakes permitted them entry into the long room of power.

No one knew how they were chosen. But those chosen had to have performed near-miraculous deeds. There had to be constant wisdom shown. There had to be spiritual power made evident in their art.

The requirements were severe, but seldom attained. Originally, it was only those who had achieved a degree of illumination, who could command spirits, enter the dreams of multitudes, foresee the future, and had a high command of their art, who were initiated as masters of the tribe. It did not matter if they were men or women. Then with the passing of time admittance was lowered to those who could accomplish one or two of those feats. It helped also if they had noble impersonality and a cosmic sense of humour.

Their powers were always in harmony with the spiritual needs of the land. They listened at the oracle of people's art. They went into the seed of things, to avert disasters, to combat evil in the place where it is born. They sought to replenish the soul of the people.

If the quality of masters fell, the tribe was in peril. There was once a time when brash individuals of low calibre dominated the council. They nearly destroyed the foundations of the tribe.

An important lesson was learnt. A people are only as great as the quality of the masters who guide them. This was never so clear as when the people were confronted with a great crisis.

There are two kinds of crisis: visible and invisible. Visible crises can be overwhelming, but at least they are seen. If they prove destructive, the people have only themselves to blame. They saw but did not take action.

Invisible crises present the greater threat to the survival of a people.

It is from invisible dangers that a people are more likely to perish. Dangers that cannot be seen. Dangers without a name, or a face. Dangers that enter a land and destroy it before anyone knows they are there. Then afterwards only a few standing stones and shards of pottery in the sands and skulls rolling in the wind give any sign that a magical tribe once lived joyfully in a land now grown over with trees or made barren with dust.

To sense invisible dangers before they bring destruction is one of the great gifts of the wise. To heed their warnings is the good fortune of a people. For it a blessing of the spirit to be able to understand how unseen dangers can bring about the end. Many civilisations have not been so fortunate. History is written with their bones.

It was such a danger, which did not seem like danger, but mere malaise, that confronted the tribe. The secret masters gathering in anonymity sensed something they did not know they were sensing.

4

THEY ARRIVED LIKE ghosts at the appointed hour. They arrived in silence. Even the old didn't rustle the night with their white capes.

Degeneracy would soon devastate the core of the land, but before the age of dust some last splendour survived. Even in that atmosphere of last days, when fireflies flickered under the spell of doom that had slipped into the earth, some glory remained.

At the previous meeting the masters had sat in complete silence, with nothing to say about anything. They sipped their harsh alcohol and chewed kola nuts and kaoline as if in a trance. Those who did not drink stared straight ahead. The opening ritual had been listless and for the first time in years seemed irrelevant. Nothing to say. Nothing seen. Nothing thought. Just silence like poison drunk in the dark. At the earliest signs of dawn they had melted like shadows back to their homes.

Not all the masters had been present. A few had not attended the meetings for years.

The last meeting infected the present one. Malaise had become the new mode. They sat again in silence. They were mostly old, but vigorous. They had lived out time in prophecies. Their skins were cracked, their eyes drained by enchantments. Their mouths had been political about the oracles and distorted the messages of the gods. Now all these masters, blended into one spirit that was the council, were silent and unable to function.

Some sickness had befallen the oracle. The well of divination had been corrupted. No one knew how. History was delivering a strange verdict on the land, a parable to future ages. And it was among the council that the enigma of history was first made clear. No one could read the signs or interpret the parable that they were living through. Does the feather feel the death of the sun?

The masters sat staring at one another's form in the dark. Silence, and nothing to say. The desert had arrived in the heart of the forest. Scattered remains of bronze busts emerging from the earth will tell a tale no one can hear. It started there. In the dark.

Then as if an invisible ray of light penetrated the walls and illuminated an essential spot, an unknown voice among the masters began to speak. The person recounted a persistent dream which they had persistently forgotten. Now, at last, it was remembered.

5

IT WAS A dream about a golden heron lost in its own dream by the river. Beautiful white birds descended on the heron and tore off its feathers and broke its wings and left it dying on the riverbank. It lay for ninety-nine years. It was wounded, but not dead. The birds had also fallen on the heron's nest and carried off many of its children. Most of them died and the others were scattered about the world in terrible conditions.

The scattered herons did not know one another anymore. They forgot that they were the children of the golden heron.

The children suffered and grew and changed in these different lands. Meanwhile the mother heron lay wounded by the river. The children left at home were not the same anymore either. They lost their way and spent most of their time fighting one another.

Then one day all the birds in the world discovered that they were descended from one bird. They learnt, to their surprise, that the dying heron was of their family. Then they realised that if the heron was dying, they were dying too.

The voice telling of the dream fell silent at this point. He did not speak again for the rest of the council meeting. The masters listened with an attentive and listless air. They listened to the silence too. They had nothing to say. No interpretations to offer. They were sunken in the malaise that had infected the dream-enclosed tribe.

With the hint of dawn at the edges of the sky, the council members slipped back in silence into the anonymity of their lives.

6

THE MAIDEN CONTINUED to suffer. Her body confused her. She felt that she shouldn't really have a body. It restricted her, prevented her flight and freedom.

She was sick, but she bloomed. She thought she was expiring, but she was in vibrant health. She felt awkward, but was graceful. Her body was heavy, but she skipped about like a young gazelle. Weighed down with unhappiness, she was often giddy with delight, her head spinning. She felt like dying, yet she loved life like a young bird in spring.

She walked about in a dream and heard nothing that anyone said. She ran her errands imperfectly and said silly and irrelevant things. She would suddenly burst out laughing for no other reason than that a bubble of happiness had risen in the pit of her belly. While listening to the drums near the shrine, or staring at the clouds, or walking in the forest, or skipping on the sands near their house, she would suddenly fall into weeping. Then for no reason she would hurry home, throw her arms round her mother's neck and kiss her, or she might start to carve a face in ebony and would stop just when its beauty was beginning to emerge...

7

THE SAME THING, in a different way, was happening to the masters in their nocturnal meetings.

They had intuitions, but no clear understanding. Haunted by impulses, their tongues were leaden. Omens flitted about them, but interpretation eluded their minds. Oracles spoke to them, but their hearts were deaf. Tremors happened beneath them, but they felt only the movement of the wind in the raffia rooftop in the dark.

They sat and stared and brooded. Dreams floated past them. In the silence they heard worlds coming to an end in the hollow cry of birds in the sleeping forests.

8

AT THE NEXT meeting the unknown voice continued to talk about the dream.

'... and the white birds realised with horror what their ancestors had done. They couldn't sleep well because of it. They wanted to change the terrible things that had come to pass. Meanwhile the descendants of the golden heron learnt about their origin. Then the scattered tribes all over the world decided to visit their ancestral home. They made a great journey back to the mother. They brought the lost time and the lost rain with them. The gifts of the centuries they brought back with them. They flew the long distances and converged at the riverbank. It was a great day in history. The mother heron was overcome with the love her descendants from all over the world showered on her. She was revived by the compensations made by the descendants of the white birds, for what they had done. And she was strengthened by the kinship and solidarity of all birds. She made a miraculous recovery and became what she would never have become without these tragic events. She became a gift of the sun. And because of her regeneration the kingdom of birds was raised higher in the scheme of things. A new cycle of history began, leading to the fulfilment of the golden prophecies.'

The masters listened to the recounting of this elaborate dream. When it was finished, silence reigned. Nothing was said.

The sense of apprehension continued.

9

AMONG MASTERS, IN the council meetings, extraordinary things sometimes happened. Miraculous occurrences give rise to tales of wonder that blind pilgrims on the path of enlightenment. It diverts them into a desire for amazing deeds and visitations and magic. Among masters great feats that lead to stories are impure. The true quest is for peace and simplicity, an intuition in which all things are clear.

Understanding is a glass of pure water. All great truths have no taste. The need for sweetness is a craving for amazement.

Among masters astonishment is suspect. A desire for glory is a sign of spiritual collapse. Soon afterwards people lose their way. Deceptions have the greatest charm to the eye.

The tribe had long been the home of myth and fabulous legends. But they forgot something which they discovered long ago: that with too much myth, an excess of magic, the road to heaven is undone. What captivates the eye blinds the soul to its true destination. When people are amazed, the inward gaze of paradise is diminished.

The masters of the tribe knew this. They knew the fatal allure of astonishment. But like all people who had been on the path too long, they forgot what they knew.

In those times, across the savannahs and in the forests, tribes danced to a multiplicity of gods. They killed and sacrificed one another. They were led astray by babblings from oracles and false priests steeped in the stupidity of men and women. In those times a clear light came from the austere images of the tribe of artists.

The old masters of the earliest times were wiser. They had a purer knowledge of the way. But the weak, the needy, the power-hungry, and the blockheads also stumble upon the path. And in degenerate times they join the council. Then impurities poison the pure way forever. No gardeners emerged to clear the weeds of the mind that would one day destroy the garden.

10

BUT AMONG MASTERS marvellous things happen. Sometimes in the darkness of a council meeting a spirit would appear. It would tell, very briefly, a tale of woe and wonder upon the earth. Sometimes a being not of this earth would become visible. It would speak of innumerable worlds, in the vastness of space, where beings dwell in a bewildering variety of forms. Sometimes such interstellar beings, in lights of blue and gold, eyes of shining stones, with transparent bodies, would tell of their civilisation and how they came to an end. Sometimes in the stillness of a council meeting a sorrowing magical animal would appear. It would gaze upon them with pitying eyes and would give them, in silence, a formula for the regeneration of the race. But the masters, saturated with astonishments, missed the simplest of formulations.

Those who fall prey to the astonishing cease to believe in astonishments. Those who are inundated with stories learn the least from them. They devour too many, when one true tale can lead to the palace of understanding.

Only one master grasped the formulation. He nourished it secretly, as one nourishes a great love.

11

In COUNCIL RITUALS, among masters, birds had appeared from the empty air. Words had been spoken from no mouth but the mouth of the unusual. White forms, singing softly in the wind, had paid visits. Kings had coagulated in the air, requesting help for their dying kingdoms. Children had become visible, seeking aid for their lost parents. Girls had materialised, crying for a change in the traditional ways that crush their lives.

In council rituals, among masters, victims being sacrificed had appeared, swearing vengeance on their people for cruel practices. A succession of the dead had made themselves present and whispered about evils in the land, the inhumanity of their rulers, and the stupidity of allowing monstrosities to pass for tradition.

Apparitions streamed past crying out for the land to be purged of its evils, invoking a curse of fire that would sweep away centuries of superstition, injustice, tyranny, infanticide, cruelty, and horrible rituals from people in whom so much was good, joyful, hospitable, and loving.

There were simple appearances too. Feathers suspended on threads of light. A child praying on the moon. A fabled creature from another land. A fairy with a blue wand. A painting of rare beauty turning in the air. A sonnet breathed on the wind. The beginnings of a tale of chivalry. A knight in broken armour. A bearded man with a luminous sword. A book whose words streamed into the partially illuminated space. A castle seen in miniature.

All these visions appeared in the silence of the council rituals. The masters gazed upon them vacantly, unwilling to interpret that which must be unseen to be seen. Unwilling to interpret what they had seen.

Such things turned into tales of wonder, beguiling them from true comprehension.

12

But they had heard the dream told in the dark. It was a time of ennui, in the last years of enchantment under the old sun. For a new sun, harsh and strange, was rising from a puzzling sky.

At the next meeting, someone suddenly spoke.

'I too had that dream. But in my dream the children of the heron did not return. The white birds did nothing but try to make themselves more powerful. Anyway, it was not a heron but an eagle. It recovered from its sickness by its own sustained effort. It became a great bird and made an excellent contribution to the race of birds.'

This voice created a pregnant mood. Another voice spoke grumpily.

'In my dream all the birds returned to the father in heaven, and then a new history began on earth.'

Something opened among them. There was a new expectation. Who else had found the same source from which this fountain sprang?

Briefly, the wind blew hard against the house of rituals. There were hooting noises in the distant forest. Unseen forms were alive there. They too were having their meeting.

A third voice spoke.

'I had the same dream. But it wasn't an eagle. It was a sunbird. The children scattered throughout the world did not return. They did not remember their mother. Many of them were ashamed that the sick bird on the riverbank was considered their mother, and they denied her. In their new lands some of her children mocked her and laughed at her. With its own powers of healing, the sunbird made itself strong and well again. It became a great bird, the saviour of the race of birds on earth.'

There was another silence. Then came an older voice. Old and not quite here. It spoke with boredom.

'All this talk about birds, when something terrible is happening which we cannot see.'

That ended the matter of dreams for a while. They returned to their listlessness. The heat weighed on them like an oppressive enchantment.

13

IT WAS THE same with the maiden. She became cloudy-headed and unpredictable. She frightened her mother, who hinted that perhaps it was time for her to marry. Her father thought she was perfectly normal.

'Her destiny is being born in her, poor girl, and her life is fighting against it. And so her body suffers these changes, like water suffers the changing lights of the sky.'

'You always talk in riddles about perfectly simple things, my love,' said her mother. 'She is pregnant with a need to be pregnant. That is all. It is time to consider her marriage. It is time to choose acceptable suitors from the poor specimens around.'

Her father laughed, but said nothing.

The maiden walked among the clouds. Curious impulses raged in her heart. She was waiting for something to speak to her and free her from the dark joys of not knowing.

III

1

EVERY LAND IS guided by its secret necessity, its essential truth. Even when a people lose their way, or disappear from the face of the earth, what lingers of them is this essential truth, this secret necessity.

It is like a dream experienced but never remembered, like a homeland forgotten, or like a love lost and found again without being recognised.

Sometimes a people forget who they are. They lose their secret necessity and become strangers to themselves. They dream up rituals and deeds upon the earth to forget their forgetting. They try to find out who they were, who they now should be. Such ventures are doomed. A skin shed is a skin shed. A loss is a loss.

They say we are meant to lose one thing so we may find that which is truer. That which we find may well be that which we have lost but which is found on a different day, when we have changed.

To forget what we are and not know it is an accursed thing. It creeps upon a people in the hundred ways that darkness steals across the sky.

Then one day invaders appear on the horizon, bearing mirrors. Then a people disappear into captivity and vanish from the face of the earth but for a few stones standing in a forest.

The stones are unseen for centuries. Then one day a child playing in the forest comes upon them. Stones without history, without a story, except for that which is glimpsed, in dreaming fragments, in the book of life among the stars.

2

How to tell the story of the tribe of artists, who are my ancestors, from visions seen in certain stones, fragments gleaned among the enigma of the stars.

They used to live invisibly. They were always on the move. But they were always perfectly still when fishing for inspiration revealed in their art.

They lived like fugitives. They never wanted to be part of the corrupting worldly structures. They only wanted to contribute to the spiritual and artistic life of the land. They wanted to be free. They wanted to be truthful to their dreams and visions, to the guidance that came to them through the mysterious agencies of life and art.

How to explain that this need so permeated their lives that it also permeated their ways of loving...

3

SUITORS WERE INVITED into the maiden's life. They wooed her with art. That was the way of the tribe.

The busiest time of the year was when suitors were competing for a woman's hand. The sounds of carving, planing, and drumming could be heard all around the square. Sacrifices at the shrine multiplied. Young men, vigorous and intense, could be seen in groups busy with artworks for the suitors they supported. Gossip sweetened the women's hair-dressing hour. They talked of little else but the suitors. They talked about their families, the rumours of recent and ancient scandals, as well as the appropriate or inappropriate behaviour of the maiden and her family.

It was a time of great creativity. Relations and friends of the maiden were wooed with gifts from the suitors. There were impromptu dances, dramatic performances, and improvised songs directed at the maiden. It was the best time in a girl's life, a time of festivity.

The whole tribe centred its attention on the girl to be married. Her worth was assessed not only by the artistic excellence she inspired in her suitors (this counted very highly indeed), but by the conduct of the girl herself, her humility and grace. They also noted how affected she was by the attention.

The tribe wanted to fall in love with the girl. If her conduct was exemplary and enchanting, she inspired greater excellence. Then the harvests would be plentiful, their art would achieve new heights of innovation, the old would feel rejuvenated, the women younger, and the men would dream of glories. As if by the special favours of a goddess, every aspect of life was enriched.

4

THIS WAS WHEN their art was most colourful. Reds and yellows, dazzling blues and deep bright greens caught the eye. The suitors would create totems celebrating the lineage of the girl being wooed, or displaying the worth of their own families. They might create sculptures showing the face of a warrior from three angles at once, or the statue of a goddess so pure that people fell in love with the art more than the girl it was made for. Suitors from rich families made bronze casts. Sometimes, in rare instances, they cast in gold.

Occasionally, a miraculous art was created. It entered legend and afterwards children were told they were born in the year that so-and-so was married, the year that a great work of art was made.

One such was the year the maiden's father wooed and won her mother's hand. The suitors were numerous, for the mother was of exceptional grace and beauty. She came from a distinguished family. Her father, one of the masters of the tribe, was an important chief and her mother was of royal descent. The suitors were not only numerous, they were of the highest calibre. Some were among the greatest artists of the land. Some were princes from distant places, who had heard the legend of the mother's beauty and charm.

Every day brought new suitors. They came with their entourage, their musicians, and praise-singers. It was a magical moment for the tribe.

The bride conducted herself impeccably. She had borne herself with simplicity and a becoming shyness. This inspired the suitors to higher peaks of artistic and spiritual endeavour. That year of the mother's marriage did more for the tribe than a decade of harvests and art. Money poured in, artworks were bought in great quantities, and trade multiplied.

Whoever won her hand would have to be truly exceptional, for storytellers would be talking about him long after the tribe had vanished from the earth.

Princes brought their praise-singers: griots prepared their sagas; warriors honed their sword skills, artists perfected their creations. Some suitors prepared in secret, others publicly. They were all of noble and celebrated stock. All except one.

No one noticed him. He was an orphan who lived with an uncle, a master bronze-caster. He himself had never been remarked as an artist of any note but he had grown wise in the service of his uncle. He had been initiated into the mysteries because of his interest in the causes of things.

If he had any desire for it, his sense of humour could have made him famous in the tribe. But years of studying the secrets of sculpture and bronze-casting had inclined him to nonchalance.

He was an outsider who had thought more deeply about art and life than any of the age. He was a master sculptor, and had made things that baffled the elect. He was one of the best artists of his times. But no one knew it, least of all himself.

He made himself a suitor for the simplest reason. He was in love. One morning, some time before, he had seen a woman working on a bust of a girl with high woven hair. He had fallen in love with the work at first glance. When he saw the woman who made it, he had fallen in love a second time. It had been a quiet love that had grown over many years. He had grown profound in his secret love. He had developed with it into a man of substantial character. His love had become the primary motivation of his life, his chief inspiration. It had given him reasons to study the laws of life and to master his art.

Through this love he was open to the way that led him into the ancient mysteries. The mysteries had been brought on golden tablets by the ancestors of the tribe, who had come from somewhere not of this earth, and whose civilisation perished under the sea. He was initiated into these mysteries and worked with the secret of the ages.

This love, his circumstances, and time had enriched him. They had made him a true man among men. He became one who saw what others didn't, intuited what others couldn't, dreamt what others wouldn't, and questioned what others felt they shouldn't. He ascended to realms others didn't suspect existed, and knew what others didn't know was there to be known.

5

NOBILITY OF BIRTH does not confer nobility of soul. Only those who strive for the highest attain it.

The maiden's father was a free man. He had fashioned himself out of dust and a love that led him to the stars.

His love was his chief qualification as a suitor. All those who knew him told him that he was mad to harbour any hope. How could an ordinary man, unknown to his peers, without a presence in the land, compete in such a magnificent gathering? But he did. He did it simply. That was his way.

Others created extravagant works. They made big masquerades, giant bronzes, stone statues, rapturous dances, rolling epics. But he did the simplest and most astonishing thing. He made a sculpture of air and sunlight which induced a sweet dreaming in the tribe. It caused an enchantment that stilled the minds of masters and children and made the women weep for its beauty. The sculpture was composed of the material of love itself. It was revealed in the open air, above the shrine.

The other suitors claimed they couldn't see it. They said that it was a fraud, that it was sorcery masquerading as art. Everyone else could see it and fell under its spell. The maiden's mother spent most of her day sitting in front of the shrine, gazing up at the work, on her face the expression of a lover lost in adoration. She declared that she wanted to spend the rest of her life with the man who had made such a dream.

Her parents also fell under the spell of the fascinating new work, though they were more cautious than their daughter.

'We ought to know more about him,' they said.

'All I need to know is in his art. I don't care if he's a beggar. This is the man I want to marry.'

'But what if he's mad?'

'Then it's a madness that pleases me.'

'You haven't even met him and you are behaving like this. What will you be like if you live with him?'

'Happy and mad for the rest of my life.'

'But what he's done is unheard of. He's changed how we do things. He could be dangerous for our people.'

'Or he might save us from dying.'

'Maybe this man has used sorcery on us.'

'Why would he do that, when he can make art like this?'

'You will bear strange children.'

'They will be unique.'

'You will have a strange future with him.'

'There is no protection against the future, mother. My love will be my guide.'

'Then so it must be.'

'But only with your blessings, my mother and father.'

'Let us prepare for a new story.'

6

AND SO IT was. The work of the unknown suitor altered something in the air. It was the first time a work of art had induced a universal experience that was like communing with the gods. It induced a sense of wonder. There was fear in the wonder.

It was something that had never been done before. It changed the tribe's history and possibilities. For the work not only transformed the tribe's art, it transformed the way the tribe saw itself. It renewed the vision of the tribe and opened up its destiny forever.

The tribe now felt its future was not determined by its past. Overnight the tribe felt that its future could go any number of ways. Before there had been only one way, and that way was related to its past. Now it had many futures. It was freed from the past.

The sense of an ongoing freedom was inherent in the work. Like a door that is never open and never closed, a door that opens both ways, this freedom was new. The work made people dream again, made them believe that they were more than they thought they were. It made them feel they shared in the glories and powers of heaven.

This was the first time that the people had been presented with an invisible sculpture that could be seen by all. It was an art composed of elements beyond the human mind, borrowing from the divine. The power of the gods had been directed into artistic creation.

There was no competition. The outsider, the unknown one, had come through. With a complex sense of humour, a curious detachment that concealed great compassion, slight of figure and strange of eyes, he had come through. Without appearing to try, silent among great and famous names, with their big noises and public acclaim, he had won the girl's heart and had been chosen. In ways it was too proud to admit, the tribe of artists would never be the same again.

7

THE WEDDING WAS a quiet one. Though they both wanted there to be no fanfare, the tribe was ecstatic in its own celebrations. Quietly they slipped into being man and wife, as if they had spent many invisible decades rehearsing for it.

His distinction had been earned by genius, hers by the greatness of tradition. Together they grew, laughed, and prospered. They bore one child, the maiden of this tale.

8

IN CONTRAST TO her mother the maiden was awkward, moody, and alien. Someone once said she looked like a beetle. Some said that she looked like a mask that frightened off evil spirits, others that she looked like a spirit that frightened off human beings. The more charitable said she was just plain. They added that girls like her, like some birds, changed as they got older and had the potential to become quite beautiful.

Some said you could never tell with her type whether her face would settle into beauty or not. But given who her parents were, it was best to assume that she would. Other people did not see it that way.

'She's not beautiful at all,' some girls said.

'So aloof.'

'Thinks she's too good for marriage.'

'As if she won't spread her legs…'

'And won't get fat…'

'I pity her parents having such an ugly daughter.'

'If I had a daughter as ugly as that, I would put a mask on her.'

'She is not like her mother, who is loved by everyone.'

'Her mother is a flower, the daughter an insect.'

'If her mother were a man, I would say that daughter is not his child.'

That is how it was. The mother was the delight of the tribe. But the daughter had eyes that saw too much. She seemed to see the future in people's faces and didn't much like the future she saw.

She was born with a perception of the world so singular that as a little girl she frightened people. Something about her spirit was intimidating.

In herself she wouldn't have drawn illustrious suitors. But as the daughter of a legendary master she was of great interest. Her suitors were not of the calibre of her mother's but they were distinguished enough.

The artistic competition for her hand turned out to be more interesting than expected. Driven to heights of inventiveness to win the approbation of the master, the gifted men of the tribe altogether surpassed themselves in artistry.

ALL THIS TIME the tribe still expected the maiden to create the work of art that would quicken her healing. All this time the sculpture with the chained figures continued to work on the tribe. An ancient ennui hovered in people's hearts.

All was not well. Forebodings danced in the forest. The shadow of unmentionable events stalked their dreams. Omens that could not be deciphered appeared among them. A bird shorn of its feathers hopped erratically beneath a silk cotton tree. The seasons were slipping their rhythms. It was hoped by the tribe that the season of the maiden's wooing would prove auspicious.

But the maiden didn't care. Suitors wooed her with songs, sculptures, and paintings, but she gazed on their best efforts with indifference. She saw no art, only artefacts. She looked upon the works of her suitors with a neutral eye and a distracted smile. What was she dreaming of? Where was her mind? What images and immeasurable moods moved in her spirit? She saw nothing but the mediocrity of her suitors, mediocrity masked by energy. Their works made her long for some incommensurable mood. This longing became a desire for freedom. She longed for an elusive something that would make her not a modern, or a traditional, but a transcendent woman. Her longing was for an impossible feat. It was distilled into the image of an earthbound eagle.

The image grew stronger. The eagle, in its sleep, thought of itself as a hen. This was the mood of her spirit. But she dreamt of the open air, of the land beneath the clouds, and of the clear heavens above, with all their stars.

The works of the suitors, their masks, their songs, their

little epics, their vigorous dances, their bronzes, and their giant sculpted goddesses were flattering, charming, and impressive. Everyone was delighted by them, but she was cool. She was unmoved by all the noise and fame attending the works that would have swept many a virgin off her feet.

SHE HAD BEEN raised in magic. Her ordinary days were touched with legend and myth. Her mind had been formed in an enlightened laboratory of the tribe. The art of the woman-spirit had been fed her with her mother's milk.

She gazed at life with the intensity of art. She saw the heart of things without trying.

She knew that true mastery comes once or twice in a hundred years. And she was not disappointed that her suitors had nothing true in their art.

She expected nothing of them. The genuine can only come from the hidden. This she intuited from her father. She awaited a sign that might come from the margins. She endured the wooing and suffered the yearning for something unknown that was coming.

11

THERE WERE MANY suitors. There was a mask-maker, a bronze-caster, and a feared image-maker. His images were used as war fetishes by alien tribes. There was a warrior and a dancer, a master musician and a courtier. There was a chief from a far-off kingdom and a few members of royal families. It made the tribe come alive again to witness an array of brave young men assemble for the hand of one of their daughters.

She was deaf to the serenades and blind to the works of ingenious inventors. She was indifferent to the gifts of gold and cows. Wealthy intermediaries found her dreamy. To her mother's pleas for graciousness, she was resistant.

Her aloofness worked wonders on the suitors. It inflamed their passions. Her otherworldliness suggested that she thought them unworthy of her.

But to her they were all a blur, all variations of one suitor.

12

AROUND THIS TIME the maiden took to wandering off with her friends to the river. Sometimes they played games. But mostly she stared at the river, at its lights and reflections. Sometimes, lost in reverie, gazing at the river flowing quietly, she glimpsed evanescent fragments of future events.

Listening to the water lapping on the shore, staring at the birds, lingering at the hinges between here and there, she dreamt things which her mind barely registered. They filled her with the delicious sadness of which her days of youth were composed.

Sometimes, in a golden dream, she would see but not register a ship tossing about on the ocean. She would smell, without locating, the stench of blood and decomposing bodies. She would feel, without feeling, her ankles in chains and agony in her wrists. She would notice, without noticing, that she was standing in a bare marketplace and being sold like a goat. She would sense the heat of the whip and glimpse the white faces. She would hear, without hearing, cries of abandonment. She would catch, without knowing, the mood of a cold land, a universe empty of hope...

13

SOMETIMES, IN THAT golden mood, conversations rose in her mind. Were they her thoughts? Such things perplexed her as she woke from those states. Then she would continue the game she was playing, the figures she was drawing with a stick on the sand, as if there and here were the same. In one of the conversations someone would say:

'Tell us a story.'

'I will tell you a story of a girl by a river in Africa,' she would say.

But she never spoke a word of the story.

'Stories can't be told in too much pain, my dear child,' she would add.

Was she dreaming or thinking a dream as she thought it? Time and eternity work on the brain. It filters things here from elsewhere.

'Do you remember the moon?'

'The moon died in the big sea.'

'Do you remember the land?'

'The land died with chains around my neck.'

'Do you remember your mother?'

'My mother died when I was sold like a goat.'

'Do you remember your father?'

'To remember is the worst form of suffering. Spirits torment me saying the past cannot be real. Only death is real. I long to die. Then maybe I will find happiness.'

And she would wake from the hinges between there and here...

She would wake into the sweet sadness of which her youth was composed, beside the great river.

14

THE MAIDEN LOVED the river so much that one night she dreamt that a god addressed her from its shore. She dreamt that the lady of the river rose in a golden mist and brought her wedding gifts of white flowers and a dress made by mermaids and a ring fashioned by the little people who worked for the river-king.

She dreamt too that her husband would be a young god from a glamorous land. She would not recognise him but would save him from death not once, but twice.

All this from the river.

The river became her dream. It was a languorous dream of past, present, and future. Her whole life was there. Many lives and deaths. Many births of moons and skies and suns in its watery surface and depth. The entire history of her tribe was there. The magic and the sadness of things sparkled in the glimmering water's face. All she didn't know was there. All that was whispered to her heart, the joy and dread of all that was to come, was there.

Occasionally she would be overwhelmed with happiness. She would weep at the strangeness of it. Once she saw in the river the face of one who loved her more than the moon. The river became her dream.

She waited for the river to yield its promises. Many moons went past but only dreams came to her.

Sometimes she travelled the river in a canoe. She and her companions sang to the mermaids. They asked the mermaids to bring them gifts while they were still young...

It was around this time, in a state of expectancy, that she heard the voice from the bushes asking her three riddling questions. She thought that the gods, at last, had kept their promise.

15

THE BEST OF the suitors was a handsome and virile man. He was a hunter, a warrior, had strong eyes, good instincts, and great cunning. He had that gap in his upper front teeth that sent young women into raptures. But the maiden was indifferent to him. This inflamed his desire to possess her. It brought out the hunter in him. It brought out the cunning.

He knew that marriage to the maiden was marriage to legend. He would be set up not only for life but also in the long memory of the tribe. She was his best chance of immortality.

He set about the conquest of the maiden with stealth, ingenuity, and calculation. He began by executing the most powerful series of sculptures he had ever managed. He exceeded the limits of his talent. He went beyond himself in his desire to win.

He was known as the Mamba. This was because of his wrestling style. What he locked his hands on, never escaped him. He had killed at least five men. He took part in wrestling competitions in distant villages, and often returned with the winner's trophy. He brought this relentlessness to bear on his campaign to win the maiden.

Before a match he studied the style of his opponent, analysing all their weaknesses. Just as he caught his opponent's neck in an arm-lock and never let go till their legs stopped twitching, so did he concentrate now on the task of wooing the maiden. He studied, from a distance, the secrets of the maiden's father's art. He paid spies and servants for information about him. He looked at as many of the works attributed to the master as possible.

His reasoning was simple. The maiden's taste would be formed by her father. She would love what she had grown up seeing in the works of her father. This would be her unconscious weakness. Her taste would be bound up in her daughter's love.

But how could he be sure that those works were indeed the work of the master? This was a philosophical problem, the dimensions of which he could not fathom. For the more the masters reveal, the more they conceal. They reveal the least of themselves, their red-herrings. They are false trails meant to mislead those who seek superficial power and fame. These the master traps in the labyrinths of false achievements. The master's true works lead to illumination and freedom from the dominion of matter. To all intents and purposes, they are non-existent and invisible. They are visible only to those on the path, whose hearts are pure. Their true works are hidden in the works that are seen.

The Mamba studied what he could find of the master's works. Then he imitated, almost to perfection, the flaws, the illusions, the errors, the false beauty, and the traps lurking in all such works. He copied them, with variations of his own. In this way he produced sculptures of twins inverted, fishes swimming in opposite directions, a great mother with stars all over her body. He made carvings of a god with a sun in his head, of a sage with entwined snakes round his thyrsus. These were images of the enlightened but the Mamba did not understand this and therefore used them indiscriminately, as with an alien language in which one speaks nonsense.

The Mamba presented the carvings for the chilly appreciation of the maiden. She looked at them, saw the poor imitations of her father's work, and went past him without comment.

The works merely confirmed what she suspected. Masters are born only once or twice in the life of a people. The truly gifted are rare. There are at best very hard workers who have found a personal language with which to say nothing profound. As her father had said for as long as she could remember, the deep can only come from the deep.

And so, while not entirely abandoning the wooing through art, the Mamba made another plan for conquering this brilliant and unattainable maiden.

He took to following her, stalking her, like a shadow.

16

ALL THE ACTIVITIES surrounding the wooing of the maiden concealed from the tribe events happening in the undercurrents of the world. It is not necessary to be deaf to not hear loud noises around you; sounds played close to the ears can accomplish this. A whisper blots out thunder. It is not necessary to be blind to not be able to see. Distraction is sufficient.

Rituals and festivities are distractions from events drawing closer that could alter a people forever. All the activities of a people hide that which is coming.

The masters of the tribe used to advocate long periods without rites or celebrations. This was to prevent people being distracted, to make them open to things that were coming, things already present but not seen.

But these suggestions were ignored over the years. The tribe had gradually lost the faculty for stillness. It was a quality that would have given them greater receptivity to signs and omens.

There was unease in the land. The people sensed it, but did not know that they did. The masters sensed it, but could not identify what it was. They were mesmerised by the power of what they sensed. They were paralysed by the future, like those who gaze into an abyss and no longer know if they are gazing or falling.

These conditions were perfect for being possessed by that into which they gazed, till they became one with it, and fell into it, through self-enchantment.

17

WHEN A PEOPLE sense their extinction they either throw themselves into orgies of distraction, or they resist the inevitable with deeds which only make happen the thing they dread. Or they do nothing. Or they create, in a fever of hope, magical works to avert disaster and perpetuate their memory, so that the earth will not forget that they once lived and were passionate under the sun.

There were those who had glimpses of this extinction and remained tranquil, as though it were a necessary part of a universal plan.

All these responses amounted to the same thing.

18

THE MEMORIES OF a land are vast and deep. They are more than the land itself. They are a realm unto themselves.

Deep were the memories of the land in the time which the tribe passed through. What were these memories?

They were births and deaths, rites and rituals, murders and wars, love stories and rape, festivities and loneliness. They were the smell of burning tapers, slaughtered chickens and goats and cows in offerings at altars and shrines and thresholds. Kaoline sprinkled in sacrifice.

They were ghosts that wander through grey timeless zones of the land, sunsets that bleed omens on dry nights, babies born in the forest and abandoned and devoured by ants. They were branded women, and slaughtered captives, proverbs of great wisdom salting the dusk, and the low moon that draws out stories from the people like the rising tides.

They were diseases and witchcraft and harvests, family quarrels about land, boys that play and discover the differences that are girls, and girls that discover the novelty that are boys. They were celebrations and the disappearance of a whole people devoured by disease or famine or wars. They were new arrivals, with old histories, in a new cycle, building abodes, fishing, hunting, farming, dying, moving on, living difficult days and hot nights.

The memories were ghosts and laughter, feathers in the wind, dust in the air, leaves from the trees, and the river's winding majestic flow. They were bones of those long dead, spirits in the forest, lions in the wild, birds that circle the air, drifting clouds, moon over the land, the sun with spears of light.

The memories were insects in the undergrowth, seeds bursting into shoot on walls, on clothes, and in the eye sockets of the dead. They were the abnormal fertility of the land, things growing everywhere, flies and flying insects pestering the new villages, and the villagers moving on. Everything moving on.

Deep were the memories of the land. Deep with tragedies, comedies, dances, silences, blood, riddles, laughter, and death.

There are spaces vast enough for more memories, millions more than have been. That is the endless depth of the land. Out of this what is to come is not hinted at. The space will accommodate whatever comes to be. Who can measure the depth of that space? Who can draw from it all that is needed for renewal?

When a people sense the end of a way, they always sense it as the end of the world.

Who can stop the end of the world?

19

THE MASTERS KNEW all things going on in the tribe. Some of them sensed all things going on in the land. One or two of them sensed all that was going on in the world.

A few of them knew that the events surrounding the marriage of the maiden were not isolated events in the history of the tribe, or the land, or the world. They knew that these events were linked to some immense catastrophe and some heroic future redemption through fire.

Some sensed that the end of time is there in the seed of an insignificant event. The full arc of stories are beyond telling. They reach from here into spaces beyond words and things. In those spaces dwell no stories, nor images, nor sounds, nor colours. Stories start in their already-existence and cease in mid-space. The rest vanish into the invisible.

Only the living and dead together can tell stories in their completeness. Even then only in isolated threads. All the gods in all the lands could not tell the entirety of a single story all the way from its pre-beginnings to its infinite end.

Only fragments are left to us. We make structures out of them. Structures full of hints that delight us in the labyrinth.

Fragments glimpsed in the invisible book of life.

20

THE MAMBA WAS a man of stone and strength. His prowess had been proven on the battlefield as on the farms. He had saved people from drowning, saved men on the battlefield, and women from the jaws of crocodiles in the swamp.

He was famous for having wrestled another crocodile that had snatched a child. With a howl, he had broken the crocodile's neck. It was from his battle with a deadly mamba, which he had wrestled with for almost an hour until he broke its neck, that he got his celebrated name.

He had dragged the mamba back with him to the shrine of the village. It was huger than a tree and as long as the village stream was wide. He uncoiled it in front of the shrine as an offering to the gods. Afterwards he fashioned a mighty sculpture of the mamba that amazed the tribe with its power.

Apart from the masters and most of his rivals, everyone admired the sculpture. The masters saw its solidity and fluency. It was a man's work. But it had no mystery and was not suggestive. It had power, but not lightness; strength, but not vulnerability. It did not have that deep simplicity that the masters admired. It amazed the eye, but did not touch the soul. It did not induce dreaming.

Its very power implied something sinister about the artist. Some masters detected in it self-mythology, and a secret craving for power.

The masters kept silent about the work. The Mamba was never invited to their council. He became bitter about this silent rejection, and brooded on it often.

21

THE MAMBA CAME from a good family. He was of respectable birth. There was some wealth in the house. His father was an esteemed carpenter and maker of images, and his mother was skilled in the art of patterning myths on cloth.

His father was not a member of the council of masters. None of their lineage ever had been. His mother was not on the council of the wise women of the tribe either. This was of no great account, for the family was liked and respected. They paid their dues, did their duties, and were much consulted in important decisions affecting the well-being of the people.

The Mamba grew up, like most people, in the shade of his father's philosophy and his mother's gently guiding stories. But with time he came to amaze his parents with his strength and cunning. He grew up to be a solid young man. Quite early the elders had begun speaking about him as a future member of the council. He would be the first in his family ever to attain such heights. But his successes made him rash. His strength made him overconfident. His success with women made him too visible. And his rude virility lent an impetuous brilliance to his art.

He inclined to the gigantic. The great size of his art drew crowds. Children clambered on them and played games of hide and seek round them. He was often chasing them away.

His art made people gape, but only for a short while. His speciality was short-term astonishments. Every time his work appeared, people knew it was his immediately. They enjoyed going to see it. They liked his unusual creations and, from the sheer pleasure of talking about them, bestowed on them their popularity. It was as though such works were needed to aid gossip among them, a not inconsiderable function in society.

This very quality and the success it brought him made him continue the same way. It never occurred to him that there were other ways of being. His popularity, his facility, his victories in hunting, wrestling, harvesting and war, did something peculiar to his reputation, but he never noticed. With time, talk of the council of masters quietly vanished.

Yet he thrived in the estimation of the people. He was, after all, a man who had built his house with his own hands, a man who had wrestled with wild animals and broken their necks...

22

THE MAMBA DRANK little and was considered sober. But there was something curious about his brooding presence, his bulk, his strong eyes. He did not speak much, but his reputation was not that of a silent man.

When he was there, he was too much there. When he wasn't there, he wasn't there at all. He was noticed when in society, but not missed when he wasn't. People talked of him, but not about him. Despite his dramatic deeds, people didn't tell stories about him.

Maybe the stories told about him didn't last. More deeds were needed to generate more stories. He seemed to live in a race against the way time devoured his deeds. He kept chasing story-making events. This gave a desperate energy to his life.

He had an unusual knack for knowing when things were being rumoured about him. Then he was in his element, radiating a charged serenity.

His eyes were always flashing, looking about to see if he was being noticed. Something in him responded to public mythology, no matter how shallow. This made him one of the most alert of men. With patience he would have made an excellent actor.

These qualities also made him do ambiguous things. He thought of himself as a good man. But his character was strange, even to himself, as if he harboured unsuspected lives, from a distant past or future...

23

HAVING CRACKED THE spine of a child-snatching crocodile, he was seen by many as a hero. But there was something diabolical about him. There were rumours that he had conjured ambiguous spirits and that this was the source of his powers. It was rumoured that his seduction of many women was entirely due to his dark transactions.

But the power of his crude magnetism didn't work on all women. Some seemed able to turn his powers back on him and make him the slave of his own sorcery. His powerlessness then to resist the spell he cast on himself nearly drove him mad. He avoided those women. There was simply no accounting for them. The curious thing was that they did not need to be beautiful, rich, devious, vulnerable, clever or flirtatious.

They were simply unique. Nothing he did worked on them. Everything he tried rebounded. They were always innocent of their power. It was something they were born with. This nameless quality was the one the Mamba feared most in women. Paradoxically, it was the quality he sought most. It represented for him the ultimate challenge, a challenge more daunting than battling a crocodile or wrestling in distant villages.

The maiden had this rare nameless quality.

24

HIS DESIRE TO possess the maiden drove him to the edge of hallucination.

At night he couldn't sleep for thinking about her. When he did sleep he ground his teeth so loudly that he alarmed his neighbours. Because of this slight madness he was constantly tense. He was always working his jaws and clenching his fists. His eyes developed an odd maniacal light, and his face twitched.

He took to brooding. Strange propensities surfaced in him. His mind developed sinister inclinations. Murders, vile notions, a desire to do something monstrous took possession of him under the influence of the maiden's composure.

Overnight, out of his brooding, there grew in him an urge to command, to compel, and to crush. He wanted to be powerful, to dominate, and to overcome all obstacles to his will. He brooded often on power and on the domination of the tribe. He wanted to rule the world...

First he had to win the hand of the maiden. He had to destroy her power over him. If he did not win her, if he did not annex her mystery into his powers, he would never be able to lead the tribe. Beginning with the tribe, then the surrounding tribes, he would make the great land his own. He would spread his legend to the furthest stars.

It is impossible to say when the notion came upon him that the maiden was the key to his destiny. She had grown so strong in his mind that he came to see that if he could not conquer her, he could never conquer anything. She became the obstacle, the antidote, the fear, the magic formula that stood between him and greatness.

When such notions grow in the mind of a man, the strangest instincts develop. There is nothing more powerful than instinct harnessed to desire.

Such people conquer the world or destroy it.

IN HIS DREAMS he knew things about people that baffled them. This ability of his made him a formidable opponent. He was able to divine people's secrets, without knowing how. He dreamt of fights beforehand and knew in advance what tactics his opponent might use. He often guessed what people were saying about him. This made him know when to take advantage of rumours and when to kill them. He had the gift of second sight.

With women, he knew where their sweet point, their weaknesses, lay. He seduced them in his dreams, and in real life he knew exactly what to do to make them surrender to him of their own free will.

But this gift was sporadic. It came and went. He was not a master of the skills. This infuriated him. Without a vision, without a dream from which to deduce a method, he was lost. He was in the dark. This made him fearful.

It meant that only when his erratic gift gave him insight could he really achieve anything. This gave him an air of enigmatic shallowness, fascinating to the naive but transparent to the masters.

He was in constant dread of the gift deserting him. For someone with ambitions this was a disaster. He couldn't conceive of being without it, but didn't want to be at the mercy of ignorance.

The fear of losing his erratic gift made the Mamba unpredictable. He was confident when he had it, but frightened when he didn't.

This made him feel like an impostor. But he discovered, as he got older, that people were hopeless. Even without his second sight he was better than most. With it, he was superior to almost everyone.

This gift was to prove invaluable in the competition for the maiden's hand.

ONE DAY HE was in the forest, cutting wood for a sculpture he hoped to make of the maiden, when he paused in his labours and fell into a deep sleep. He dreamt that the maiden was spied on by a slender creature with doe-like eyes. In the dream he saw that she fell in love with this stranger and wanted it for her husband. In the dream the tribe was horrified that she wanted to marry an animal that no one had seen before. This caused such outrage that the elders were dispatched to the Mamba to beg him to kill the creature and free the illustrious tribe from this threat of abomination.

In the dream the Mamba set off for the forest, hunted the creature for seven days, and brought it back alive to the village. Then in full view of everyone he set the creature free and challenged it to an honest wrestling match. During the match he broke its neck with a crack so loud that it caused astonishment. The creature died instantly. The Mamba became a hero, celebrated in songs and dances.

But on the seventh day of the celebrations, the creature rose again. It had changed into a man. It stood like a colossus in front of the shrine. It stood there silently. The clouds passed across his soft face, now obscuring, now revealing it. There was the most unnerving stillness in the village while the colossus just stood there. It stared in perfect serenity at the Mamba. The Mamba felt tiny in the presence of such gentle might.

He woke from his dream and knew he had to do something but he did not know what. His world was in danger. He was sure the tribe felt that its world was in danger too, and did not know why.

First he needed proof of what he had sensed. He began to spy on the secret life of the maiden.

DRAWN BY HER mystery and cut by her disdain, the Mamba stalked her.

In public places, he had no need to spy on her. Public eyes did that well enough. He was kept informed by daily gossip. But when she stole away to the forest, or wandered the sepia path to the river, alone or with companions, he stole after her and watched.

He preferred to follow her when she was alone. He wanted to catch her at an unbecoming habit or vice, some act of nature that would demystify her, something that would shatter her purity. He wanted to catch her squatting or making the kind of natural noises impeccable women are not expected to make. Then her reverse spell might cease to work on him. He would break his enslavement to her mystery. But the maiden was as irreproachable in private as in public.

This made him madder, made him more obsessed. His visions and hallucinations grew worse.

He magnified her. Multiplied her. She became many people in his mind. He suspected her of sorceries and invested her with witchcraft. The fact of her solitude was for him a sure sign that she belonged to a coven.

Then he suspected that she was perhaps the priestess of a goddess, a handmaiden of the great mother, a devotee of the mysterious one. She was gentle and walked with wayward grace. She had an air of special protection. She seemed to live under the aegis of a divine being. Who was she? he wondered. What did she worship?

The Mamba interpreted everything she did as a sign, a votive deed, an act in an unknown series of rituals, in a great worship. He expected that at any moment the focus of her worship would be revealed. He half expected to be blinded by the power of this unveiling.

On the other hand he also half expected to be brought to the edge of terror by what he might witness.

Which would it be?

Her mystery and prestige filled him with fear.

28

HE WATCHED HER speak to the birds in the forest. To spiders in their webs, she sang a song. She whispered flirtatiously into the trunks of trees.

Sometimes, she threw her arms up and exulted in the rich bank of green above her and the cool shade of the baobabs and irokos. Then she would pick up a snail and move it from the path, urging it to be more careful where it strayed.

Sometimes she just vanished. He would panic. Then baffled, he would find her in another part of the forest, as if she'd been lifted there by unseen hands.

Once he saw her surrounded by fairies. They were yellow and blue and golden. They were tiny and bright, with green silken wings. She was sitting on a fallen tree and telling them stories.

29

Sensing that she had made a pact with solitude and with the little creatures of the forest, the Mamba was surprised one day when her direction changed and her feet wended towards the river.

He walked in her footsteps, hoping to steal her powers. But his big feet only splayed and destroyed the shape of her footprints on the white sand. It left him briefly confused about why he was following her.

He touched the flowers she touched, and they wilted. When he tried telling stories to the fairies he found an evil-looking bird studying him from a tree.

He followed her and then lost her in a gentle mist. When he next saw her she was wearing white. The forest had darkened and a magenta glow had come over the river. His heart pounded with dread. Was he going to catch her at last at her secret activities?

That twilight evening he saw her with her companions, at the riverbank, singing to the goddess of the river. Where had they come from? The girls wore dazzling white shifts. He saw them all in a circle, their hands linked, dancing and spinning round so fast that they rose from the ground. Their sweet voices filled the forest. The Mamba sat down against a sycamore tree, in astonishment. When he got up he found that he was almost blind.

For two days he could not see. The golden form of a ring burned in his eyes. Then, from his room, they heard screaming. Neighbours said he screamed for no visible reason.

30

WHEN HIS SIGHT improved, he went back to spying on the maiden. He was shocked one day to find that he wasn't the only one spying on her.

Then one day she appeared to be in a dream or a ritual. She stood there beside some bushes, near the river, head bent, humble in her attitude, listening to someone. He distinctly saw her speaking, but no one was there. Was she speaking to the air?

He was struck by her beauty. She had dropped to her knees and was answering questions which the air had asked. Her body radiated the quality of the morning sun. Limned by the light, a holy fire seemed to concentrate around her slim form. The Mamba gasped at her luminosity.

He drew closer to listen.

'Come back here the same time tomorrow. Come alone,' he heard a voice say.

He saw how the words in the morning wind made her shine.

He was instantly suspicious. It occurred to him that one of the other suitors might be behind this trick. There was a rustling in the bushes. He saw the form of a man disappear behind the cover of acacia. Amazed at the audacity, he hurried in the direction of the rustling. He took a longer way, so as not to be seen by the maiden.

When he got there he caught a glimpse of a horned animal vanishing among the trees in a beam of sunlight. The animal dazzled in gold, and evaporated into the shade. For the second time the Mamba was blinded.

31

HE LAY THERE on the floor of the forest on a sweet-smelling heap of leaves. A slow drip of late morning dew fell on his neck. He listened to the footfalls of invisible creatures in the forest. He lay quite still, waiting for his sight to clear.

In the distance a wild boar was rooting around in the dry brush. He heard the steady hum and the mingled sounds of tiny insects above his head. High above the obeche trees a woman was singing in a sweet voice. The river roared in his veins.

He began to formulate an act of revenge. He felt humiliated. He was blinded and he was tricked. He couldn't get what he had seen out of his mind. Whenever he thought of that other spy, the horned animal came to mind. It refused to leave. What was he to do? He was owed vengeance. That was sure. A great rage swelled in him like a river in spate. He let it swell. He waited for it to subside. When it did he knew exactly what to do, not only to win a bride, but also to begin his journey towards power.

Dimly, he felt his way towards the river where he washed his face and eyes. Then he lay in the sun. He slept, and when he woke his eyes had cleared considerably.

32

HE MADE HIS way back home. He grunted in a bad-tempered way when anyone spoke to him. People accepted him however he chose to be. It was the advantage of reputation. He could cloak his vulnerability beneath a growl.

Back in his abode he brooded on what he was going to do. With the sure instincts of a warrior who knows when his moment has arrived, he set his plan in action.

It was simplicity itself. Like wandering notes of dissonance that never die, its consequences were incalculable.

33

THE MAMBA DID two things. First he put it about that the maiden was having illicit relations with a horned animal by the river. Nothing travels faster than an evil rumour, and rumours are the easiest things to make. Like magic, they appear. They take on the garments of truth – a truth everyone wants to believe because it makes them feel better about themselves.

This malicious rumour travelled fast. Soon everyone believed that the unattainable maiden had made love to a beast in the forest.

Good news travels with the speed of a gazelle. Bad news travels with the swiftness of the wind. A sculpture depicting acts of bestiality appeared outside the shrinehouse. It depicted, in miniature form, the coupling of a horned animal and a girl.

The second thing the Mamba did was to inform the maiden's parents that a mysterious figure, an outsider, was spying on their daughter and ruining her chances of a good marriage.

The Mamba thought that by this action he would earn a special place in their affections.

Meanwhile the maiden was completely unaware of the appalling things being said about her. She bore herself with peaceful dignity. When with her friends, she sang. When abroad in the community, she was silent.

She did not notice that her circle of friends was gradually diminishing. She did not notice the nature of the silence that came upon people when she entered their midst. The voice that had spoken to her by the river had brightened her consciousness. It had lifted her mind to realms of tender contemplation. She did not notice the change in attitudes towards her.

She gazed upon the world with a lovelorn sweetness. There was a great love in her heart but no one to whom that love was directed. It made her a floating being of tenderness. Her happiness made her giggle and then weep and then gaze sternly about her and then fall into a state of vacancy. Like a sky with constantly changing clouds, she became a changeable being of infinite sensitivity.

As she had no idea what to do with herself, she made things. She carved, drew figures on wooden panels, made up songs, and invented new dye patterns on cloths. She ran long errands for her parents and neighbours. All this she did to try to stop her feelings from tearing her apart inside.

Significant events happen, and are almost invisible, and yet are quiet catalysts that alter a life. The night after the maiden's encounter with the voice at the river, she dreamt of a young man. It was a fleeting dream. She barely noticed it at the time. But the brief appearance of the prince in her dream remained somewhere in her mind. It awaited events that would strengthen its presence.

In the dream she saw a figure, whom she took for a prince. He stared at her, saying nothing, doing nothing. He was watching and not watching her, as if she were a work of art he wanted to learn to look at, but never understand.

34

THE MAIDEN LIVED her life in gentle absent-mindedness. She was as far removed from the clamour of suitors as from the rumours. The same was not true of her parents.

When her father learnt of the man at the river who was spying on his daughter, when he learnt of the rumours being whispered in the tribe, he knew he had to act swiftly to protect her reputation. He had no choice but to make her disappear from the tribe. He was aware exile might be bitter for her.

But he was a man of mysteries. He never acted without listening to the oracles and the masters who have gone beyond. He never acted without consulting the ancestors. And so he set about the rituals by which things unknown are revealed.

From the ancestors he received signs that things must first decompose if they are to produce the immortal fruits of time. From the departed masters he learnt that evil must triumph for a season if an even greater good is to come into being. That good, in its gentleness, needs its character and resolve tested and primed by the suffering that evil brings. Only then can it transform the world.

From the oracles he learnt that only the one who is not fit to be a suitor can win the hand of the maiden. Only the lowly can be high. He also learnt from the oracle that a surprising contest would decide all things and that the future is a dark hole beyond which, in time, a great kingdom of unimaginable splendour will be found. Through pain and sorrow, all will be well. All will be transfigured. Redeemed. A joy beyond description will crown all stories. These things the oracle told.

The maiden's father was comforted. He acted with perfect tranquillity. He ignored the rumours and set about making a long-term plan. He was a man who regarded present problems as excuses for long-term preparation, long-term vision.

He began thinking of the future of the tribe, beyond its disappearance. He began preparations for its rebirth out of its decomposition. He dreamt a life after the apparent death of the tribe.

But first, deep in the night, he summoned his wife. They made plans together for the safety of their child and the future regeneration of their people.

Only those who have accepted the death of their people can dream a miraculous future. Only one who has accepted death can see the impossible things that can be done beyond the limitations of the world.

35

It FELL TO the mother to inform the maiden that she had to leave right away.

That night, the mother and father talked about the future. The father suddenly said:

'It's time for her initiation into the mysteries of womanhood.'

'And into the mysteries of the goddess,' the mother added.

Her eyes were large and sorrowful.

'What a difficult time awaits her, in the middle of her dreams,' she said.

'But afterwards she will be a woman like no other, but like her mother. She will be a woman not even kings deserve.'

'But the suffering and the dying?'

'And the shining face of the new woman when she emerges from the cave.'

'But the darkness and the loneliness?'

'Yes, my love, and loss of fear and wisdom in her spirit and strength of mind. And if she is lucky, gold in her soul, gift of the goddess.'

'But these things take a long time to reveal themselves, if ever. Most of the girls go through the initiation and are not changed by it at all.'

'Not our daughter,' the father said. 'Everything meaningful works on her. She is ready. It may take time to flower in her, but she will drink in the experience as the earth drinks rain. Then one day, when the times call for greatness, when all around are paralysed by fear, the power of the goddess, the power of our ancient ways, will rise in her and she will do extraordinary things. She will be amazed at what magic lives in her.'

'I know you are right, my love,' the mother said. 'But

children don't always live up to the possibilities their parents see in them. We have witnessed it in lots of families. The early brightness doesn't always bear fruit. All the careful guidance can just disappear in them. I don't want to expect too much of our daughter and spend our old age shaking our heads in silent disappointment.'

The father smiled.

'Have faith in her,' he said. 'She seems not of this world, I admit. But there is something in her which yearns to understand the mysteries of life. This is a special gift in itself.'

The mother stared thoughtfully ahead for a while before she spoke.

'Many want to understand, but few have the character for it,' she said, at last. 'And it takes character to receive. It takes character to wait, to listen, to learn, to master, to keep on the right road, to make mistakes and to correct them before they have gone too far. It takes character to always remember, beyond wealth and success, what the most important things in life are.'

She paused and stroked her husband's arm.

'She might want to know what the most important things in life are and yet she might settle, as most people do, for the most average things,' the mother said. 'She might not have the stamina to become a true woman.'

'Why do you say that?'

'I fear her oversensitivity. It might spoil her. It might make her want a soft and easy life. It might make her cruel. She may fail to see that the best things are the most challenging and the hardest to get. Or not.'

'Or not?'

'I have seen too many girls ruin their lives because they wanted what was easy, against the promptings of their hearts.'

The father began stroking his wife's arm in return.

'Our daughter is not like that. She has her mother's spirit. But in a different form. I think she was given to us to show

how a different destiny can lead to the kingdom of the blessed. Anyway, what have we to lose?'

'What do you mean?'

'If she turns out all right, she'll be a gift to the world. If she doesn't, she'll at least live an interesting life, because of the ways of our tribe. Already she has seen and learnt enough to give her plenty to think about for the rest of her life. She knows more than she knows that she knows. I don't fear for her.'

The mother laughed. Then she stared deeply into her husband's eyes, and said:

'What about all these rumours?'

It was now the husband's turn to laugh.

'We both know who is behind them. We both know why.'

'Yes, we do.'

'Rumours can destroy only that which is not true and deep. Rumours are like rats that eat away at the foundations of a house. If the foundations are not strong, the house will fall, with or without the rats. These things can work for our ends. We must let them come and go.'

'They will go.'

'People are seen to be greater if they survive the lies told about them. Especially if the quality of their lives proves the lies are lies. Out of a secret shame the world raises the stature of those it has maligned. But only if the maligned turn out to be worthwhile. Our daughter's integrity will turn these rumours into praise, into legend, one day. Those who tear down her good name will be forced to build a palace for her future fame.'

'You trust your daughter so much.'

'So do you. She has your special nature, but with her own strange gifts of the soul.'

'I know. That's why I'm hard on her in my words,' the mother said. 'I love her too much. These may well be the best days of her life, the purest days under this difficult sun. I want it to last. She doesn't know how happy she is. I want her to always have these happy times.'

The mother was now looking beyond the wall of their room as if she were seeing not the night but images etched in clear sunlight.

'I want her to always wander by the river and talk to snails on the path and laugh suddenly because happiness shakes her like the wind in the cornfield. I want her never to walk on nails, or to wake up in the bottom of a well, or to see the world turn into a cage. I never want her to see the road narrow to a tiny path, or to see monsters everywhere, or to become full of doubt and fear, or to become suspicious of those she loves, or to see evil in the good things of her life.'

For a moment it seemed that the mother's eyes reddened. She turned her face away a little. But her husband knew her gestures, and held her hand with gentle strength.

'I don't want her to ever drown in sorrow,' the mother said quietly, 'or to no longer see the sky with gladness. I don't want her to forget what love means, or to hate her life because of all the trouble that living brings. All I can do is prepare her for all the troubles to come, and to awaken in her a love of truth. All I can do is show her a mirror in which she can see her future self and be surprised by it and perhaps rebel against it; and in rebelling take such twists and turns that will lead her to the right way.'

She turned back to face her husband, who held her gaze.

'We will be gone by then,' she continued. 'But she will look back and see these as magical days. They will be days that are waiting. And she will find us inside her, growing in her struggles, flowering in her realisation. We will be in the best fruits of her life.'

Then she rested her head on her husband's shoulders. He encompassed her in his arms.

'I must show her, without showing her, how to make time a friend, a guide, a magician, by using the art of delaying. It is something the new generation is forgetting. But now I must be the wicked mother and bring swift changes into the sleeping life of our daughter. My dear husband, why is this always the mother's task?'

They both laughed deep into the night at the wonder of these things.

36

ON THE DAY that the maiden was to keep her promise to the voice by the river, her mother told her in a hard tone that she had to go away. It was supposed to be a day when the gods would show her favours she could hardly imagine. She had been quivery with anticipation.

She had no time to think about it and no time to pack. She had to leave as she was. Something urgent had come up. For her good she had to leave immediately.

'But mother,' she cried, 'do I have to go now?'

'Yes, my dear.'

'But I have barely woken up from sleep.'

'All the better.'

'Do I have to go this moment?'

'Yes. Now. As you are. We should be leaving as we are talking.'

'Does father know about it?'

'Of course.'

'What does he say?'

'It's his instruction. I am merely carrying out his orders.'

'But why?'

'There is no time to explain. Take what you need, the fewer things the better. Take them now or you will regret not paying attention later on.'

She was in a state of confusion, her mind in disarray, her world seeming to collapse about her. In a daze, she quickly gathered the clothes and slippers and comb and the little bust of the queen she had made. She was on the verge of tears, but was too confused to weep.

The notion of the end of things, the end of the world,

swooped down on her. She didn't know what to think. She was distressed at leaving so suddenly, of breaking her promise to the god of the river who had favoured her with speech. This filled her with a sense of panic. What would the god do? Would he be angry at her disobedience? Whom should she obey, the voice of a god, or the dictates of her parents?

She was in turmoil as she threw all her things into a bundle. How could she get word to the river that she was being taken away suddenly, against her will? And if she found a messenger, would the god listen to anyone else but her? And how could the messenger speak to the god when the god had chosen to speak to her, the maiden, alone? Could she – should she – explain all this to her mother?

But there was no time. For time was collapsing all about her. Things were vanishing. She could not find half the items that she sought. Her life was disappearing. What was happening to her?

The mother noticed her perplexity. Thinking that it must be because of the suddenness of her departure and the surreptitious nature of her journey, she began to speak a mother's words to her.

'My child,' she said, helping her to tie her bundle, 'this life of ours is an inscrutable story that only the gods can read.'

TIME PASSED IN a swift dream. Listening and not listening to her mother, she felt her life diverted into a new course. She felt lifted out of one life and lowered into another.

She felt obscurely assisted, propelled through time and space and destiny. Then she was under a low sky. The village passed by her. Faces stared. She found herself in her father's workshop. She was kneeling and he was pouring out a libation, invoking the gods and ancestors. He was asking them to protect his daughter on this journey that she was undertaking into womanhood, into the mysteries.

The prayers had a powerful effect on her. Suddenly, briefly, she saw the spirit of inspiration smiling at her. Then it was gone. Her mind faded a little and she found herself walking the long path out of the village. She saw tiny ritual sculptures along the way. Someone must have put them out in the night. She gazed at them, somewhat spellbound.

The road led up to the hills. A cloud of green hovered about the village below her. Then her mother was beside her again. She disappeared, then reappeared. Sometimes she was in the front, sometimes she was at her side.

The maiden walked on the earth and then was floating in a dream. Flashing swords shone down from the sun. The heat and the sharp rays sent her mind revolving. She went beyond the environs of the village, above the river, and high into the sacred hills. The grottoes of the gods abounded with legends. She walked for a long time, listening to the wind. Eagles and sunbirds flew over her head. She listened to the whirring of their wings.

She was led into a world beyond her dreams, beyond her horizon, into valleys of stone and brush and wild green plants with tiny yellow flowers. The rocks had faces like old masters of the tribe gazing into this world from another. Vultures perched on high outcrops. Strange animals rustled along their paths.

How long had they been travelling? Were they going to the world's end, to the domain of spirits? Was she, for some unknown reason, being led to a sacrifice? She had heard of such stories. A maiden is taken away because the god has chosen her to avert a disaster fatal for the world. Am I going willingly? she asked herself, and couldn't answer.

She felt that she was borne along by a power greater than her. She dreaded it all, but was calm in her terror.

38

SHE DISCOVERED THAT she loved the world she was leaving. She hadn't looked at it enough. The hills were rugged and beautiful. They were brown and slate-grey with patches of green. She stared at a dry mahogany tree on the hillside. The rocks were strangely shaped, like giant skulls. Here dwell the spirits, she thought. The hills are gods.

Looking up she saw the clear, bright blue of the sky. It was as if the heavens were closer to the earth. She could smell the fragrances of all the herbs and plants she had ever loved. They were in the wind. The ground she walked on was old. Ancient stories of tribes that had long vanished told themselves to her feet.

She saw bearded magi and elongated sorcerers. She saw burdened women. Warriors with spears skulked past her. The spirits of young children flashed by. Laughing fathers and sons loped through the vision. The tribes had gone into the rocks. They lingered in the air. She felt the blood of wars and ritual sacrifice.

She knew at once that she had lived and yet had not glimpsed what life was, what it meant. Had lived and not lived. She gave a sudden cry. Her mother appeared at her side and began speaking.

39

'My child, my child, be still. Be comforted,' her mother said. 'This is what a woman's life is like. A life of constant change. What is stable in this world anyway? Nothing. Everything changes. Everything goes. One day you are a girl, proud as a goddess, confused as a millipede counting its legs. The next day you are a woman, a mother, too busy, a little mad, quite helpless, and yet strangely powerful. The body changes. The world changes. Every day the earth is taken away from beneath your feet. The man who loved you yesterday, is he the same man today? One day you are loved, the next day not. One day your mother is there, the next day she is gone to join the ancestors. Who knows anything? All is like the wind, changing like water. Things disappear.'

They were climbing a path in the hills. The path was narrow and the earth was red. Plants with spotted flowers pressed on them from either side.

'A woman must learn to be still. A woman must learn to make things stay, to make things remain, to inspire things to come back, even when they go. A woman must learn the art of making time stand still. Of stretching time out. We must learn to make time wait, make it linger.'

The path was so narrow now, with rocks close by on either side, that they were obliged to walk in single file. The mother, walking behind, saw a flower of intense blue growing from a rock. She plucked it delicately.

'You must learn to make time live in your house, while history is being made. Keep it under your pillow, with your dreams. Make time a great friend. And how do you do this? This is something you must learn for yourself. It's the only way you will learn it. But I will tell you why you must learn it. It's because everything goes. Beauty, earthly power, fortune, wealth, happiness, clans, tribes, empires. Everything goes away. Disappears. But you can make them disappear more slowly. You can make them wait longer. You can charm them to stay for one more day. And if you do this, day after day, then you can manage a modest eternity. Only with love can you do this. But not an ordinary love. A love greater than life itself.'

She put the flower in her daughter's hair, slightly to the side, with one deft touch.

'Even things that go, you can charm them back, their fragrance, their spirit. If their spirit is here then they are here too, and soon their form will return in another way. These are women's ways. But not all women know them, my daughter, only those in whom the ancient wisdom of women is alive, only those who have been initiated into the mysteries of the great mother.'

40

THESE WORDS WERE meant to distract the maiden from the fear of the journey. They were also meant to prepare her, to bridge the distance between home and the unknown.

Did the maiden hear a single word? She did not. The mother knew that her daughter had not heard a single word. But she knew that her daughter's spirit had heard the spirit of her words. The spirit of the words had gone into her daughter through unusual channels, and would wait in her. One day it would give birth to wisdom.

The mother had long mastered the art of planting words in people through invisible channels. She knew that people resist words because they hear them. But the spirit of words can't be resisted.

The mother knew the art of the spirit of words. She knew the art of the spirit of things. In this she was rare. She specialised in these arts, and wove her words in and out of her daughter's mind, as she walked to the place of initiations.

41

As she staggered along in her sleepwalking way over rocks and harsh stones, the maiden did not hear anything. Her mind was full of foreboding. At the back of her mind was a terrible sense of loss. She couldn't reconcile herself to not keeping her promise to the voice by the river. She was certain she would suffer because of it.

It was only much later she learnt that in life there are many destinies. She would learn that we fail to keep an appointment with one destiny so that we can fulfil another. There are many alternative destinies waiting in the wings of failure.

This knowledge would not have consoled her then. She stumbled along the hot paths of the ascending hill, crushed by the sun and obliterated by the sky. Her feet were raw on the earth. Exhaustion wore down her mind. She felt herself fading into hallucination.

But she thought only about the voice by the river that she was leaving behind forever.

42

THE MAMBA DIDN'T know that the maiden had gone. He kept up his malicious campaign.

He spoke out, in an obsessed manner, about sinister foreigners invading the lives of the people. He seemed to forget that the tribe was always open to outsiders, that it relied on a continual flow of people who brought trade and art from distant kingdoms. Without them the tribe would have no idea what the rest of the world was doing. It would be isolated from the currents of art and thought and trade.

As a people they thrived on wonder. There were few things they appreciated more than a new sculpture from an unknown race, a carving in which the human features were scrambled, an unfamiliar way of representing the world. They loved nothing more than to be amazed by a work that they did not understand.

It was essential to their pleasure that they did not at first understand the art that came their way from the trade routes of the world.

They saw better when they did not understand. For understanding stopped them looking. Consequently they liked to delay their understanding. They felt that things had more presence when not grasped.

Even when they understood a work, they sought out in it the things they did not understand, could not understand. This they held up as its core mystery. When this point of mystery moves, as it does through time, under the light of unexpected events, it also altered the centrality of the work's mystery. But first it had to be a significant work.

Like women admiring new clothes in the marketplace, or the fruits of a rich harvest, the tribe gathered round like children and admired the new art which traders brought from the wider world. There might be knives with ivory handles, figurines of fired clay with displaced eyes, reliquary figures and animal forms sculpted from rock. They might be drawings on scrolls, handwritten manuscripts from prosperous kingdoms, paintings on parchment, vivid colours on absorbent wood. There might be the seeds of bizarre fruits and the skulls of strange animals. Often there were objects that were magical because they were inexplicable and beautiful, or potent in the ideas that their forms breathed out. These works created a great and lasting excitement in the tribe. They were a vital part of its creativity.

They freely adapted the possibilities in these works of art. They transformed the objects they encountered. They absorbed and they acknowledged. They did this in the art they made, the quotations, the displaced reference, sometimes even the scrambled homage. For them acknowledgement was an expression of gratitude. It made their higher creativity possible. They believed that the gods of creativity disapproved of unacknowledged influences. Artistic barrenness was believed the punishment for this aesthetic crime.

43

IT WAS AGAINST all this that the Mamba found himself pitted. In his obsession he forgot the basis of the tribe's creative and commercial success. They relied on the purchase of their works by traders, who were outsiders. He found himself up against the fear of a loss of trade. He also found himself up against the other suitors for the hand of the maiden.

Soon he became isolated and didn't know it. He was outside the current but no one told him.

In the tribe silence was often the highest form of condemnation or appreciation. But silences are different. A mad man shouts obscenities from dawn to dusk and people are silent. The mad man becomes madder and one day is heard from no more. There is a silence that swallows up those who talk too much.

44

THE MAIDEN'S FATHER had not learnt of the rumours from the mouths of people, from friends, or from relations. He had learnt about them from the hints that the tribe was expert at making.

He heard songs in the marketplace with certain references and sly images. He intuited their references. It was always indirect.

He saw certain works of art, noticed certain sculptures near the shrine, overheard certain words in conversation. He noticed a suggestiveness in certain glances. With an insolence previously unthinkable, someone might linger too long in a stare.

The unspoken speech of these acts wasn't hard to hear. The unsaid things thundered in a hundred other ways than through speech.

When he sent his daughter away he didn't do so secretly, but in daylight, so that everyone would see and therefore not see.

When he acted, he acted in the highest spirit.

45

HE AND HIS wife had talked into the hour of the dwindling stars.

They talked about their daughter, while seeming to talk of other things.

'One does not become a woman by getting older,' his wife said.

'Nor a human being just by being born.'

'To be what we are takes time.'

'And no time at all.'

'Those who use only their brains cannot get to the mysterious depths of these things.'

'The present will not last.'

'People see only that which has gone.'

'They don't see what is here but invisible.'

Man and wife spoke of these things, into the hour of the awakening sun.

46

THE DISAPPEARANCE OF the maiden raised her stature with the suitors, and fuelled more rumours about her.

As rumour took the place of fact, filling an absence, it allowed people to be creative in the stories invented. They said the maiden had gone mad, that she had contracted a fatal disease, that something bad had been foretold about her fate.

They hinted that she had been impregnated by the horned animal she copulated with and had to go away. They speculated about the nature of the man-beast to which she might give birth. Would it wander about the village in broad daylight?

Some thought that the pressure of creating the work of her own healing had wrecked her sanity. Some wondered if she had crumbled under the strain of the relentless wooing from the suitors.

There is always an element of truth in collective rumours, even if the grain is allegorical or symbolic.

The wise few who suggested that the maiden had gone away to be spiritually fortified were closer to the mark than they realised.

47

SHE HAD BEEN taken to the cave of awakening, in the hills of the gods. In that cave her real life began.

She was buried alive, left for days, allowed to die, and then she was raised.

It was in the cave that she began to dream of a dying prince.

48

ABOUT INITIATIONS ONE ought to be silent. They are sacred and private events. The rituals belong to the initiated. They should not be bared to the world. Their power is destroyed when they are revealed. Noble initiations ought to have great silence and a ring of fire around them, so that the initiated may undergo the rites of their transformation in the privacy of that sacred space. That is how it should be for those who make the ritual changes from darkness to light, from boys to men, from girls to women, from chrysalis to butterfly. Wisdom ought to guide these processes of liberation.

About the maiden's initiation, though I saw it in the book of life, I shall be silent, in my revealing kind of way. I shall conceal by revealing. She passed through it with difficulty and suffering. She dwelt alone for seven days in the cave of transformations. She was buried alive for several nights. She gave birth to herself in her death and emerged from the earth in a disorientated state. She had nothing but water, fruit, and herbs. She dwelt among the rocks and awaited the goddess. She recited the prayers of light that had been given her till she broke down and wept for a whole day. Then she felt like dying and lay down to die on a white rock in the blazing sun, with her lips all broken and her mind quite cracked.

Then a blaze of light encompassed her and in the light there was a bird and she followed the bird into the heavens and wandered in halls of pure white glory. Then she saw a prince waiting for her at the door of golden splendour and he reached out his hand and she held it and together they entered the chamber of angels.

They were silent there among the angels and they were both

happy in their bliss beyond mortal dreams. They dwelt there in love and harmony for a small eternity. Then time tugged at her and she found herself alone, listening to the goddess in the hall of the holy. The whispers were not words. They were beyond words.

Then a flash of red light fell upon her and she awoke and found herself alone in a cave. The girls who had changed into women were singing outside. They were calling to her to come out of the cave to be a new woman and give birth to a new world.

49

SHE EMERGED FROM the cave into the light. After much coaxing and encouragement, she danced the dance of the new woman and she was taught the rituals of birth. Her blood broke then and ran down her legs and they celebrated her as a woman who with blood bears the weight and wisdom of the world, who with blood makes the earth beautiful and rich with meaning, who with blood brings forth souls to emerge into history and time, who with blood incarnates myth and legend.

She danced and ate and was fed excellent food with the new women. She learnt proverbs and the power of silence and the legends of the land. She learnt the histories of the tribe and the sagas of families. She learnt the ways of women that dissolve the stubborn and short-sighted ways of men.

She was taught to see men as allies in the universe created by the supreme being to make noble the future of the race and the earth. She was taught the art of indirectness, the science of herbs, the marvels of decoration, the proper place for agreement and disagreement, and the higher ways to accomplish things. She was taught that wisdom is greater than force, grace more magical than power, love stronger than hate.

She learnt that bitterness and food do not mix, that a pure heart is more beautiful than a pure sky, and that discord is the enemy of prosperity.

She was taught a thousand other things which will be forgotten and then remembered and passed on from generation to generation, longer than the life of the hills.

With the new women, she danced and grew and learnt and unlearnt. She changed and didn't change. She had no idea what her initiation had made her become. Her face in the mirror of the lakes looked odd to her. She had acquired a new face, with a new look in her eyes. She feared her new self, feared its power and wisdom. She kept it hidden for a long time.

50

SHE WENT TO the hills an innocent girl, and emerged from the caves a profound young woman. She was sweeter and more self-contained than before. And odder.

Initiation had made her more deeply what she truly was. She had not really changed. The greatest experiences do not change the soul. They only reveal what was there in the depths of the spirit. They make a person what they really were all along.

When people say an experience changed them, they mean that it brought forth their real nature. Under the impact of significant experiences, people only become what they really are, for good or ill.

But initiations are different. If they are noble, they transform a person into their higher selves. They see themselves more clearly.

Initiation unveils. Transformation is self-revealing. The maiden was revealed to herself and did not yet know it.

51

THE MAIDEN DESCENDED from the hills.

The world she left was not the same.

She saw things she had not seen before. She heard things she had not heard before. She did things she would never have done before.

And yet could it be said that she had changed?

52

IN ACCORDANCE WITH tradition the tribe welcomed the maiden back with songs and dances reserved for heroines. They embraced her into their heart. They treated her as a special being. They created an arch of palm fronds for her to walk under, as if she were a priestess returning from the oracle with good omens for the world.

53

IT WAS WHEN she returned from her initiation that, in a sudden inspiration, she created the sculpture of the dying prince.

She had not long returned when she began haunting her father's workshop. She wandered among the sleeping wood and the unsummoned spirits. She was seen walking in the forests. She was searching for something which could not be sought, but could only be received.

One day, in her open-minded state, she encountered an old man who was sitting on air. His eyes were piercing, his face young, and he had a gentle smile. She said nothing to him. He stared through her. But as she went past him, in silence, she heard him say:

'What you seek is the foundation.'

She went straight home. The next day she found the perfect piece of ebony wood near the shrine, as if it had been placed there for her. The wood shone with the mystery of dawn.

She took it home and slept with it by her pillow. Then on another day, in the middle of her duties, unaware of all things, she saw the dream of a face in the wood and surrendered to it completely.

She asked no questions, sought no answers, forgot all techniques, discarded all craft, abandoned her heart, left behind her mind, ceased to be a woman, or even human, became blind, refused speech, and in complete emptiness, like one without beginning or end, she received what emerged from her dreaming in wood.

When it was finished she placed the sculpture of a dying prince in front of the village shrine.

54

BEAUTIFUL AND ROUGH, rich in pathos, touched with humour, the work caused consternation in the tribe. But it caused more problems in her.

It troubled her. She had no idea what made her create it. She pondered it often and stared at it whenever she could. Sometimes it was like staring into a mirror. Baffled by the strength of her own creation, she began to fall in love. It was not the beauty or the work she fell in love with. It was with the things the figure suggested. She fell in love with the languid youth in wood.

The tranquil sadness of the dying youth became a fascination. The mystery unhinged her a little. She began to seek a man who was like the sculpture. She searched for him in all the faces that she met. But she found no one who rivalled the beauty of her own creation.

Then she dreamt that the youth would wake from his death-slumber in wood and stand before her as fresh as a flower touched with dew.

It was a vivid dream. Blood returned to the pale cheeks of the dying prince and he stretched his limbs and sat up. Then he turned and spoke to her with a voice so familiar that it caused in her a tremor of delight. The dying prince stared at her a long time. He had doe-like eyes of liquid sadness. His lips were gentle and red and his nose was fine, but his jaw was strong. He stared at her and did not speak. His eyes seemed the centre of the universe and his breathing the centre of her love. He filled her with an ache which she could not locate, a desire from which she could not escape.

He made her want to weep for the tragic condition of the world. But not one word emerged from him.

There was just his quiet stare. The intensity of it touched her to the core.

Then slowly the prince lay down again and assumed his dying repose, returning to his condition of a sculpture in wood.

55

SHE HAD THIS dream several times and each time she woke she was disconsolate. The prince never uttered a word to her and till he spoke, she felt she could not speak to him. His awakening from his imprisonment in wood was the miracle that would free her.

The maiden carried this secret around all day. She wanted the prince to wake from wood into flesh. She wanted him to speak, so that she could learn to love.

She was a prisoner. She could not be free till he was free. Her return from the hills, which should have made her stronger, now made her susceptible to impossible fantasies. The creation of the work of art, which should have healed her, now made her ill.

She fell ill because life was not as subtle as art.

THE TRIBE OF artists were troubled by her work. They had expected from her a healing image, an image of beauty. They had expected a work potent with her distinguished lineage, her unique personality.

They had hoped she would be the oracle of a new generation, that her art would mirror the broken rhythms of the times, that it might somehow interpret the omens perplexing the tribe. They hoped that with new and uncontaminated eyes she might show them that which they could not see, the fate pressing on them, invisible but palpable as a tragic premonition.

Centuries of art had made the tribe sensitive to the links between a work and its creator. Like those who can read personality from handwriting, they could detect the mind behind certain works. To the mind of the tribe, the face of the creator was in their art.

When the sculpture of the dying prince was found, first there was puzzlement, then controversy, then rumour, then intuition. The signature of personality was deciphered. A maker was deduced. Then there was consternation.

The work was perceived as an outrage. It seemed irrelevant, a conceit, an aesthetic indulgence. It was devoid of prophecy or vision. It did not relate to anything that anyone could care about. It was beautiful and sad just for the sake of it, an exercise, a display of genius.

It did not address the need of the times. Nor did it reflect the mood of the tribe. It did not soothe or guide. Nor was it the voice of a new generation speaking with the authority of youth.

The maiden's art brought no new techniques that required an altered way of seeing. Secretly they had hoped for a work that would begin their liberation from a destiny they could all feel but could not name.

Maybe their sense of outrage was caused by the fact that the work was the image of liberation. Maybe they knew it without knowing they did.

The work bypassed direct expression and worked on their souls. It worked on the foundation and depth of who they were as a people and as individuals.

Their outrage was real and almost became violent.

MANY HASTILY EXECUTED works were displayed ridiculing the sculpture of the dying prince. There were songs satirising its inadequacy in drinking places, at the farms, in workshops, marketplaces and communal kitchens. The ridicule was unprecedented, the number of works mocking the sculpture surprising.

Wise heads wondered if the people, encompassed by invisible tragic fears, did not feel it necessary to find something to laugh at, to relieve themselves of the weight of foreboding. Ridicule seemed a way of dealing with a larger, oppressive bewilderment. It seemed the hysterical laughter of the doomed.

58

THE RIDICULE PASSED, but the consternation remained.

They had expected a clear healing image, and had placed great hopes on the maiden. They hoped that she might be their eyes till sight returned.

Instead she had given them this ambiguous image. There were no princes in the tribe. What had this to do with them? they asked, infuriated.

She was startled by the fury, taken aback by the ridicule, the incomprehension. She was shocked by the abuse and the threats of violence, amazed at how quickly she became an outcast, shunned and denounced.

Her talent was declared worthless, her father's reputation fraudulent. There was this sudden desire to demonise her family. At the same time there was an increased fascination in them.

All this had been touched off by the simple image of a dying prince.

She was caught between two absurdities, one public, the other private.

59

THROUGH ALL THIS her father was silent. He made his art with his usual serenity.

He appeared not to register that anything unusual was going on. He didn't seem to notice the fury directed at his family.

He went about his business as though he lived in a separate realm. In that realm the significance of events was radically different from that of the real world.

He was invincible. This strengthened his mystique, and magnified the power around him.

When his daughter came to him about it all, he smiled at her gently. With mild eyes, he said:

'The moment people are unjust to you, they have lost the fight. The moment they attack you, they have lost the war. The moment they try to humiliate you, invalidate you, or destroy you, that moment they have lost the truth. Then they lose all spiritual protection. That moment they surrender power and authority to you, but they do not know it.'

'Is this true, father?'

'It is one of the laws of life.'

'But sometimes people attack and win.'

'Only for a short time. In the long run they lose. It's just that the loss comes about in a roundabout way and they don't make any connection between their injustice and their eventual failure.'

'But sometimes they are unjust and the injustice stays.'

'It only seems that way. Justice takes its time. Its power is unfailing. No one who is unjust ever wins. In the end they lose.'

'But father, sometimes they succeed and people are destroyed.'

'A bigger destruction always comes upon the destroyers. But

it takes a thousand mysterious forms. No one ever escapes the injustice of their destruction of others, even if it takes a thousand years.'

The maiden became thoughtful.

'The moment people try to hurt or bully or disgrace you, that moment they have lost the true magic of life. Without knowing it they pass the magic to you. Their end is certain. Their defeat is inevitable. The rest is time's work.'

'Is this really so, father?'

'It is. Carry on your work. Be serene. Follow your conscience, and have no fear. The laws that operate in the world are invisible laws. But they are greater than the force of nations. You can depend on these laws.'

'Can you, father?'

'Yes, my daughter. Some people kill a little thing and invite a mighty storm on their heads that wipes them out. Take pity on those who try to destroy you. Try to forgive them, for what they call down upon themselves is more terrible.'

The father paused. Then the tone of his voice changed. It became faraway and strange and sorrowful.

'Perhaps it's better to endure their stupidity than to let a whole people be wiped out. Sometimes, for their own good, it's better to fight them.'

'Why?'

'Better to fight them and stop a greater and more terrible army doing the fighting for you. Sometimes, when you fight them, you do it out of pity, and even out of kindness.'

'That sounds strange.'

'I know. But it's true, and so, for now, go about your business. Let's see what time brings.'

Much comforted, she went about her business. Like some flowers, some babies, she had an air of innocent invincibility, as if she knew that she could and could not be destroyed. As if she knew some simple secret of eternity. A new smile appeared on her face.

60

ON THE NIGHT of interpretations the masters gathered to contemplate any signs that had come to them from the innumerable agencies of the oracle.

These signs could be the words of a madman or child. It could be words overheard somewhere or the last words of a dying man or woman. It might be a phrase heard in thunder, or the roar of an animal in the forest. Incalculable were the forms of the oracle's speech.

They came together to tease out the meanings of new parables, paradoxes, stories, songs, or inexplicable sayings. They also gathered to interpret any work of art that perplexed or would not yield easy revelation.

For them the desire to understand a work of art was often a presumption. It got in the way of seeing. For them seeing was endless.

They believed that once a work was thought to be understood its magic was dimmed in the person who thought they understood. Such people become closed to the light of the work, closed to its power for regeneration.

In this way the world is diminished a little, a source of light hidden.

The masters sought therefore only to be open. They made themselves open to the work's secrets, its language, its inspiration, its guidance.

61

No one missed the night of interpretations. Not even if they were ill. Even the dying were known to have attended. It was considered greatly auspicious to be there on that night. It was considered a high honour to die on a night of interpretations, for it was believed that then the soul went straight to the happy land of the ancestors.

On this night the masters convened to contemplate the image of the dying prince. The wiser ones among them had stayed above the ridicule. They had sent the maiden signs of support. The masters knew there could be no hasty response to a work that had come from one newly born in initiation.

The masters knew they had to look deeper into the phenomenon. They had to wait till the work spoke, or till the world gave it one of its unexpected meanings.

On this night they waited for the work to speak, but it didn't. They pondered its meaning. They could find none. Or they found too many.

Was the land a dying prince? Was their way in danger? Had they lost their way under the sun? Was their freedom dying and they couldn't see it? Was their conscience perishing and they did not know it? Was the spirit of the tribe in peril? Was their art fading?

The masters were baffled and concerned. The more they probed, the more baffled and concerned they became.

But the work itself did not speak. The work itself said nothing.

62

MEANWHILE THE SUITORS persisted in competing for the maiden's attention. Meanwhile the Mamba redoubled his campaign of rumour and seduction. Meanwhile the maiden became more obsessed with the enigma of the dying prince. She didn't eat and roamed the forest for long hours and soon fell ill again.

It was feared that her sculpture was exercising undue magical influence on her and that she was dying with the dying prince. She was falling under the spell of her own creation and nothing could be done about it.

It was thought that she had to go through this condition if she was to emerge as a greater artist. She had to develop psychic protection against the forces of her own mind. She had to acquire an immunity to the laws of art as it affects its creator.

For the second time in her life the maiden surrendered to death. She became ill with her own mystery and died for seven days.

63

SHE DID NOT die as such, but she did not live. She was profoundly ill, yet in strangely good health. Lean and languid, an ineluctable yearning occupied her days. She longed for an impossible, indefinable condition. She yearned for her original homeland in a faraway constellation, where life had been unimaginably beautiful.

To parents and suitors she seemed detached. Broken sentences fell from her lips. She spoke only of a love beyond reason, a love sweeter than madness. Or was it a madness sweeter than love?

She slept most of the time. She slept like a calf, wherever sleep took her. If it came upon her near the river, she would curl up on the wet bank and sleep. If it crept upon her in the marketplace, she would arrange herself on bales of cloth, on heaps of oranges, and sleep the sleep of the innocent. It was as if she had been put under a spell.

64

SOMETIMES, IN HER father's workshop, she would be listening to the tale his hammer told as it beat upon the chisel. She would listen to the dream being wrought from the resistant wood. Sometimes she would curl up among the masks and images. The images were of beings never seen on earth, faces from remote galaxies. She would drift off to sleep listening to tales being told across the vast spaces, carried by waves of light that were everywhere.

She would fall asleep in her father's workshop and wake up in the marketplace. She could drop off to sleep at the foot of the goddess or in the alcove of the shrine and wake in her mother's kitchen, her head on her lap, listening to stories from ancient times. Stories of lost secrets from a fabled land beneath the sea.

She would fall asleep as her mother plaited her hair, and wake to find a bucket balanced on her head as she returned from the river, with water to purify the goddess on the day of celebrations.

Whenever she slept, she dreamt of the dying prince, who gazed at her and never spoke.

65

THEN ONE DAY, in her dream, the dying prince sat up and stared at her. He looked at her as if she were the first flower he had ever seen. It was as if he were trying to see the flower properly, to understand what about it so moved him.

He stared at her as at a work of art that was beyond understanding. She bore his gaze for a long time, waiting.

Then it occurred to her that it was she who must speak. He was her creation. If the creator did not speak, how could the creation? Her speech would free him into speech. She had to invest the dream with life. For too long she had been mute. What a failure in a creator, she thought. If the creation was to have the vitality of the creator then its soul must be awoken with love.

The prince had sat up. He was looking at her simply. She realised that she must seem the most impenetrable mystery to him, because of her silence. Unless she spoke, the prince would remain in his unknown condition. He would be unconnected to her, the sole focus of his being. He would have nothing to say to her. And she would never know herself through the eyes of another. She would remain a mystery to herself.

She realised that she needed the prince more than the prince needed her. Her reality depended on being known and loved by another. If the prince did not speak, she might cease to exist.

Then she understood his stare. He was looking at her with love. A love without suffering, without story. A love that did not know itself. The love of a pure thing that had not lived.

That was what she saw in the prince's eyes. The purity would have to be broken if the prince was ever to speak or be free. He must be free to love her not as her creation, but out of his own necessity. He must be free to love her as himself. He must be awoken from his enchantment.

Then the maiden, in her dream, spoke to the dying prince.

'Who are you?' she asked.

'I am that which was and now am.'

'What is your name?'

'My name is written in your tears.'

She realised then that she had tears in her eyes.

'Why are you dying?'

'Because I'm not living.'

'Why are you not living?'

'Because I don't know what love is.'

'Do you know what love is now?'

'Yes.'

'What is love?'

'Love is life.'

'You talk back and forth.'

'It is back and forth.'

'Why are you a prince?'

'Because I'm the son of a king.'

'Who is the king?'

'The king is the king.'

'What is he king of?'

'A kingdom.'

She paused and stared thoughtfully at him. The prince gazed back at her.

'Is it a kingdom of heaven or earth?'

'What is the difference?'

'Am I of that kingdom?'

'Yes.'

'How can I be? I made you.'

'Did you make me or discover me?'

'What's the difference?'

'Sometimes we make what we discover. Sometimes we discover what we make.'

The maiden was perplexed. Then she had a strange notion.

'Am I dying too?'

'You can only make what you are.'

'So I am dying?'

'Maybe.'

'Why am I dying?'

'For the same reason I'm not living.'

It was like catching a glimpse of herself in the clear mirror of a lake and finding she did not look the way she thought. This was going to take some time to get used to.

That was when it occurred to her that she must delay her life. She must delay till she knew who she was, till she gained some wisdom and self-knowledge. Till she learnt how to live.

She was not going to make any hasty choices about who to marry. She was going to take life slowly. Take time to learn.

The prince was silent again, looking at her with candour and simplicity. In the depth of her dream she found peace.

66

AFTERWARDS SHE BEGAN a slow recovery. She slept less and went about in the village more. She became calm and humble and less strange.

She listened to everything. It was as if whatever life had to tell her would be told her in between the sound of things, in the least expected ways.

She became attentive. She was as attentive and aware as she had previously been distracted and unaware. There was much she didn't see because she was trying to see. She wore herself out with her intensity. She couldn't sustain it long and she became alert and quiet. She was waiting for life to teach her.

Her father saw all these changes with an inward smile. Her mother fretted.

'We mothers are built this way,' she said to her husband. 'To worry even when we know.'

The suitors were exasperated by the maiden's delay. One by one they fell away. Till there were only six suitors left.

67

TIME PASSED SLOWLY. The river imperceptibly changed its course. The tribe imperceptibly changed its ways. It quietly lost its centre. No longer did it make art as though it were the most essential thing in the world.

People died and were born. The gods perished silently and no one saw it happen. The world impinged on the land and no one saw the shadows approaching in the distance, like the evening.

Lost in its dream. The land was lost in its dream. Lost in its rituals, its cruelties, its superstitions.

It was lost in its ancient ways. Lost in its power, its wickedness, its enchantments. It did not hear the music of the world outside.

Time passed slowly, as in a dream where things are changing. The dreamer is unaware and yet alert. They are asleep and yet awake. They see what is coming and still are blind to what they see. They are deaf to their own prophecies. It is as if they are cursed not to know that they are cursed, blessed not to know they are blessed.

68

Time drifted slowly down the dreaming way. And many things were forgotten even while they lived.

The image of a dying prince was forgotten. The scandals were forgotten. Because it got worse, and therefore imperceptible, the unease was forgotten. Rumours were forgotten. Suitors were forgotten. Purpose was forgotten. The rituals were dimly remembered. The masters slowly succumbed to oblivion. Their existence became a rumour of conspiracies, of sinister secret societies. The shrines were unremembered.

All this happened in the space of a dream. It happened in no time at all, or in the time it takes for a people to change and be lost. Then one day, inexplicably, they vanish off the face of the earth. As if they had never existed. As if they had been taken away and repositioned in another realm, in another constellation.

Then something unusual came to pass.

69

On a clear day on which nothing unusual happened, this happened. Mysterious laughter was heard throughout the land.

It was an immense laughter, booming, inexplicable, deep, happy, sad, sublime, light, mocking, ironic, sane, and wise.

Everyone in the tribe heard it in their dreams. They heard it when they were absorbed in their work. They heard it in their passionate moments. They heard it in their silences. The masters heard it in their meditations. The river and the birds and the trees heard it. Children and babies heard it with a special clarity. The deaf and the dumb and the blind and the crippled and the sick heard it. The dying heard it, and it aided their peaceful deaths. Criminals heard it and shivered. The evil ones heard it and trembled. The Mamba heard it and felt a chill come over him that presaged the dissolution of his powers. The suitors heard it. The shrines heard it and the unknown priestesses within echoed the laughter.

The maiden heard it and fell into a trance. Her father heard it and was inspired to create one final work of sculpture, after which he would sculpt no more. Her mother heard it and was visited by a prophecy concerning the future of the race, which she was forbidden to communicate.

In their different ways, they all heard the celestial laughter. It shook the foundations of the tribe. They never stopped hearing it. For it pervaded the land and became a permanent force in the air, constant in the renewal of things.

Long after their world came to an end, the laughter remains.

BOOK THREE

The White Wind

I

1

MANY ARE THE wonders to be lived, without knowing it, in the book of life among the stars. Many are the horrors deprived of their tragedy, evils deprived of their cruelty, deaths deprived of their sting. Many are the lies stripped of their power, sufferings stripped of their excesses, agonies drained of their depths. Many are the loves that still haunt, betrayals that still shock, and the stupidities of men and women in the empty vanities of their days. All stripped of that which made them absurd.

Many are the great events drained of wonder. Many are the wars which seemed so significant, but which now are moments in a panoramic dream.

Many are the moments unnoticed: babies in conversation with angels, spirits of the dead drifting past the love-making forms of the living, the earth seen by the stars through gaps in the trees. Many are the secret joys: young girls brimming with the ambiguous happiness of life, drummers lost in wild joys of syncopation. Many are the losses: passionate lovers who destroy their love through fear of loving. Many are the moments when dust dreams and lives adventures in the dim mirror of illusions; and within the living an immortal light shines, unseen.

Many are the lives that speak to one another across the vast spaces of the universe, connecting and not knowing it. Many are those who think they are alone but are in constant speech with others in remote constellations, asleep and awake and in the depths of their spirits where time and space cageth not the soul.

Many are those who do not see the wonder of things in the blind realm of mortality.

All this to be lived, in sublime ways, beyond the brain's knowing, in the magic spaces.

All this to be lived, in a flash, in the book of life among the stars.

2

DURING THAT TIME there was an uncommon plague in the kingdom.

The kingdom was so large that it did not know its own parts. Many of its parts did not know they belonged to the kingdom.

The kingdom was sprawling and vast and within it were many sub-kingdoms. The kingdom was so extensive it did not know itself. The king knew it only through the cartography of his dreams.

He dreamt all the corners and obscure places of the kingdom. He knew the great variety of people, the huge forests and mighty rivers, the innumerable creeks and hills and valleys, the multiplicity of traditions and the incredible number of languages.

The King knew them all in dreams. He ruled this unruly, undivided, yet much divided kingdom, through the agency of dreams. There was no other way.

Terrestrially he had chiefs, emissaries, deputies, spies, messengers, and sub-rulers. They travelled the vast lands carrying laws, decrees, legislations, edicts, proclamations, instructions, and dictates. He had an extensive hierarchy of chiefs and sub-kings who ruled the lesser kingdoms in his name and spirit.

But to rule them all by land was impractical. To rely on messages sent by couriers, edicts sent by messengers, was insufficient. Often weeks passed before messages were received. The messages were often out of date by the time they arrived. Laws were no longer valid by the time they were made and received. Time devoured the possibilities of ruling the immense kingdom; distance mocked the reforms and the decrees sent forth; space distorted them on arrival.

The only thing that time and space could not distort, but would enhance, was the way of ruling through dreams, through thought. The king sent forth his laws at night, on the wings of sleep. And all over the kingdom officials and chiefs and sub-kings woke up at dawn knowing what to do. They would enact the laws as if they were their own ideas.

3

THE DREAMS OF the kingdom were laden with instructions and urgent laws. The night trafficked in edicts and reforms, praise and corrections.

The kingdom was busiest at night, when people were sleeping. Then the king, sending off a round of new laws, would visit the sleeping forms of his people. He would listen to their dreams, and question them about their needs and fears. So extensively did he speak to and listen to his people that he was thoroughly involved in their lives as though he were one of them.

And they felt he was one of them, that he knew their hearts and they knew his heart, though they didn't know they did but felt it intimately.

So profoundly did the king listen to the courtiers, the elders, the criminals, the butchers, the market women, the farmers, the traitors, the orphans, the enslaved and the servants, the abandoned and the hungry, the rich and the broken-hearted that he knew the desires of his people more sensitively than if they had come to him in person and he had granted them an audience. In this way he knew their anger and their hopes.

But he did it through dreams. He listened to them and queried them and paid attention to them in their dreams. He tended to them in dreams too, sending them solace and guidance, advice and suggestions, protection and blessings. He was often dispensing powerful spells and incantations into their inner worlds, to strengthen them in their daily lives and to make sure they didn't feel abandoned. He wanted them to know that their king, though far from them, was also closest to them. He made sure that they knew that he never dozed and that he kept their needs always in mind and always worked for their good in thousands of ways that they never suspected. He did this equally, whether they were good or bad, as if they were all his children, which they all were.

They all belonged to the vast kingdom without a name.

4

THE KING RULED without ruling. There were many who had no idea that they had a king, many who had no idea what a king was. There were many to whom the king existed as a dim rumour, a figure made up from many stories. To some the king was a personage who dwelt on a mountaintop, or at the bottom of the sea, or in a cave. To others he was one who sometimes came to the village in disguise, an old man with a strange beard, or an old woman with youthful limbs, or a child with a golden cane, or a beautiful young woman no one had ever seen before, or a white antelope covered in light. To some he came disguised as the wind, as a cloud, or as the night itself, and sometimes as the sun.

Many were those who never thought about their king, but who worked very hard at the forge or in the farms, from dawn to dusk. Many were those who lived lives that didn't seem like lives, but one long toil and drudgery, like beasts, for no purpose, save to feed their families and drink under the moon and sleep without resting and wake without pausing. But the king knew them all intimately. From their dreams he knew their desperate truths.

Many were those who did not think the king existed, but acknowledged their local chiefs, the elders of their clans, and the figures of authority of their villages and their lands.

5

THE KING SEEMED absent in the kingdom when he was most present. He left them in freedom to be how they best can be. He left them free to choose how they wanted to be.

The only way the king was known was by his mysterious laughter. This laughter was heard everywhere that solace was needed. Through this laughter all things were connected, corrected, answered, acknowledged, balanced, embraced, and touched with enchantment.

The only other way the king was known was by the silent figure in the people's dreams, the one who is always there, taking part and not taking part, observing and never observed. The one who sometimes makes a suggestion, which is rarely heeded because such listening has often not been learnt.

But then the next night, in the next dream, that silent figure would be there again, humble, and unknown, paying attention to the most important or trivial things in the spirit of his people.

6

MANY THINGS WERE happening in the kingdom that were baffling to the people. An unusual plague came to the land. At first it appeared as a new wind that blew over from across the great sea. It was a cold white wind and wherever it blew it created empty spaces. At first it was a pleasant wind, bringing melodies and fragrances and lovely dreams. At first it was a soothing wind that brought new visions of the earth and the heavens. It seemed to clear the sky. Stars that had always been in the heavens were seen more lucidly.

The wind was, in the beginning, cleansing and bracing and fresh. It cooled the humid air of the sun-loved land. The white wind brought coolness to the skin and the mind. It brought a new way of being and wider worlds. New dreams travelled on the white wind to enrich the dreams of the land. It unveiled new horizons.

At first the white wind was a thing of wonder, a phenomenon strange and delightful to experience. It swept through the land changing the appearance of things. It brought new colour to the bright light of the day and new hues to the brilliant darkness of the night.

Then, imperceptibly, the nature of the wind changed. It began to erase that which it passed over. It erased hills and valleys, towns and villages, forests and rivers, animals and flowers, gold mines and whole portions of the lands and the memories of the people.

Slowly, mysteriously, things began to disappear. The weather changed. The seasons were altered. Songs began to vanish. Artworks evaporated.

Then, most strangely of all, the gods disappeared, one by

one, from the pantheon. For a long time no one noticed the momentous silence of this event. The silence of the gods was taken as a sign of the serenity of the people. It seemed a sign of good fortune, harmony, and plenitude in the land.

7

THERE WERE THOSE who remembered a great malaise coming among the people. It made them sleepy, in-turned, argumentative, and slow. The malaise made them superstitious and sluggish in the reading of signs.

The first thing some remembered was a strange new failure to decipher the signs that multiplied in the land. There was an unwillingness to heed the omens. The people seemed to lose the desire to interpret their dreams, to listen to their prophets, or to pay attention to the artists.

The land was always abundant in signs and wonders, in omens and warnings. They were always receptive to hints and messages from the gods and the ancestors.

But with the advent of the white wind a mental lassitude fell among the people. It was as if the wind had erased their will, their need to interpret. It introduced a sleepwalking quality into the land.

The first god to be erased from the pantheon by the white wind was the god of interpretation.

8

THE GOD OF interpretation was always slightly removed from the other gods and never fully noticed at the best of times.

There followed the disappearance of the god of questions. People who were as much prone to contestation as silence stopped asking questions.

They stopped asking why and when and how and why-is-it-so and why-can't-it-be-otherwise. It seems they accepted the world as they saw it. They accepted what was there. They accepted and believed what they were told.

This was a new kind of sleep. It was a sleep of the mind. It was a sleep brought on by the white wind when, in its sweetness and enchantments, it lulled the spirit of the people into slumber.

The god of questions vanished from the pantheon and no one asked why or how or what it meant.

9

THEN VANISHED THE goddess of harmony.

There had always been battles between tribes and villages and clans and families. There had always been discord and enmities. But these existed in harmony within the kingdom, the way different colours exist in nature, the way different animals coexist in a forest. Beneath the differences were harmonies. Even if it was the harmony of people maintaining their unique spaces.

But with the advent of the white wind the people saw one another differently. The white wind stripped the air of the obscurities that shroud a people in a respected mystery. Suddenly they all saw one another too well. Mystery was dispelled. Suspicion took its place. Then came fear, rumours, misinterpretations, rivalries, then politics, and open antagonism. The conditions were created for future wars too vile to contemplate.

And so the goddess of harmony, invisible at the best of times, was erased from the pantheon.

10

AFTER THAT THE rest was easy. The god of memory was forgotten. He vanished. The goddess of mysteries was laid bare. She turned into dust. The goddess of love was defiled, and passed into the air. The god of thunder became a murmur. The god of sacrifice perished at the altar of change.

All the mother deities and the goddesses of women fell into silence. They became cults practised in hiding, in lowly conditions.

Even the great father god succumbed to the etiolations of the white wind. Because of his great seriousness, he proved the easiest to efface. The white wind made him seem ridiculous and unlikely and soon no one believed in him.

When the people stopped believing in the father god, he was forgotten and became a shadow of a memory.

His form was occupied by another nothing that came in the wake of the white wind.

11

THE PEOPLE WERE to pay a great price for the loss of their gods. They were to suffer immeasurably for allowing their gods to disappear from the pantheon. But because they became a different people, they would never make the connection.

They could never be the people they had been again. They had lost their gods forever. They could not resurrect that which they had allowed to die.

They became a people without the gods that made them.

In time, though, through art, through dreams, through surprising deeds, they would find the energy of the pantheon. But till then confusion and plagues and suffering and chaos and all the troubles of a people who have lost their way descended upon them.

Tribes will vanish, many languages will fall silent forever, and the secret knowledge of the people will be lost. Clans and little nations will disappear from the face of the earth. When gods die great things in a people die with them.

There are some who believe that much later something greater than the gods will be revealed. And that greatness will be born in the people.

12

THE ONLY GOD not effaced by the white wind was the trickster god. He was the god of paradox, transformations, illusions, chaos, change, and humour. He was a god tinged with the dangerous and the sinister.

This god was not effaced because he was both in and out of the pantheon. He had long escaped the serenity of the pantheon and had become without form. The trickster god found it more congenial to be part of human life, to seep into reality, into the ever-changing condition of things.

Change was his home. Whatever the circumstances, the trickster god was at home. He was part of life and of change itself. The people never wholly understood him. He was too nebulous and intangible. It was hard to worship him.

As an agent of the supreme being, he wanted to have unpredictable effects. Everything he did had flashes of celestial danger in it. His riddling and paradoxical deeds drove people mad. Everything he did was designed to bring people to the edge of the mind's abyss, the edge of things, and to tip them over. They might fall into a white emptiness where illumination awakened them to higher things. Or they might perish in the wilds of the spirit.

The trickster god turns things inside out, upside down. He fools the intelligence, to awaken something greater than reason.

The trickster god loved the white wind.

The white wind brought the perfect condition for his mischievous flowering.

There is no telling where the trickster god is working.

The trickster god was effaced, but is still here. Effacing him simply made him more powerful, more present.

Perhaps even now he is working with these words on your mind...

13

THE WHITE WIND was the first sign of the plague that came upon the land. The white wind was the beginning of the plague.

First the gods vanished, then trees, philosophies, and traditions. It became most noticeable when healthy young men and women began to disappear.

This was a sinister mystery. The young men suddenly began to vanish. No one knew what happened to them. Whole villages lost their young. No one knew how. No wars had devoured them. But there were tales of people being lured away by spirits. No one knew where they were lured to. They never came back. Their bodies were never found.

Those tales did not satisfy the people who had lost their children...

14

SOON IT WAS rumoured that white spirits had come into the kingdom. It was rumoured that they bought and kidnapped the strongest and bravest of the land and carried them off in big ships to faraway lands or to the cities at the bottom of the sea.

There was some talk of farms on which the missing young people worked from dawn till dusk, in captivity to the white spirits at the bottom of the sea. But only children believed these tales.

The plague of spirits was a mystery and brought fear to the land. No one had seen these white spirits. To see them was to be lost. To see them meant you were captured by them. Those who saw them were already caught.

Only a few isolated sages and masters, only the occasional oddly gifted child, saw them in their dreams and spoke out about what they saw. They spoke of iron chains, of instruments that spat lightning and death, of people in long lines being flogged and gagged. They spoke of chains binding their hands and ankles, of blood on the chains. They spoke of seeing the bound men and women dragged away by white spirits. They spoke of a kind of water which they were made to drink which wiped clean their memories. There were trails of blood on the sand as they were dragged off towards big ships, into whose mouths they vanished. The trails of blood ended at the sea.

15

THESE WERE TERRIBLE rumours and visions. So fantastical were they that no one believed them. No one believed that even evil spirits could be so wicked to human beings. People dismissed the visions as rumours made up to conceal bigger problems in the land.

The king held meetings of the elders to discuss the disappearances. Everyone was baffled. During these sessions the king listened and said nothing. At night, while these fears grew darker, and the plague grew fatter, the numinous laughter of the king could be heard throughout the kingdom.

16

THE DISAPPEARANCE OF the young continued. The land began to empty of healthy young men and women. In many places those who survived were the lucky, the scrawny, or the sons and daughters of kings, chiefs, and powerful people. Those under the protection of influential elders also survived. Tribes that lived far from popular routes and trading centres, who lived in the deep inlands and the weird hinterlands, protected by murky creeks, vile insects, and legions of mosquitoes did not even hear about the plague.

The fortunate were those far from coasts and ports where the white spirits did the best of their inhuman business. They drained the kingdom of its young, its future hopes, its glory, the strong, the brave, the criminal, the war-like. They took many of the gifted ones of the happy land.

17

IN THE MEANTIME the prince hovered in the land of death. He did not know the effect his dying was having on the people. He did not hear them or see them. He dwelt in the grey terrain between life and death.

He lay there in his room. Courtiers and handmaidens and the women of the palace mourned around him. He lay there, on his bed, without moving, for many days.

They believed he was dead, and yet there was softness and the faintest sign of a smile on his face.

While he lay there the crowds that had gathered to pray for his recovery had grown so large that many feared the village wouldn't be able to support their numbers.

They poured in from all over the land and from distant realms. Never before had a prince had so great an effect on the hearts of a people. His fame was a thing in itself.

Emissaries of grief were sent from kingdoms across the continent, and across the world.

Those who had no idea who he was, where his kingdom was, were moved by the idea of this gentle prince, loved by all, who was dying, and who attracted great crowds. People made pilgrimages to the village, just because others did. Strong women and tender-hearted girls, hardened men and fierce warriors joined the mass of people who journeyed to keep vigil for the dying prince. Most of them couldn't stop themselves weeping for the sweet sorrow of this death taking place in the middle of their lives.

So singular was the phenomenon that long afterwards people referred to anything that happened in that period as 'that which took place during the great gathering for the dying prince'. Musicians and griots composed poignant elegies and epics and haunting melodies to that inexplicable moment in the story of the land.

THERE ARE SOME rare people who, though they have accomplished nothing visible in the world, move the hearts of the populace by their fate.

It was widely reported that while the prince lay dying people were prone to spontaneous weeping, to great sorrowing and trembling of heart. An overpowering sensitivity to suffering swept over the land. The force of an irrational sadness dwelt in most hearts for reasons they couldn't explain.

There was a strange flowering of art, of rock paintings, of architecture, of stories and sculpture. They sprouted all over the land. They were born from the currents of a sweetening grief that circulated in the dreams of the people like the breezes of a hidden paradise.

19

THE PRINCE HOVERED in the area between life and death.

His father, the king, would sit by his side all night. He sat in silence. And in silence his laughter spread into all the realms of his kingdom.

ONE DAY A soothsayer made his way through the crowds around the palace. He made his way to the gates and demanded to be presented to the king. After much delay and many lengthy interviews with courtiers, he was granted an audience with the king.

'Your son is dying because of all the evils in the world,' said the soothsayer. 'Only love can save him.'

The king laughed.

'You think there is no love in the kingdom?'

Rocked by the laughter, the soothsayer felt chastened.

'That is not what I meant, your majesty.'

'What did you mean?'

'The only thing that can save your son is if you find a maiden of the tribe of gold-makers.'

'Gold-makers?'

'Bronze-casters.'

'Bronze-casters?'

'The hidden tribe of artists.'

The king stared at the soothsayer a long time, till the poor man squirmed.

'How do you know this?' asked the king.

'I was told to tell you this in a dream.'

'Who told you?'

'You told me.'

'Me?'

'Yes, you, the king.'

The king looked deeply into the frightened eyes of the soothsayer.

'Did I tell you anything else?'

'That was all, your majesty.'

The king thanked the soothsayer and weighed him down with many gifts and a dun-coloured horse to bear him back home.

THE KING SENT his emissaries all over the kingdom looking for the tribe of artists. They travelled the length and breadth of the land. They went deep into the interior, to the remotest communities, to villages near shallow creeks, to people who lived on hillsides among the ritual caves.

They went to the water people, the desert people, the savannah people. They went to the people of the masquerades, to wandering tribes and shepherds, to those who lived on the caravan routes, and those who bought and traded goods throughout the land. But they could not find the people they sought.

No one knew where to find the tribe of artists. No one knew where they were or even who they were. The strangest thing was that all over the land the most beautiful artefacts, medals, sculptures, shields, statuary, pottery, decorated calabashes, bronze figures, and gold ornaments could be found. But when the people were asked how they came by them they just said the objects came from the tribe of artists. They were objects bought in exchange for goods, services, food, clothes. Often they were commissioned. But the people who had them couldn't say how, or where, or when. The objects had just appeared in their lives when they were needed.

All this was difficult to understand.

It began to seem as if the tribe of artists had designed their lives so they couldn't be found. They would create and share their work and enrich the life of the land but they would be invisible. They would be unseen. They would dwell in a separate realm.

The king sent messengers and servants everywhere. He promised rich rewards for anyone who could find the tribe of artists. The messengers put out word of important commissions for works of art. There were announcements of competitions to find the best artist in the land. Many beautiful works were executed, many came forth and entered the competitions. But no one came from the tribe of artists. They remained as elusive as ever.

IT SEEMED AS if they didn't exist. As if they had never existed. They were a rumour, an invention.

It was as if the tribe of artists were a myth that the land needed to explain its own creativity. Now they had ceased to exist. They had evaporated into the moods and stories of the land. They once were, but were no more. They were a people who lived only in dreams. Or that was how they seemed.

The crowds gathering in vigil outside the palace heard about the quest. They lived in hope that the tribe would be found so that the prince could be restored. But none of them knew anything about the tribe. They just hoped it would be found. The news that the tribe could not be found deepened their sadness. The fact that the tribe did not exist filled them with a hopelessness they didn't have before.

Their hopelessness contaminated the air of the village with gloom. The gloom was dense. It soon spread a sort of pestilence and many in the crowds fell ill and some died. Cattle withered and died too, and people came down with a malaise and deadly lethargy of spirit. Melancholy drifted about everywhere. The crops drooped. The children became pale and stopped laughing. No birds were seen in the air. The economy of the land suffered. The crowds, in their pestilential malaise, were becoming fatal to the atmosphere of the village and the palace. All because the tribe of artists could not be found and did not exist.

When the king was told that the tribe of artists did not exist, it was reported that he laughed hard and long, as if it were the best joke he had heard in a long time.

BUT THE PEOPLE kept pouring in. Some had run away from home just to be part of the saddest phenomenon taking place in their lifetimes. There were spirits and inexplicable beings. People brought goats and horses, camels and baby elephants. The crowds swelled.

The fame of the dying prince threatened the life of the village. The place was overrun. People camped out in the farms. The villagers found themselves hemmed in by the crush of pilgrims and well-wishers. The kingdom ground slowly to a halt. Too many people had abandoned their posts and come to express their sorrow as at a great shrine.

The elders put it to the king that people must be turned away or the kingdom would be ruined. They insisted the crowds must be sent back home and that life should return to normal in all levels of the kingdom. They suggested that the people should be told that the prince was recovering and that he desired them all to return to their normal lives. They proposed a secondary fiction: that all the healers had made it clear that returning to their former lives was the only way to help the prince recover. It was recommended that these fictions be softened with praise for their devotion.

With these formulas they hoped to restore order to the kingdom.

The king listened to the elders, but he did nothing. The elders discerned a silent laughter in his response. They took this as their mandate to act.

24

THE ELDERS MADE the announcements. They sent out respected figures to mingle with the people and spread the word.

The people did not believe the elders, nor did they trust the announcements, nor were they seduced by the praise lavished on them.

But in their own conversations they arrived at the same conclusion. They realised they were having an unfortunate effect on the village, and that they might be bringing the life of the kingdom to a halt.

They knew they had to return to their normal lives. The time of sorrowing was over. The magic of shared sadness was gone.

They wanted, however, to know the true condition of the prince. The elders, through their intermediaries, promised the most extensive reports about the prince's health as it became known to them.

Slowly, unwillingly, the crowd dispersed. Most people returned to their homes. Some didn't. They founded new villages near the village of the dying prince. These became enclaves for those who longed for escape, for new beginnings, for those who never felt at home in their old lives.

They were not the same people who had originally set out from their homes. Like a rocky hillside altered by hosts of marigolds, sorrow had changed everyone.

The prince, who lay in silence in his room, never knew the subtle effect that his dying was having on the world. He remained oblivious to his own fame. He had no idea of the transformation his condition had wrought on the people.

ON A DAY without a name, a day outside time, the dying prince dreamt about the maiden.

'Why are you dying?' she asked.

'Because of all the evils in the kingdom.'

'What will make you better again?'

'If all the evils go away.'

'Will you take the evils away?'

'Yes.'

'Will you suffer the evils, in yourself, to cleanse the kingdom?'

'Yes.'

'It shall be so. You shall be well again.'

'What must I do?'

'What you must do.'

'Is that all?'

'Yes. Whatever befalls you, never forget who you are and all will be well with you and the kingdom.'

'Who am I?'

'You are a man. You are loved.'

'And who are you?'

'I am your destiny, and you are mine.'

'Will we be happy together?'

'In life and beyond.'

'Then I am well. I am no longer ill.'

At that moment the maiden vanished from his dream.

26

IN THE MORNING he opened his eyes. He lay there on his bed and felt as though his life had changed course. He felt he had been given a new consciousness. He felt more awake than he had ever felt in his life.

Whatever he gazed on was clear to him. Whatever he thought about was transparent to him. He had in him a new light that pierced everything. All difficulties became clear and simple. He glimpsed the meaning in all things. The wall he gazed at was as open to him as the furthest star. He understood all the space that wasn't space.

He seemed to know all things, not because he knew them, but because the new consciousness in him was a pure light that knew all things simply and without words.

He had left the world and now he was back. He lay on his bed with his eyes open. His mind was tranquil. There was a smile on his face. This smile would always be a part of him now, even in the greatest suffering.

27

THE KING CAME into the chamber and found his son awake like a newborn thing. His son had a smile on his face as if he had achieved a great feat without knowing how. The king was very happy.

He was so happy that he declared a seven-day feast throughout the kingdom.

There was joy and feasting throughout the land. Happiness swept through the kingdom at the news that the prince had been restored to health. It was as if the people had been given a new life, a new beginning. It was as if everything had been restored to a familiar state of enchantment that they never had before.

The happiness lasted seven days. Like a rich rainfall, the happiness sank into the spirit of the people and lay there in the underground rivers of their joy, while life returned to normal.

When the king came into his son's chambers and found him smiling, he gave a strange new laughter. The laughter echoed in the hearts of his people and in the underground rivers.

28

THE PRINCE'S RECOVERY was swift and wonderful. He found a reason to smile at life and now understood the nature of his father's laughter.

He knew clearly what he wanted and who he was. He had seen his end. He had travelled his road to the inevitable abyss and had seen where all stories come from and where they go.

In his death he had witnessed his life in advance. He had lived it all. Had lived it through. Had suffered it, endured it, and been granted the mercy of forgetting it. But he remembered it as a faint melody heard a few moments before it is played.

All this was clear to him. He had done it all in advance, in death. Now his body had to catch up with what his spirit had already transcended.

To those who have been awoken from death this is a peculiar grace and a unique burden. They are unsurprised by the great events in their lives.

They live a constant state of déjà vu.

THE PRINCE STAYED in bed and listened to the world. He asked his father how long he had been away.

'Long enough for you to be ready to play your part in the scheme of things,' the king said.

'How long is that?' the prince asked.

'Long enough for the land to be changed.'

'But how long is that in moons or tides?'

'Long enough for people to no longer think of it in moons or tides, but in stories.'

'That long?'

'Not long, concentrated.'

'What do you mean, father?'

'It can't be measured in time, but in enchantments. Be content with this answer.'

'Yes, father.'

'And as soon as you're strong enough to get around, go and thank the men and women of the village. Thank the courtiers and elders too. Thank them for all their prayers while you were ill.'

'I shall.'

'The people showed you much love. Now you are well they will not want to show it.'

'Why not?'

'Great events bring out unexpected feelings in people that they are too shy to acknowledge afterwards. Thank them simply. Then go about your life in a normal way, as if nothing happened. That way you will reassure the people, and stability will return.'

The prince was thoughtful for a moment.

'But father,' he said after a while, 'does normal mean not doing anything?'

'It means being your true self.'

'Whatever I am?'

'Yes.'

'Whatever death has taught me?'

'Whatever you have become.'

'For good or ill?'

'There will be no ill.'

'And this will be fine?'

'It will be fine. The people will trust your truth.'

'I don't know if I have the right to be what I am.'

'It takes a long time to know who one is. Death has quickened it for you.'

'I hope it's for the best.'

'A blessed providence watches over these things. How do you feel?'

'I feel strangely free.'

'That's how it is after a return.'

'I feel ready...'

'Whatever life brings, keep this new spirit.'

The king paused. Then he stood up and went to the window. His voice had a new emotion.

'It's not being a prince or a king that is special, my son. It's being alive to the mystery of life.'

The prince sat up in the bed.

'Knowing yourself is greater than being a king,' the king said.

'I believe that now. Stories can't be told about it.'

'Storytellers have tried. In the end they have found it wiser to speak indirectly. Or to be silent. Only the deep can speak to the deep.'

THE NEXT DAY the prince woke with a new zest. An unbounded vitality made him leap out of bed. With his arms stretched out wide as if to embrace the world, he faced the rising sun.

He breathed in the new air and the magic rays. He breathed deeply, seven times without counting. He gazed into the heavens and over the earth. A prayer of thankfulness rose in his heart. Being alive filled him with joy, and he wept.

He thanked the great surge of life for the good fortune of being alive. He thanked the air for breath, the sun for light, the world for variety. He thanked life for giving him eyes to see, ears to hear, heart to feel, and a rejoicing soul. Animals and plants, the newborn babe and the elderly, beauty and ugliness, received from him expressions of gratitude. He gave thanks for rivers and storms, for food and hunger, for trees and flowers, for song and for dance, for mothers and fathers, and for all contradictory things that make up life.

He breathed deeply and made himself aware of all parts of his body, from toe to head. He felt life all over him inside and out and was grateful for every inch of himself. He fetched water from the well. He held the gourd up to the sun and drank with a smile. He bathed.

When he had washed, he put on plain and graceful clothes. Then he went around the palace and thanked everyone for their prayers. He thanked every single person there was to thank for the part they played in his recovery from death. He thanked the women, the cooks, the servants, herbalists, messengers, gardeners, cleaners, elders, chiefs, and babies.

The prince sent a simple message of gratitude to all the people, in all the regions. He said their prayers were so powerful that even the king of death was moved and allowed him to return to them healthy and renewed. He sent messages of thankfulness beyond the kingdom, to other realms. He sent these messages through ordinary routes and through the route of dreams, like his father.

31

THEN THE PRINCE went round the village. From hut to hut, from house to house, knocking on every door, he thanked all the villagers. He shook their hands and embraced them. The men were surprised, the women bewildered, the young men were moved, and the eyes of the young girls sparkled.

He spent many days thanking people. He left no one out. He thanked the old men who were now blind and the old women who didn't remember who they were. He thanked the anchorites and hermits in the forest, the witches and wizards, the criminals and the mad, the diseased and the sick, the outcasts and the dying. And he prayed for them too.

He thanked the fishermen on the river and tappers up in the tall palm trees. The hunters in the woods and the farmers in the fields, the women in the marketplace and the town-criers on their rounds, all were surprised by his gratitude. He thanked the warriors and sages and priests of shrines.

He sought out a fabled old woman of the forest who lived in isolation, away from society. He found her in a foul mood and he thanked her too. He got an earful of curses. He didn't mind. It was an adventure meeting a fabled being. Afterwards she said powerful prayers for him.

He sent apologies to anyone he had neglected to thank.

He was seen thanking the goats and dogs and cows and the trees and the river, as if they had all, in some way, helped bring him back from the land of death.

The prince spent seven days thanking people and things. By the time he had finished he was due another recovery. He stayed at home and convalesced from his exhaustive gratitude.

When the king heard the prince had taken to his bed to

enjoy a second recovery he found it so funny that he laughed all through dinner at his son's tenderness.

While the prince slept, the king watched over him, and chuckled into the night.

32

ON THE FIRST day of his recovery, after he had performed his new rites, greeting the rising sun, the prince set off into the forest. He had a longing for a dawn that seemed now so ancient in his memory as to be something that happened in another life.

He stole away from the palace and made his way to the edges of the forest. At first he walked slowly. He took his time. This way his life had often drawn him. In what seemed like a dream he had found his true happiness on the invisible path through the forest to an appointment that wasn't kept. There was someone he hadn't met who he knew was the love of his life. This loss of her had somehow led to his death. Here he was again, on the same path, risking another death.

As he lingered at the edge of the forest, thinking about this woman who he loved without having met, he wondered if love doesn't lead to death. When you love does your old self not die? And out of this death is a new man or woman not born? Love does not lead to one death, he thought, but to several. With love one must die and be reborn. Is that why the storytellers say there are few real loves in the world, because people fear another death that love brings? They count the deaths they have undergone and say, 'So many and no more, so far but no further. I will not die again in this love. I will stay who I am, how I am, here in this fixed place.'

The prince sensed there was no end to the deaths and rebirths that love inspires. He thought: each death makes us freer, stronger, simpler, more human, more spiritual. Till we become unique, beautiful, regenerated, refined, a dream of light.

The prince thought all this without words, in a shudder, and then plunged into the cool shade of the forest.

33

SPIDERS' WEBS, BEADED with dew, enmeshed his face. He was assaulted by the smells of the forest, the sleeping earth, the breathing trees, rotting leaves, and the fragrance of vegetation. The sun dried the dew on the grass. He passed through the mood of tranquil spirits, overcome with the maternal odours of the forest which he had forgotten while he had been in the kingdom of death.

He had forgotten the path and where it led. He had forgotten his favourite place by the river. He took the first path that appeared to him. This led past wonders that he sensed but didn't see, and which made an impression on his new spirit. He would see them later in his dreams, and would ponder where such visions had their origins. He passed through many worlds in the forest. All of them were invisible and all of them were real. These things too are written in the book of life among the stars.

The prince was still weak, but he had a big appetite for life. He had a great hunger to live, to see, to feel. No longer did he want to dream. He had done all his dreaming in the land of death. He had dreamt his life through, dreamt it to its dregs. Dreamt everything in advance.

He knew, somewhere in himself, that some of what he dreamt was provisional and could be changed. It all depended on what he did, what forces he put into motion in his life. But there were things that could not be changed. In spite of them, he wanted to live his life right through.

He wanted to live it all with open eyes and an enlightened spirit. He wanted to live the challenge of his life, to square the impossible circle of destiny by the feat of his loving will and vision. He wanted to be the conqueror of his own life. Others were famous for conquering territories. He wanted to conquer himself, transcend his fate, with the simple power of love.

34

HE WANDERED THROUGH the forest for a long time. The rays of the sun shone through the leaves and branches. The forest was new to him. He lost his way and found new paths. He pursued a dimly intuited course in a direction that was as vague as dreams that disappear upon awakening.

Lost in the forest, he wandered paths that pleased him. He made many discoveries. He came upon a few isolated huts. He saw an old woman, sitting outside the door of her hut, watching him with peaceful eyes. He greeted her and she smiled but stayed silent. When he passed another hut he saw an old man, who also watched him with serene eyes. This happened a few times. He began to think he was passing the same person, now a man, now a woman, sitting outside a hut, smiling but never speaking.

At last the forest changed. Innocently, he passed through the dead at their crowded feast. Many there had loved him as a child. They watched him wander through their feast and were sad that he couldn't see them. After he had gone past he shivered, stopped, and looked back. One of the dead wanted to go after him and tell him how much they loved him as a child, but was restrained by the others. They watched him go. They knew he would join them soon, for time is short among the dead.

The prince was done with dreams. He wanted to be, to act, to do.

Then he broke through the confusion of paths and found himself by the river, among the wild flowers. He found his familiar spot in the bushes. It was much changed now. The rains had made the vegetation luxuriant. The parting among the branches where he nestled and watched the shore was quite overgrown. It had forgotten him altogether.

With a heart beating to a new expectation, he waited to see if a dream would come true on the first day of his liberation from death.

35

THERE BY THE river, still weak from his recovery, he fell into a mild hallucination. He saw a shrine sailing down the river on a yellow boat. He heard the oracle babbling. The shrine of the oldest god flew in the air.

Strange beings were holding a meeting on the riverbank. A white form danced on the water, scattering its radiance everywhere, sweet to blinded eyes. When it was gone there was darkness.

Men with chains on their legs and wrists trod painfully on the shore. Men the colour of clouds, with guns under their arms and hats on their heads, led them away. They had servants who carried luggage and kept the chained people in control. The men in chains were frequently whipped. Then they were dragged on to boats that took them away into the blinding reflections of the river. He heard their poignant lament beyond the horizon, as if they were drowning in the place where the sun went after it had left the kingdom.

The prince did not understand what he saw, and took it for another vision. He walked a familiar route back home, more troubled than before. What he had seen had awoken an unease that had been sleeping in him, growing while it slept.

36

THE WORLD THE prince saw after his illness was not the world he saw before. Much had been subtly altered.

Something had changed in the air. There were more gaps between things. There were more gaps between trees, between huts and houses, and between people. He noticed these gaps everywhere, and didn't understand.

After a while he wasn't sure if what he saw were absences, or if they were actual things. Were the gaps real things or were they simply spaces?

This bothered him.

37

THE NEXT DAY he went into the forest again, bound for his watching place by the river. He still hoped that the girl would return. On the way he noticed the gaps again more clearly. They were everywhere.

He saw gaps spreading between the trees, slowly obliterating them. He saw gaps along the shore, erasing the edges of the river. He saw the shrinking of the waters on the shoreline. He noticed the gaps among the bushes and the flowers. He rubbed his eyes. He was convinced that he was dreaming with eyes wide open the gradual disappearance of the natural world. It continued to happen. He continued to see gaps proliferate between things.

Holes appeared in the river. He expected the water to drain away, but it didn't. Holes sprouted on the shore. Gaps appeared in the sky. Birds flew into those gaps and never reappeared. This troubled him. He hurried home to ponder this new phenomenon.

When he got home to the palace, he went straight to bed. He covered himself with a blanket and shut his eyes. But even in his sleep, the gaps appeared. There were strange gaps in his dreams.

38

THE NEXT MORNING he performed his rites and set out into the kingdom. Instead of going to his watching place, he went about the kingdom like a beggar, looking at everything. He used his eyes as he had never done before.

What he saw astounded him. The gaps were growing. He saw gaps in people's faces, in their eyes. He heard gaps in their voices, and in their words. Mothers had given birth to babies that were part human, part gaps. This frightened him.

'Where are the gaps coming from?' he asked out loud. 'Have they always been here? Am I just noticing them now? Or are they recent?'

He asked people the question and realised their minds were full of gaps. There were gaps in their history, gaps in tradition, gaps in their reasoning, in their knowledge, their laughter, their suffering, and their happiness.

He saw people whose hands were disappearing, whose faces were becoming gaps. He saw a man who walked on one leg. His other leg had been eaten away by the gap, but he didn't know it.

No one else saw the gaps.

The prince saw them multiplying. There were gaps in the dances, the drumming, in the farms. He said to the people:

'Where are the gaps coming from?'

No one knew what he was talking about.

Then he sought out the wise men and women of the kingdom, to find answers to his questions.

39

THE WISE MEN and women did not want to be found. He made enquiries and was directed to this hut or that house. But when he got there he would find that the wise man, hearing that the prince was looking for him, had disappeared, had made himself scarce. The prince was struck by this.

'Why do the wise flee from me? Are there gaps among the wise too?' he wondered.

When he sought the wise they were not at home or had been seen leaving their abodes by the back door or had moved or had gone away on long pilgrimages or were reputedly performing great feats of the spirit in a remote part of the kingdom. Not a single wise man or woman could he find.

Maybe their wisdom consisted in not being found, he thought. But this left him with no one to discuss the phenomenon of the gaps.

He wandered back home that evening, lost in thought. Occasionally he strayed into holes of contemplation.

When he came back to himself he saw the darkness gathering. The stars shone between indigo gaps in the sky.

HE SUMMONED THE elders the next morning and asked them about the gaps in the kingdom, the gaps in tradition, the gaps into which people disappeared, never to return.

The king listened to his son's questions. He was radiant with pride.

'Gaps? What gaps?' one of the elders said. 'There are no gaps in our tradition, our history, nor our people. There are no gaps anywhere. We are fine. Our foundation is secure, the house is stable. We are solid. We have no gaps among us at all.'

Another elder stepped forward.

'We have a proverb: "Only the person who sees the world as mad is mad." We don't mean you, our dear prince, nor do we mean any disrespect. But you have not been well. You have not given yourself time to recover. You're looking at things too hard when you should be convalescing. Maybe the gaps are in you.'

The first elder, more emollient, said:

'I would not go so far myself. But maybe you need to get better, my prince. Then you will see that the land is fine. Our traditions are secure. You will see that there are no gaps among us.'

The prince did not press the issue.

But his unease continued. On the following day he saw birds in the sky flying into nothingness and becoming invisible. He saw children playing near the stream. They were running and laughing when they completely vanished into the wavy whiteness of the air. He saw drummers. They were beating out complicated, beautiful ideas in cross-patterns in the white heat of inspired syncopation. Then they drummed themselves into invisibility, the more intensely they played, as if obliterated by their own harmonic discoveries.

He saw strips of the palace crumble into the air, wiped out by effacing clouds. Portions of farmland vanished into nothingness, and farmers with them. He saw a shrine evaporate into the trembling heat haze of an intolerable afternoon. Only the ghosts of the resident gods quivered in the space above the shrine. Then they too were blown away into a tremulous sky.

He beheld these things and kept his counsel. He knew now that no one would believe him. But having to be silent about the momentous things he saw became unbearable to him. They tormented his sleep and stalked his dreams. He could find no solace anywhere.

To SEE THESE things and have no one with whom to speak of them introduced a new sense of alienation into his life. He felt isolated, an outsider in his own land.

The people seemed happy enough. The elders carried on as usual, scheming and intriguing. The king remained silent and mysterious. Only his laughter gave any sign of his presence. It could be heard from the rooftops. It trembled on the light breeze in the long afternoons into which the gods, one by one, were vanishing.

The prince found himself alone. The world was being obliterated by a mysterious phenomenon which no one else saw and he did not know what to do. He thought he was going mad. Then he thought everyone else was mad. Sometimes he thought the world was dreaming.

He began to think he was living in a perpetual dream in which nothing was real. Only the gaps seemed real. They seemed real because no one else saw them.

There were times when he thought he had died and was seeing everything through the eyes of the dead.

IN THIS STATE of mind he might have done something dreadful to himself if one night the king had not appeared to him in a dream, dressed in his full regalia.

'My son, seek the maiden of the tribe of artists,' the king said. 'Be a servant to her father, study the daughter, then win her heart. This will not be easy. But eventually your children will be the saviours of the land.'

The prince woke up with the distinct feeling that something had changed. He was still uneasy, only now he had a clear sign of what he had to do.

Every day, at dawn, after his morning rituals, he set off to wait at his hiding place by the river.

But he also sent emissaries round the kingdom to find the tribe of artists. The emissaries returned with the definitive information that the tribe of artists did not exist.

From the freshness of dawn till the blazing heat of the afternoon, the prince waited for the maiden. He waited every day. He waited with hope in his heart like the dew on the grass. He waited through the light that blinded all things, to the plunging dark of the evening. She did not return to the river.

He feared that his encounter with her had been imagined. Maybe it had happened in another life, when time was young and beautiful and true.

43

SOME OF THE elders were not delighted by the recovery of the prince. There was one who had spoken first at the meeting convened by the prince, when he asked about the gaps. This elder's name was Okadu. He was chief among those who were not thrilled.

Chief Okadu was enormously pleased with his abilities as a strategist and organiser. He was an efficient man and a great sycophant to the king. He had crocodile eyes, discoloured lips, and a manner that was somewhat slimy. His complacency was based on having secured for himself the economic management of certain aspects of the kingdom.

He had no power himself, but he had the ear of the king. He despised the people. He believed in hierarchy only if he was at the head of it. He believed in anything only if it would benefit him. He was given to striding about the village with his hands in his pockets as if he owned the world. Chief Okadu was foremost among those who were displeased with the restoration of the prince's health.

He was also the one most threatened by the notion that there were gaps in the kingdom, in tradition, and in history. He hated the idea of gaps. Ever since the prince had raised the subject he had gone around to the elders and asked them if they knew anything about the gaps of which the prince had spoken. Without exception, none of them did.

'I don't see gaps anywhere. What does he mean by gaps anyway? Do you think he was referring to us?'

The elders went about the village and made their own investigation. They stared at the world. They spoke to the people the prince had spoken to. Then they reconvened to assess their findings. They still did not see gaps anywhere.

While they discussed this, Chief Okadu's eyes grew more sinister than ever. He had been acquiring, in his silent opposition and his grasp of the underlying conditions of the land, a strange power over the minds of the elders. It was a power that had been growing all along with his sycophancy to the king and his general mode of appeasement. But now he was the force behind the elders. They held him in silent awe.

All of a sudden, they realised that they feared him more than they feared the king. Silently, in whispers, in the bushes, in the dark, Chief Okadu came to be known throughout the kingdom as the Crocodile. They called him 'the Crocodile whose eyes never shut, whose jaws never sleep'.

Under the Crocodile's insistence, the elders came round to the idea that the prince was talking in code. He was hinting that they, the elders, were the gaps, or had created the gaps, that they were corrupt, had distorted the laws, misused their powers, stolen from the people, impoverished the traditions, and were somehow a negative force in the kingdom.

'It seems to me quite clear,' said the Crocodile, in heavily accented menace, 'that we are the ones the prince is referring to. The way he is going he will sooner or later want to get rid of us as a class. He is our natural enemy. We wish him nothing but good, but he sees us as the cause of destruction in the kingdom. We have much to fear from that prince when he ascends the throne.'

The Crocodile paused. Then in a low voice that instilled fear into the mesmerised elders, he said:

'Unless there is no longer an accession…'

He paused again. He gave a sign to his minions to blow out the lantern in the hall where they met in secrecy. Darkness fell on them like a thick mantle. Then in a whisper that could almost not be heard, he said:

'Or a throne.'

44

THE GAPS, WHOSE existence they denied, began to haunt the elders. It created gaps in their minds.

They began to suspect that the prince had found things out about them, their hidden activities, their corrupt practices, their ritual sacrifices, their secret societies, their collusion with kidnappers, their illegal levies on farmers, market women and traders, the profit which they kept to themselves, at the expense of the kingdom, while so many suffered.

The elders were for the first time troubled by revelations they feared would emerge any moment.

They did not like the prince's recovery, his new awareness, his clarity, or his courage.

Above all they were not pleased with the great love the people bore him.

45

THE ELDERS DID not know what to do with the gaps that the prince had insinuated into their minds.

They hated the notion of gaps. It revolted them. It threatened their establishment. It undermined the foundations. It sabotaged their grasp on reality. Because of this, the elders over time became involved in a series of weird rituals meant to tighten their grip on the power structure of the kingdom.

Like cultists performing dread operations, they went around at night, with lanterns, and tapped at things. They tapped on walls, buckets, trees, buildings, floors, and people's heads. They tapped to find the gaps. They tapped with their knuckles, sticks, canes, bones. They tapped with ritually treated objects. They listened to the sound of the hollows. They noted the spaces between buildings, trees, earth, and sky. They studied the spaces above the river and between people. They were overwhelmed by the spaces that led to the stars. The multiplicity of spaces flummoxed them.

46

THE ELDERS BEGAN to have bad dreams. They had nightmares in which the spaces oppressed them. They contemplated
filling up all the hollows, blocking up all the spaces. They
wanted to eliminate all gaps. But in doing so they didn't want
to create bigger ones. They became obsessed with filling up all
the gaps. Wherever they saw a gap they saw a force undermining their foundation.

They dreamt up ways of jamming up all the empty spaces
with things. But they couldn't find a way to block the spaces
that led to the stars. As they associated these vast accusing
spaces with the prince, they began, for the first time in centuries, to scheme against the throne. They began to devise ways
to get rid of the king.

They no longer heard his laughter in their hearts.

II

1

WHEN THE SUN was new born in the golden mists of the east, when the birds competed to wake him with the obscure message of their melodies, the prince rose from sleep. He tried to remember his dream. He performed the rites which he had devised to keep him alive to the wonder of living. Then like every other day since his recovery, he set off into the forest. He was not seeking adventures. He was seeking that which he had lost before he nearly died.

The vision of that which he had lost had grown much more in meaning with each passing day. The love which had lain sleeping in him stirred with a restlessness that made his life intolerable. But he was not aware of it. He was not aware of the love that possessed him like life in his limbs.

As he made his way deeper into the forest he suddenly saw a white and golden antelope through the trees. Its head was turned towards him. Then it bolted. He found himself pursuing it through the undergrowth of the dark forest.

The antelope led him past a stream he had never seen before and past a white house. Inside the house he heard a girl singing a song so beautiful that he nearly broke out in tears. He followed the antelope past a well in which he saw not water but a crowded cluster of pearls and diamonds. He didn't stop to investigate but kept on the trail of the antelope.

It led him past a village in which he was worshipped as a god. When the villagers saw him they fell in mass prostration. In a screaming ecstasy they cried out that they had been blessed with a glimpse of their divinity. The prince didn't linger to taste that ambiguous power. He kept firmly on the trail of the antelope. It led him into a maze of trees and flowering bushes. In the centre of the trees was a hole in the air the exact shape and brightness of the morning sun. The antelope leapt into the hole, and vanished. The prince hesitated at the threshold of this mystery. Then without thinking, with the courage of youth, and with a quick prayer, he leapt into the sun-shaped opening.

He found himself in the forest, not far from the river. His head was clear, but he was a little disorientated. He remembered only that he had left the palace, entered the forest, and was now at his favourite hiding place in the bushes, near the river.

How had he got there?

HE HEARD THE laughter of young women in the wind blowing over the waves. He listened to them teasing, to their sweet songs, their half-told stories, and their games. He listened to their names being called out. He felt he was in a moment from childhood.

Like a faun waking from sleep, the prince woke from his half-dreaming state. There was the haunting melody of a rainbow in the sky. He hurried to his hiding place among the flowering bushes. When he looked out from the white and blue and red flowers that surrounded him on all sides, he saw the river aflame with sunlight. Then he saw girls all in white, dancing in circles on the riverbank.

They had yellow flowers in their hair and strings of cowries round their necks. They were performing a magic rite to the season of flowers and to the gift of green after the gloom of death had passed over the land.

THE GIRLS HAD bronze bangles on their wrists and gold threads round their ankles. They danced along the shore, in the beauty of their youth, in a time without memory, in a happiness that could not last. They were like the image of beauty that the gods had conjured there by the river to celebrate all creation. The prince gazed on them with wonder. They were singing a song that seemed to make the river smile. That's how it appeared to the prince.

> If you touch me
> And I touch you
> This is true
> And that is true
> Too.

The last word detached but also connected to the other words in the song had an odd effect on the prince. It made him aware of one girl who stood apart from all the others. Apart but connected. Her form made his heart quiver. The world changed and the lights darkened a little, as at an eclipse. Then it was brighter than before and richer colours were restored to all things, as though a veil had dropped from his eyes.

He watched the girl. She stood apart from the others who were dancing. She stood apart, but was not aloof. She stood in a pool of water on the shore, staring into the horizon, spinning the stalk of a blue flower in the palms of her hands, so it was the flower that danced, while she stayed still.

There she was, as in a dream that time forgot, in the perfect enchantment of life. Upon seeing her the prince wept silently, with a smile in his soul.

The young sun was in its moment of early gold.

4

AT THAT MOMENT, the girl who stood apart called out to her companions. They gathered about her in a circle.

'I feel a special sadness today,' she said. 'It is as if a god has given me all I ever wished for. But I can't see it, because I am such a fool. How can this be?'

Her friends giggled at her riddle. They danced round her in a circle, singing their sweet songs with charming melodies, without giving her an answer.

She turned and turned as they danced, till she was quite dizzy. Then she danced herself and they all began a game of chasing one another up and down the shore and into the forest and back again.

The young women had come to do their washing on the stones of the river. The morning had cleansed away their tasks. Their games, which were a celebration of their task's end, were over. They had eaten fruits and laughed and talked of suitors. They had mimicked the various male characters in the life of the tribe. They had shared dreams and hopes and now they lifted their buckets on their heads and started back to their homes.

Then the prince realised that she was now alone. Only she lingered by the river, as if she were waiting for something. She waited and sang a little to herself. She looked about her expectantly. The wind bore down on her, making her tremble. When nothing else happened, she began to return home.

She had three flowers in her hand, which she played with. One was yellow, another blue, and the third was red. She loved them all.

She seemed in a half-dream as she made her way through the bushes and flowering plants into the forest. She had a happy smile on her face.

5

WHEN SHE LOOKED about her so expectantly, the prince had wanted to speak to her, but a wiser urge made him stay silent. He was learning the lesson of the heron. When he wanted to express that which was beyond expression, he kept silent.

As he watched her his soul joined her being forever. But he kept still. He breathed gently the sweet life of the sun. When she wandered away from the river, he followed. He had no idea if this was the right thing to do or not.

As the moon draws the tides, as the sun setting draws the heart homeward, so did this dream of his life draw him through the forest.

She moved gently among the shadows. She alone of all the girls bore no bucket on her head. She had come to keep her friends company in their tasks. She had come empty-handed and was leaving with flowers. Her slender form and smiling walk delighted the invisible beings of the forest.

6

SHE WANDERED DREAMILY. The prince followed her through the trees. Her presence made everything magical. Everything she went past changed with her passing.

He followed her through new villages where there were sculptures of him around the shrines, to aid his recovery. He saw them without seeing them. She went down a valley and emerged in another forest that was blue within the shade of its trees. It was a complicated journey.

Often she would stop to gaze at a tree as if looking for someone within it. Sometimes she would feel the trunks or she would tap on them and listen to their interiors. Her actions intrigued the prince.

She came to a junction where many paths met. There were whispers in the air and a clear view of the sky. Then she did something amazing. She stopped and became alert, like a warrior waiting for the sign to go into battle. She looked all about her. Then she stepped into a luminous hole in the air between the trees and disappeared completely, like a dream fading in daylight.

He hesitated for a moment before he went through the hole in the air. On the other side he found himself at the same place he had been before. It was the same but different, the same world but more lucid. The shadows were still blue. The junction where the paths met looked the same as it was before he went through the bright opening. But it was not the same. He could not tell how it was different.

He saw her white dress through the trees. She was singing to herself. The forest path that she walked on was a subdued ribbon of gold. Around her were banks of green and thorn-bearing bushes and tall obeche trees. She stooped to talk to a snail on the path. He saw her place it among the plants.

Not long afterwards he went with her into a sublime village.

7

FOLLOWING THE PRINCIPLE of the heron, the prince wandered through the village without drawing attention to himself. He saw what building she entered, and guessed it was her home. He made discreet enquiries from a man going past, who had a basket of eggs on his head, and learnt something about her family. He learnt that the girl's father was something of a marvel, and that he was feared. He explored the village and lingered in palm-wine bars and asked further questions from fellow drinkers. He discovered that this was the tribe of artists. Here is where they lived secluded and made their magical works, in the unseen spaces of the world.

He thought about spending the night at the edge of the forest. But he had visions of eating tuberous roots and not sleeping for all the noises of wild animals in the dark. He imagined himself devoured by a wild beast as he dozed. He decided to go home.

He was lucky. As he set off home he saw the girl leave her house. He followed her round the edges of the village, past the shrine, into the woods. She stepped into another opening which shone like a little moon barely visible in daylight. When he stepped through the ghostly opening, he caught sight of her vanishing into a long wooden house. The door had an eye in its centre. She didn't come back out.

As he was about to go away he had the curious feeling that the eye in the middle of the door was staring at him. Then the door opened and a man came out and looked around. He had eyes like those of an eagle. He gave off the impression of a man in the fullness of his power. He looked about him, sensing something in the air. Then uttering a potent incantation, he withdrew into the wooden house. But he left his form outside. The form kept watching, then it faded. Then there was just an afterglow.

The prince didn't linger a moment longer. He hurried home the way he had come. He was careful to go back through all the luminous holes in the air. That way he made sure he left nothing of himself behind. He didn't want to get trapped in the forest, lost in a world of legends he did not know.

8

THE MORE THE elders tried to fill the gaps, the more gaps appeared. This precipitated a crisis among them and in the kingdom. The elders caused many evils because they feared that the gaps revealed by their paranoid scrutiny were actually real in the world and in the tradition. If there were gaps in tradition then the world was not as they saw it and their place in it was not as stable as they had always believed.

With each passing day doubts grew in them about the truth of everything. They were no longer sure when a certain innovation became a tradition, or whether that tradition had been there since the beginning of the world. Their earth became shaky.

With the prince's recovery one of the things he liked doing was talking to the young. He wanted to talk to children and listen to what they had to say. He arranged for children of the servants and the market women to be brought to him so he could tell them stories and share food with them. On one of these visits a seven-year-old child asked the prince about the earth and the stars.

That was when the elders overheard the prince telling the children in the palace that the world stood on air and that nothing held up the earth in space. He told the children that in a dream he had seen the world as a shining blue bowl in a sea of nothing, surrounded by stars.

'The earth is held up by nothing, by mystery,' he said.

'How come we don't fall off then?' one of the children asked.

'Because it's the same nothing that keeps us on the land. Some people walk upside down, and they don't fall off into the big nothing. An invisible power keeps us here. It's not our power.'

The children were silent.

'The earth stands on air?' one of them said.

'On nothing,' the prince replied, smiling.

This overheard conversation began another bout of fevered discussions among the elders. It awakened more fears. They met at night and gazed into the heavens. They could not see what held up the earth in space. They saw more gaps which had to be destroyed.

9

THE CHIEFS AND elders, unable to sleep, watched the gaps growing in the kingdom. The phenomenon paralysed them.

Chief Okadu was heard screaming in his sleep. His wives assured him there were no gaps in the world. But his raw red eyes could not unsee what he had seen.

The paranoia of the chiefs was made worse by the horror of the news that they stood on air, that their world was held up by nothing. This threatened the potent mythology by which they controlled the kingdom in the name of the king.

They thought of having the prince poisoned. They enlisted the support of the most disaffected of the king's wives.

Three times they attempted to poison the prince but each time the food was eaten by an eagle or a dog or a monkey that appeared in the prince's chamber before he was ready. Three times he saw empty plates on the table where his food should have been. Three times he saw a dead eagle, dog, and monkey near the palace. No one could explain how they had died. He took this as a sign to fast.

He fasted till he received another sign. He took the sign to mean that it was time to meet the family of the maiden; but in disguise at first, following the principle of the heron. The sign came in the form of a dream in which he was sitting at the foot of the master. The maiden was at the door, looking out at a group of dancers with a masquerade in the street.

The prince informed his father that he would be away for seven days and would return every night. His father nodded and asked no questions. He didn't laugh, but there was a twinkle in his eyes.

10

THAT MORNING THE prince, in disguise, made his way through the forest and passed through the brilliant openings in the air. He went down the yellow valley and back into the blue shade of woods near the village of the artists. Then he went directly to the workshop of the maiden's father. He sat outside its unremarkable door with the single eye. He sang a song that went like this:

If you cannot find it on earth
Seek for it in the sea
If you cannot find it in the sea
Seek for it in the sky
If you cannot find it in the sky
Seek for it in the fire
If you cannot find it in the fire
Seek for it in your dreams.
If it isn't there
Then it is nowhere.
This is nowhere.
And I like it here.

The prince sang in a voice unused to singing. He had no particular talent for music. But the mood of the song soothed him and he sang himself to sleep. He still sang in his sleep, his head resting on a wooden pole in front of the workshop door.

When the maiden's father arrived for work that morning he saw a strange and beautiful youth at the entrance to his workshop. The youth was singing in his sleep.

Before he woke up, before he spoke, the master knew that this young man was going to play an important part in his life. He knew, instantly, that this unknown youth had already altered his life, the life of his family, and the life of the tribe.

11

As the master scrutinised him, the young man woke. The master saw the future in the frail form of the youth. He had eyes like one who has not decided whether to live or die.

'What do you want?' said the master gruffly.

The youth gave a shy smile.

'Sir,' he said, 'your fame is great, but your art is greater.'

He paused. The master, serene, said nothing.

'I have travelled a long way, sir, past the regions of death, to come and serve you. I ask nothing in return.'

He paused again. The master remained still.

'I do not even ask to be taught. I dare not ask so great an honour from so great a master as you.'

He looked up with his soft intense eyes.

'I desire only to serve you in any way you want. In the evenings I will return to my own land. I will do this till you no longer desire my service, sir.'

Something whispered to the master that he couldn't refuse this modest request, even from a stranger. He sensed the youth was of unusual birth and might not be as he appeared.

Under the sway of a kindly power, the master said:

'I don't know why I'm saying this, but I accept.'

He paused.

'You shall serve me as I instruct you to do. But you must only do what I ask of you.'

He paused again.

'Nothing else in my household is your business.'

A severe pause followed.

'You will learn nothing of my art and I will teach you nothing.'

The youth nodded.

'You will sit and serve till I decide otherwise. I have no need of a servant and I don't know why I am doing this.'

The youth nodded again.

'At night you may do as you wish, only don't disgrace me in any way. You must not reveal anything of what you see here. I demand of you silence and discretion.'

The master looked sternly at the youth.

'You must not speak to my daughter.'

The young man bowed his head.

'Thank you, sir,' he said. 'This is the greatest honour of my life.'

THE MASTER WAS discomposed by the young man. He had not felt like this for a long time.

In some obscure way he felt that it was he who should be thanking the youth, that it was he who was being honoured.

His confusion annoyed him. Few things ever did. The master was encountering something that eluded his powers of intuition, that silenced his guiding spirit. For the first time in years, he knew a delicate kind of fear, a terror trembling with illumination.

'Who are you anyway?' the master asked. 'And where do you come from?'

The young man gave a half-smile.

'I am a poor lost person, sir. I was separated from my family during our journeys, and I found myself here.'

'I thought you said you had come a long way because...'

'A long way, sir, I have travelled because of your art and your fame, past the land of death even. The earth itself can bear witness to this. The wind will speak for me. The stars watched my journeys with keen eyes. You may ask them, sir, when I am not around, and they will bear me out.'

The master fell under the spell of a disquieting amazement.

'Who is your father?'

'One who laughs, sir.'

'I see. And your mother?'

'She is happy among the stars. She flew to heaven when I was young.'

There was a pause. Then the master said:

'You begin today.'

'May you be blessed, sir, for the greatness of your heart.'

The master stepped into his workshop with his new servant.

13

WHEN THE MAIDEN came to visit her father that afternoon she did not notice the new servant.

He sat in a corner, close to the wall, among statues and images. Light poured in from a chink in the wall above his head. He sat in absolute stillness, as he had been instructed.

The maiden's father worked in silence, among stones, among blocks of wood, at a table. With quiet intensity he was dreaming new beings into form, as if he were praying.

His daughter sat at her favourite chair and spoke thoughts that came to her mind. She was partially aware that her voice had a nice effect on the mood of the workshop. In the dark the statues listened, as if to a loved one. She had been to the river that day, she said, and had found it barren.

'There was nothing there, father, and I could not understand. The river was the same, or maybe it wasn't. The shore was the same, though I am not sure. The sky hadn't changed, and all my favourite flowers are in bloom, but it was all empty, as if the spirit of things had gone away from them.'

She looked up at her father. His back was listening to her.

'When my companions sang, they didn't please me. When they danced, they were clumsy. I did not feel like being with them. The wind wasn't sweet and the river was like rock. I wandered into the forest alone. It was without colour. I couldn't see the green of leaves. Everything was flat.'

She paused again, lost in thought. Her father turned and looked at her and smiled. He resumed his work.

'Normally when I go into the forest nice things happen. Sometimes a butterfly lands on my shoulder. Sometimes I see a beetle on the path and we have something to say to one another.

Sometimes, while I'm walking, I dream. Maybe some fairy has made me a princess and I'm smiling among the trees. Sometimes I see in front of me a perfect image that I can make in wood or bronze. When the vision goes away it reappears in my dreams. Sometimes I hear a suitor singing on the edge of a dream while I am coming home.'

She sighed.

'But these days, today especially, nothing happened. The world is flat. The stars don't shine, and even my heart beats as if everything is normal. Has something changed in the world that I haven't noticed?'

Her father was silent. He worked quietly. Now and then he moved wood on the table or drew symbolic designs on stone. He breathed as wooden statues do, gently, as if not wanting to disturb the air.

The maiden stared at the statues in the workshop. She stared without seeing. In that semi-abstracted dreaming state she made out the shapes of spirits going about their tasks of bringing new forms into being, under the precise instructions of the master.

She watched the dimly visible forms of the spirits out of the corner of her eyes. For a moment she noticed a new one among them. But when she looked to ascertain, it was gone. It had faded into the half-light of the workshop, in the shadows, where the most important things happened.

14

THE MAIDEN DIDN'T notice the new servant, even when she dozed in the workshop and dreamt that one of the statues was alive.

Sometimes she would be awake, listening to her father carving. Sometimes he carved shapes in the air. She listened as he spoke to his spirit-helpers, describing a form he wanted in the wood he had prepared for its new life as art. Sometimes he talked to the wood itself, as he planed it.

The new servant would stir under the wall and cough gently. Breathing in wood-dust irritated his throat. But even when he coughed the maiden didn't notice him.

Once while the maiden dozed with eyes half open the new servant crept across her field of vision. He received his instructions from the master, went out, returned, and whispered in the master's ear. He passed her form in the chair again. Then he sat among the statues in the dark, his back pressed to the wall. Still she did not notice him.

The master may have cast a spell of invisibility over the new servant so that he could not be seen by his daughter. He may also have cast a spell of incomprehension over his daughter so that she could not see the new servant. But then the new servant may have cast a spell on himself, that he would not be noticed by her, raising the principle of the heron to the pitch of an enchantment.

15

WHEN HE SAT there in the dark, his back to the wall, many things came in to the mind of the new servant.

He once fell into a dreaming state and passed through a golden opening in his sleep and found himself in a place where he was a slave. He had no idea what had brought him to this condition in a faraway land. The people of the land were the colour of the sky just before evening comes. He was a slave working in a cotton field from dawn to dusk, along with many others. Some of them were from his kingdom but he did not know them. While they worked they sang lamentations for a life that was gone.

Another time he was half-naked in a marketplace, being sold for less than the price of a dog.

Then he dreamt he had three children that were not his colour and his wife's eyes were cold like the eyes of a dead fish. In the dream it was hard to find the golden opening back to the workshop. When he did return, he was puzzled.

Fragments of lives, fantastical and real, descended on him as he sat there among the statues.

16

THE NEW SERVANT sat quietly. He learnt the art of statues, their stillness, their repose. He learnt to absorb energies and moods into his being. He learnt to radiate moods in silence.

He learnt the absorbency and radiation of statues. Learnt, like them, to be present. Like them he learnt never to insist. Not moving, yet seeming to move. Never changing, yet seeming to change. He changed with the light, or with the angle.

He learnt the simplicity of statues. He learnt how simplicity makes them monumental in the mind. He learnt the immobility of statues, and how this helps them enter minds who have never seen them. He learnt the humour of statues, their indwelling mystery, their inward smile. They keep their best secrets to themselves.

He learnt like statues to dwell in mystery, to live in its secret light. To listen to truths whispered inside the form of things.

He learnt the openness of statues, gazed on without being understood, and not minding; offered to all eyes, all souls.

He learnt the tranquillity of statues, content simply to be, wasting no energy, unconcerned.

He learnt the power of statues, occupying and not occupying space.

He learnt from them the art of experiencing every part of his being, aware of all that is, in the universe.

17

FROM THE STATUES he learnt that all things participate in all things. No one thing is really isolated from another.

He learnt indestructability. He learnt that forms persist in the memory of space.

He learnt the oblique art of happiness, and that statues reveal their inner art in the dark, among themselves, when no one else is around, when they can be most true. Happiness was a by-product of all the statues knew, their inner certainties.

It took some time before they admitted the new servant into their exalted ranks. He had to be tested and then initiated into their mysteries.

Many things the new servant learnt from them without knowing it.

His time among statues was one of the greatest adventures of his life.

To serve, the prince became a statue in the master's workshop. He seldom moved.

18

MEANWHILE THE CLAMOUR of the suitors grew worse. Their competitiveness intensified. Many of them stayed in the village and put forward their suits through influential intermediaries.

Herbalists had been recruited into their ranks. On the payroll of one of the suitors, the herbalists would insinuate their way into the maiden's household and whisper hints about the evil things that might befall the family if so-and-so were not chosen as the bridegroom. If there was an illness in the family, and a herbalist was consulted, it would often be suggested that such and such a suitor was responsible, or that if a favourable decision were made in the direction of so-and-so then the epidemic, of which the illness was a forerunner, might be spared the family, if not the tribe.

On all sides the family was pestered and hounded by the frustrated suitors. Their frustration began to have an unwholesome effect on the people, on their good will.

People found themselves being drawn into one camp or another, into supporting one influential suitor or another. Those who sold fish or meat or trinkets or vegetables or bales of dyed cloth in the market would whisper to anyone the name of a suitor they favoured. This name would make its way, circuitously, to the mother, and then eventually to the maiden herself.

But she wouldn't consider any names. Nor would she hear the word 'suitor'. She had developed a deafness to the whole subject. She acquired a trenchant absent-mindedness.

She preferred to sing, or dream, by the river.

19

THE MORE THE suitors clamoured, the more elusive she became. Almost unnoticeably, she grew more beautiful. She developed the art of passing among people without being seen, slipping through crowds without being noticed. She learnt not to see what she didn't want to see.

As the suitors began to make themselves fixtures in the village, she learnt to see less and less, and to hear less and less of them. She withdrew into dreaming and wandering.

The suitors infected the village with their rivalries. The families of other young girls of marriageable age started to complain.

'Why doesn't she choose one man and have done with it?'

'Is she the only girl in the world?'

'Why doesn't she think of others?'

'Because of her the village is being ruined by strangers.'

The Mamba, who made this theme popular, increased the pitch of his campaign. He slandered the other suitors, maintaining that their wealth and their alien ways were corrupting the spiritual integrity of the tribe. He said that the maiden's inability to make a sensible choice would bring fragmentation and death to the people.

This kind of talk grew in strength. Many picked up on it. The masters were alarmed enough to feature it in their meetings.

20

FOR THE FIRST seven days the new servant did as he was told. If he was told nothing, he did nothing. He never spoke, only listened. He never knew there was so much to listen to, so much to hear, in the universe.

At first listening in this way, to ants climbing the wall, to the wind in the forest, was alien to him. It was very difficult. He experienced it as a kind of agony. Then he noticed that if he slowed down the workings of his mind, if he forgot himself, there was a rare pleasure in listening.

He began to hear things he would never have been told. He heard stories and rumours about the kingdom. He learnt that the land had a king no one had ever seen. He heard that in the king's court they were plotting the removal of the king and the division of the kingdom. He heard that the prince had died and that a false prince had been put in his place to placate the people.

He heard that on all sides the kingdom was being invaded by shadows and white spirits. He heard that the land was being devoured by darkness. An evil had come among the people and was snatching the young men and women and stealing them away into a dark place beyond the seas from which there was no return.

He heard the cries of the ancestors, the wailing of the legion of unborn generations, the howling of the dead. He heard the collapsing houses, the crumbling palaces, and the crashing down of the great pillars of the land. He heard the angels singing of the new ages that would emerge from the appalling destruction.

He had no idea how he heard these things. But when he learnt to listen there seemed no end to the things to hear.

He learnt to listen without fretting, without acting.
He learnt to listen, and to hear, the way statues do.
He realised that the more he listened, the more he heard.

21

WHEN THE DAY'S work was done, he would rise from among the statues and bow silently to the master. Then he would pick his way through the wooden busts, the statues of gods, the host of images, and out into the village. He would make his way through the thronging artworks along the village streets and paths, through images in stone and wood, images in mixed materials of nails and feathers and blood and cowries, works that crowded the thoroughfare. The works changed shape with the fall of evening.

He made his way past them all, listening to the murmur of voices. Without looking at any faces, or dwelling too long on any one sight, he would glide through the busy village, drawing no attention to himself. He found his way to the forest, and slipped through the ambiguous openings between trees.

Often the fragrance of the evening-breathing trees filled him with childhood memories. They gave him a feeling of great freedom, and his heart would sing with a ruby-dark joy. He felt fortunate to have the kingdom of the forest all to himself. He would linger among the trees and sing to the birds and recite lines of ancient verse to the forest flowers.

Sometimes he would lie with his back against a tree and allow himself to drift into a realm of elementals.

On one such occasion he had an extraordinary dream about a baby who, on the very same day he was born, became a man, married a wife, had three children, fought valiantly in a great war, travelled to all the continents, was initiated into a secret brotherhood of universal masters, healed the sick, redirected the course of world history, cleansed half the earth of its corruption by diverting through it the wonderful river of Venus, yoked the oxen of the sun to the dry unfruitful earth, fought the seven-headed monster of the deep, restored the neglected garden of the race to its pristine beauty, and then died at the midnight of his first and only day on earth.

He had no idea what the dream meant. But he drew strength from thinking about this child who accomplished so much in one day.

22

EVERY EVENING THE new servant experienced something unexpected on his way back home. Sometimes he learnt the taste of fear as he walked in the dense shadows of the trees and listened to the birds.

Sometimes he tried to listen to the language of trees, to hear what they had to say about life. Sometimes he heard whispers that death lived in the forest. Its house was all the trees and all the shade and all the darkness and all the earth. Its womb was life too, if you could find it. The whispers made no sense to him.

Whatever he did, however much he lingered, he always made sure that whenever he was returning home he found the exact opening between the trees. He always passed through it quickly and in a firm spirit.

It was some time before he realised that this opening might be the reason the emissaries had been unable to find the tribe of artists. It occurred to him that the magical tribe was not on any map or in any territory, but in a separate realm. It also occurred to him that the tribe had ways of making itself visible when it needed. The prince was not even sure if they were of the kingdom.

The opening that he passed through changed shape from day to day. It was never the same. Sometimes it was like the moon. Sometimes it was like a fire. Once it was like a clear mirror of water sparkling in the air. Another time it was the shape of a woman.

But whenever he passed through the opening he felt somehow other. Different, but also the same.

On the journey home he became the prince again. His head shimmered with a new clarity. He often felt as if with eyes shut he glimpsed half the universe.

23

A<small>FTER SEVEN DAYS</small> of going back and forth between the worlds, the prince asked his father for permission to stay longer on his mission. With a hint of mischief in his eyes, the king said:

'I consider it part of your duties as a prince to be first and foremost a human being. You should be richly grounded and properly rounded.'

The king laughed, perhaps at himself.

'A season of humility will do you good. A season of humiliation would put power in your veins and some ripening rage in your heart.'

The king was no longer laughing.

'To be all things is to be human. Exile, slavery, warfare, madness, folly, grandeur – these are the food of the brave. All will be tasted at the feast before you become king. But the greatest fruit of all, my son, is love. If through love you learn the art of being human, then you will be a great prince and a joy to the gods.'

The prince was taken aback by this strange speech. His father had never spoken to him like that before. By the time the prince recovered from the surprise, his father was gone.

24

THAT EVENING, DRIVEN by an inexplicable passion, the prince summoned the elders. Under the silent empowerment he sensed from the king, he demanded answers from them about the gaps that were multiplying in the kingdom, the gaps that were undermining the foundation of things.

His questions enraged the elders more than ever because they had no answers. They could do nothing about the gaps that were spreading through the kingdom like a nameless disease.

25

THEY WERE GATE-MAKERS, masquerade-shapers, dreamers. The prince lived among them. He lived with the tribe of artists as an ordinary, invisible man.

He worked as a servant to the master. He also worked as a servant to the maiden of his heart. He worked with the master for seven seasons. Often, with permission, he stole back to the palace.

In all that time he never spoke to the maiden. She never spoke to him. She didn't see him. She didn't notice him. He never looked at her directly, but he watched her in his spirit and listened to her soul. He studied her heart and followed her ways. He absorbed the peculiar philosophy of her being, the tangents of her mind.

She was one of the gifted ones who did not know how strange she was. She took her strangeness as normal. The new servant learnt that she was not much interested in the reflection of things. Her own reflection did not fascinate her. She was more interested in being than in things. Yet she avoided people and hid among things. She was more interested in fruits than in roots. Other people probed what lay behind things, where people came from, where they stood in the hierarchy of things, who their ancestors were. But she was interested mainly in what people produced, their fruits, their art, their deeds.

The new servant often noticed how with a glance at someone's art she took in all she needed to know about them. With that glance, her silence spoke. Nothing was more revealing to her than the signature of a soul in the art they created. In this she had the severity of youth.

She could read the interior of minds in their art. Everything lay bare to her, like a covert confession, in every work she saw. She could glimpse courage, humour, patience, the capacity to grow, freedom of spirit, meanness, hidden greatness, cowardice, a mystical inclination, their state of health, how long they would live, their trustworthiness, their capacity for love, the kind of husbands or wives they might make. She intuited many more things in every work she encountered.

This was a strange gift she had, a witchcraft of the eyes. It was almost a curse. It weighed her down. The tribe feared her eyes for this reason. This power had grown more acute since her initiation.

To look at most people's art, for her, was to suffer. She saw too clearly the inadequacies of the best. Very few works ever affected her, ever struck her as going beyond. Those that did affected her like a wound, like a mental breakdown. They were like a revelation in which she was somehow destroyed. She craved this destruction. Only through such a destruction did she get a sense of the unspeakable truth of life, which raided her daydreaming hours.

26

THE NEW SERVANT, in his stillness among the statues, studied the maiden's heart. She was difficult to read. He studied her ways.

Using the power that death had given him he listened to the philosophy of her being. He roamed in her spirit.

It was his primary reason for dwelling there in the shadows, in that realm where he was unknown and unseen.

All he wanted was to live in her spirit. More often than he realised, he did.

He sensed that she saw straight to the heart of people. But she seldom believed that she saw what she saw. Sometimes seeing clearly obscures itself.

27

Often her mind would drift to another world, a world faraway. In that world she had long conversations with beings of unusual beauty. They were beings of many colours, yellow and blue, red and gold. Their forms were pure.

To them all things had gods. All things were philosophies. To them science and technology were pre-historic. They believed, for a civilisation to be great and creative, it was important to forget. They had been through eons of excessive memory and it paralysed them for millennia. Their forgetfulness was not forgetting, but acts of genius. They knew that everything that ever was ever will be. To enshrine history was to commit a tautology and to clutter the future. All things that were important found their way to the present. They were masters of the present moment. In the present all things, all worlds, all possibilities exist. Their sense of irony was inexhaustible.

These beings showed the maiden many wonderful notions that filled her heart with delight. They showed her the past and the future, under the aspect of sublime irrelevance, seen from the perspective of the stars.

28

THE MAIDEN LOVED the hours she spent wandering in the forest and dreaming along the shores of the river. She loved her conversation with those beings of a remote place that was her true home.

Once they conversed about the art of misunderstanding.

'Misunderstanding is all that is possible between you humans,' said one of the beautiful beings. 'It is simply not possible for you to understand one another.'

'Why not?'

'Because of the way you are made.'

'How are we made?'

'You can only experience the world through your senses. But your senses are inefficient for experiencing the full nature of reality. Do you think someone with only one faculty, like hearing, grasps all of reality?'

'No.'

'That is how you humans are. You think your senses perceive all that is, but they don't. How can you live a life or have a philosophy from such a limited structure?'

'Maybe for us what we experience is true.'

'True for you, but false about reality.'

'Is that bad?'

'You do not hear what can be heard. You do not see what can be seen. What you say is not what you intend. What you intend is not what you say. How can that which does not know itself know what it is saying, or what it wants to say? Nothing is as you sense it. Your bodies are inefficient for experiencing truth. All you can do is misunderstand. You may as well make an art of it.'

'How can we make an art of misunderstanding?'

'By assuming that nothing can be understood, because nothing is what it seems.'

'But where is the art?'

'Making misunderstanding the very tool itself.'

'Like people who talk different languages and yet do good business in the market?'

'Yes.'

'Is that what art is?'

'Yes. Being misunderstood and yet speaking clearly to the spirit.'

'Is that what life is?'

'Yes. The great misunderstanding.'

'Is there any hope for us?'

'Begin with the art of misunderstanding and find your way to the gate of illumination.'

'What is that like?'

'Everything will be simple and clear. You will realise the beautiful oneness of all life and you will be beyond death.'

29

THE MAIDEN SPENT hours in the company of those beautiful beings, her true people. They were constellations away and yet as close to her as her thoughts.

Their conversations were far removed from her life and were useless to her except as refreshments of the spirit. Sometimes they gave her signs of things that were to happen. She caught these signs in her art and then forgot that she did. In this way, almost sleepwalking, she added to the enigmas of the race.

Sometimes a figure from that distant realm would pay her a visit. They would come to her in a form she didn't recognise, in that kingdom where artists are not seen...

30

WHILE ALL THE stars in the galaxy revolved, while the story of all things approached the ultimate secret of their ends and their beginnings, while death crept over the kingdom, and darkness stole into the name of that realm, the new servant sat quietly among the statues.

Drums broke their silences in the evenings, holding the beat of the public festivities. On the sides of the drums were embossed cameos of figures driving death back to its cave with the power of their drumming.

Deep voices sang. Dancers shook the earth. Libations were poured into the cracks. Laughter rose among the flute melodies. Some of the melodies sounded like newborn babies.

The new servant sat in the silence of statues till spiders wove their nets about his face. They entangled his hair, imprisoning him in their fine webs from which he did not stir.

How quickly did the spiders work?

He would come in and take his place and be still. He would wander in the delicious philosophy of the maiden's being. When he came to he would find himself enmeshed in fine-spun threads of darkness. He would hear the king's laughter in the irony of it all, and smile.

31

HE WENT ON seeking a magical way into her spirit, into the sweetness of her being.

In the world of thought he lingered with her by the river, when she was doing errands. In the world of thought he learnt through her the art of weaving stories on cloth, of dyeing tales on sheets. Symbols and signs, figures and forms, hints of dreams and shapes of prophecies were patterned on bales of wrappers which the men and women wore on ceremonial occasions; and he learnt them all through her spirit.

The maiden, her mother, and the gifted women dressed the tribe in prophecies. Ambiguous fishes, beings with eyes of moonstones and gold, dancing angels of brilliant colours, were charmed on to the cloths. Divinatory cowries, a garden of stars, men in space among the stars, embracing the universe, were patterned on to materials that would become blouses, dresses, wrappers, coverlets. The tribe would be draped in dreams and visions and playful myths, in divinations and inscriptions to the future.

The maiden loved working on cloth with her mother. While working they laughed and told stories and challenged one another in images and inspiration.

When evening fell, and the day's work was done, the maiden would go to the farms, with water and refreshments for the farmer-artists as they prepared to come home.

Often the new servant, in the world of visions, would see her wandering among the golden sheaves of cornfields, leaning against a tree, lingering among the cassava plants, or gazing at a remote constellation.

Then he would be surprised to see her burst into tears, as if she had lost a lover to the stars.

Then, just as suddenly, she would be composed again. She would join the women returning from the farm, carrying a basket of yams, or dangling a child in her arms while its mother rested a moment in the shade of an obeche tree.

THE NEW SERVANT sensed a profound restlessness in the maiden. One day she burst into her father's workshop and said:

'Father, something is supposed to be happening to me, but isn't. What is it?'

'Are you ready to make your choice of husband now?'

'No.'

'Then what do you mean?'

'I'm supposed to be happy or sad, but I am not.'

'What are you then?'

'I don't know. Do you?'

The master said nothing. The silence lengthened in the workshop. The new servant could hear the statues whispering. He could hear the spirits at work. They were enchanting the forms and statues, polishing them with the invisible wax of myth and infusing into them moods of amber and unfinished stories. The spirits breathed an odd quality of life into the master's works till they fairly bristled with a mineral and lifelike condition and became alive in a troubling and dreamy kind of way.

The new servant listened as the spirit-servants made finishing touches to the statues and figurines, giving them an immemorial ancient mood, under the master's precise instructions. They worked on the masks too. The masks would later adorn the masquerade's faces. They would *be* the faces, on the day of the ancestors or on feast days, when the chosen ones are possessed by the gods.

These masks took on their true personalities only when in motion, only when in the ritual dance. When motionless the masks had a tense, active stillness. This fusion of motion and stillness would transform the art of civilisations across the seas.

The master's spirits infused into these masks the eternal longing to dance, to be free.

AMONG THE SILENT statues, the new servant listened with the maiden for her father's reply. But the master didn't speak.

Then the maiden wandered absent-mindedly among the statues in the workshop. She wanted to see how they were coming along. She also wanted to see how much they were altered just by being there in that space, immersed in the radiance of the master and the atmosphere which deepens them with dark and wonderful notions.

The maiden lingered at each statue. She gazed at them dreamily. Then she came upon the new servant. He sat motionless against the sepia wall, among spiders' webs and the wood of royal old trees. She was startled at this new perfection of the master's art. A sense of the unknown king of the forest came over her. She drew in her breath and cried out, half-enchanted and half-horrified at this seated statue of a beautiful young figure from another world.

Her heart was beating fast. Something flooded her head. For a moment she went quite blind. Then a white light, like the brilliance of the sky, conquered the top of her head. Everything suddenly cleared. Her mouth was dry, her vision renewed.

She drew back, shaken, astonished at what she beheld. It seemed incredible to her that her father had now created a work so real that it had become practically human. If there was any flaw it was that there seemed something altogether too kind in the face, too adorable about the lips.

Overcome by the sorcery of the accomplishment, the maiden feared that her father had gone too far. This time, in his perfection, he might have challenged the gods with the greatness of his art...

34

SHE WENT TO the far end of the workshop. The corner where the new sculpture sat was for her now a place of dark magic. She wanted to forget that beautiful, unsettling experience. There was something unnatural about the charm of that face that she didn't want to think about.

She had also forgotten the question she had asked her father. She sat in a mild confusion, feeling scared and miraculously altered, but not knowing why. Soon the mood of the workshop crept over her in its fragrance of old stone and wood. She was listening to the whispers of the spirits when she drifted into a deep and wonderful sleep. In her sleep she was far away from the workshop, in a remote constellation, playing like a child with the beings of her other homeland.

As she slept her father rose and went towards her. Above her form he chanted ancient tribal spells, reality-altering incantations. He spoke to the master-spirit within her.

'Forget that which does you no good,' he said. 'Remember things in a manner that is best for you. Open your heart towards your marriage. Choose only he who will best help you fulfil your destiny, and whose destiny you can most help fulfil. Whatever those destinies are.'

He intoned another ancestral spell and went back to his work.

35

WHILE SHE SLEPT, the master summoned the spirits of the workshop. Then he gave them fresh instructions about the new work he had been gestating. The spirits set about their tasks.

The new servant hadn't moved. He breathed gently. He felt the spirits working all around him. They were enriching the air with ideas, opening dimensions to other worlds and other ages. They worked on the atmosphere. They impregnated the air with ancestral wisdom and future realities.

This charged atmosphere, seeping into the statues and masks and carvings, was what created the highest mystery in the works. When finished, the works were not complete. They needed to absorb an atmosphere richly treated in enchantments and sorceries and dark beautiful suggestiveness. They needed to be treated in ancient moods.

This was the most important work that the spirits performed. They steeped the finished sculptures in enigmas.

It wasn't long before the new servant realised that he too was being cooked in enigmas...

36

THE MAIDEN WOKE with a shock and sprang out of her chair. She hurried out of the workshop and went to her mother.

'I'm in love,' she said, 'but I don't know who I'm in love with. Why?'

The mother was bewildered. She was dyeing images in cloth when her daughter joined her. Together they were making a collection of dye images of trees and hills and children playing. The maiden added an image of the sculpture of the four bound people. Among the images she had made little cameos of the suitors, with their traits and gifts and the art each had created. She worked in silence with her mother. It was their way of dealing with things too difficult to talk about. As faces and forms emerged, each one represented so carefully, the mother wept at her daughter's wonderful talent.

'Why are you weeping, mother?' the maiden asked with a smile.

'You're so talented and you don't value it.'

'Oh, mother.'

'I just pray that you marry the right man.'

'I will do my best, mother.'

'A talent like yours needs the right man.'

'Where is he to be found?'

The mother looked at her.

'You're the strangest daughter that God could have given a mother.'

'And you're the loveliest mother that God could have given a daughter.'

'I'm serious. I just don't know what to do with you.'

The maiden laughed and then she wept on her mother's shoulder, like a little girl.

When the dye was set, and the cloths were ready, they were distributed to the suitors. Their faces adorned the wrappers and the dresses and the shirts, worn in the season's festivities. The cloths were seen beyond the tribe, carried to distant lands by merchants who found their way to their realm. Instead of pacifying the suitors, the gift made them more determined to succeed in winning her.

37

IN CREATING THE images on cloth, the maiden made a discovery. She was not remotely in love with any of the suitors. And yet she knew, from all she had heard, from all the tales of the heart that she had been told, from the happy and alive way she felt, that she was in love.

There could be no other possible explanation. Either she was in love, or she was possessed, or she was going mad.

How could she love without an object?

These questions troubled her.

She could not sleep. She brooded round the outskirts of the village and hung around the shrine and lingered in her father's workshop, staring at statues slowly coming to life.

Privately, she consulted the priestess of the shrine. They gave her riddles, prophecies, and obscure words that confused her even more.

When that which is not seen is seen,
When that which is dead comes to life,
When stone turns to flesh
When the yellow river bears
The prince and princess into distant lands,
When darkness has come and gone
Over the world
And we understand the meaning of the sun
And we realise what a human being
Is among the stars
Then all your questions will be answered.

The whole world is a seed;

Inside the seed we dream.
One day the seed will sprout
And what we will see will be
As great as heaven.
What you love is right in front
Of your eyes.
But you can never see it
With your eyes.
Only with your heart,
Only with your tears.

This they told the maiden in songs, woven with choruses.

38

MEANWHILE THE NEW servant was woven in cobwebs. The spirits worked on him.

To serve, he became a statue. He slept there in the workshop. He was inducted into the mysteries without knowing it. For statues, in their purity, know the secrets of the land. They absorb them simply. They store the secrets in their form.

The new servant absorbed the lessons he had to learn from the master by being still. He almost never moved. When he did move, he did it silently, like a shadow or a ghost. He ate his simple food quietly. He never troubled the air or shifted the mood. He moved with the simplicity of the dead. Then he would return to his place under the wall, in the dark, among statues, as though he were occupying a space he had never left.

He began to suspect that a part of him moved, but another part of him remained behind, unmoving. The unmoving part stayed with the spirits and the fragrance of wood.

He thus acquired a delicate patina from the air of the master's workshop.

39

FOR A LONG time the master had not required much of the new servant. He didn't ask him to do anything. At first there had been simple errands, but even these were forgotten.

The master worked in silence at his great new work. It demanded utmost stillness and concentration. For the master, concentration was a form of humility. An acute receptivity.

The master had to cease to be so he could see what needed to be. It was a new mode every time.

Sometimes, to make a new work he had to turn into a lion and roam the forests hunting for a dream that dwelt among the spirits there. It was a dream that could be seen by noble beasts, but not by men.

Sometimes, to drag back a form that would endure for thousands of years he had to change into an eagle and fly to villages in remote lands and spy on the rituals of the daughters of an ancient mother. The children of the ancient mother, scattered about the world, didn't know one another anymore.

Sometimes he felt great trouble in the world. He felt the giant wound that an entire race will suffer. He sensed that a special art was needed to help to heal it in advance. But to create this art he had to first, with sorcery, turn into a shape abhorrent to humans and journey to the realm of the dead. Then he had to drag back writhing evil forms and change them into beautiful new images in the darkness before the light of the sun reached them. He would fashion from this a new work of art to stun and awaken.

Then for many months afterwards he would have to learn to be human again. All this converted his vitality. The dangerous journey expended and shortened his life.

It was only by regenerating himself in the invisible stream of light that flows from the centre of the sun to the centre of the earth that he managed not to die before his time as many artists do who work with such terrible materials of the soul.

He regenerated himself with rigorous spiritual practices, with dreams and meditation and prayer.

40

NOW THE MASTER was preparing himself again. Slowly, he let go of the world. Slowly, he let go of desire. Slowly, he freed himself of the need to create, command, will, or dream. The world must do without him.

He was in prayer, within a magic circle, in his workshop, surrounded by an invisible light. Protected by the seven spirits who ward off all intruders, the master set himself adrift into a world where all forms and ideas and unexplored possibilities dwell in a constellation bright as the fire of jewels sparkling in the sun.

The master released himself into this realm. He surrendered himself to its currents and found the gates to higher worlds, where he made new friends, and attended the convention of master artists from all the universes. While there, he might as well have been dead.

The master often went off like this, without informing anyone. He forgot all things and left the new servant without instructions.

41

THE NEW SERVANT sat under the wall and dreamt and discovered new gaps and was silent. Then he found that he was learning and being taught in the silence.

Things and beings and artworks were whispering to him. The masters of the tribe, who saw him in their meditations, whispered secrets into his heart. Spirits of the workshop came and explained the workings of things to him, the hidden art of bronze-casting, the kinetic magic of mask-making, the golden art of harmony in wood-sculpting. They revealed to him the public and sacred history of the tribe.

It was whispered to him, by unknown beings, from realms inaccessible except to travellers in dreams, that the artworks of the tribe were prophecies of one kind or another. The tribe did not know that their works were prophecies, or what the prophecies were.

Sometimes, in the silence, the new servant found himself elsewhere. He might find himself in the village square. He might find himself at the shrine, being shown sculptures and paintings of wars between tribes, wars fought across the seas, invasions of continents by strange-looking people, unsolved murders in distant lands, secret intentions of governments faraway. They were all given clear artistic form.

Traders on caravan routes have been shocked to recognise among the artworks of the tribe the face of one who had been crowned king of their land just as they were setting out on their journeys. They might see the face of one of their famous sages who never travelled. Things the tribe of artists could not have known about.

The new servant gathered, in the hints in the air, that the tribe of artists were listeners in the universal realm of events. They had access to a place where all things that happened in the universe were registered.

They knew of invasions planned on sleeping lands, of world wars that would happen hundreds of years in the future. They knew the faces that would unleash monstrous pogroms and mass exterminations. They knew these things without knowing that they knew.

The new servant learnt to see in the artworks of the tribe great events to come and those long gone. Happenings and possibilities were coded there in their art. The future of the world was encoded there. The tribe knew great and intimate secrets.

Time seemed a river in which past, present, and future were all one. The artists bathed in that stream, drawing from it inspiration without end.

42

THE NEW SERVANT was astonished to learn that the tribe of artists were not interested in prophecy. It meant nothing to them.

They were only interested in creating different kinds of beauty. They were interested in weird beauty, the sort that lurks in chaos, that hides in disorder, that sings in destruction. They were keen on beauty found in the least expected events, materials, elements, or combinations. They sought beauty in ugliness, or the beauty that exists in a seemingly horrible-looking work only when you stop looking at it. They were drawn to the beauty that a work creates in the mind. They were fascinated by the mental and spiritual beauty created by the work but not residing in it. They were indifferent to beauty.

They had no word for it in their language. They had banished it centuries before because the word got in the way of the infinite suggestion that was true art. It got in the way of an inducement to higher states of consciousness. They were interested only in what exalted states the work of art could induce.

Prophecy was merely a covert accessory. It was hidden and incidental. It accompanied the peculiar beauty that their art embodied.

43

ALL THIS AND more the new servant learnt in silence. The semi-darkness was invaluable. So was the stillness in which he learnt to be free. He learnt more in the silence than in years of being told things.

After some time, he realised he was learning about the kingdom, the palace, the traditions, the gaps, the white spirits and their silent invasion of the land. They invaded with mirrors and hidden fire.

He learnt about learning.

Everything in the workshop was eager to teach him. Stones yielded the secret of structure, spiders the secret of making, walls the art of the vertical. The air taught invisibility, feathers taught flight, and the light that came in through chinks in the wall revealed to him the underlying secret of all things, in hints and fragments of illumination.

Time was different in the realm of the workshop. Sometimes it was long. Sometimes it was short. Often it did not exist at all. Time there was timelessness.

Everything was eager to teach him. He was eager to learn.

44

MEANWHILE DARKNESS GATHERED in the greater kingdom. First came the white wind that made people disappear. Then came the darkness.

The old sages say that it came with words. They were words wielded as an incantation to distort the land by those who wanted to use and conquer it. They say the words created the darkness and then the darkness hung over the land and the people did not know it. The darkness thickened among them and the elders did not see it.

When the darkness made them more visible to the outside world, the white spirits came and took from the kingdom its young ones, its virile men, its beautiful women, its gifted children. At first no one noticed. They didn't notice because of the darkness.

45

About this time the new servant made infrequent visits home through the openings in the forest. He noticed that there were more gaps than ever. This filled him with alarm.

In the palace he saw changes in the air. The women were more silent. He peered into the faces of his people and saw a new doubt there.

He asked them questions and they spoke of their dreams. Many dreamt that their bodies were taken from them in the brightness of day, in the middle of their tasks. And without knowing when, they had become spirits who were performing empty duties in a place where nothing happens. Their bodies had been snatched from them and were working on white fields of blood in a sleep of horror. They tried to get their bodies back, but were stuck in that place, working the farms of the strangers.

Many reported having the same dream. They were spirits in the other world. Some said they managed to get their spirits to reunite with their bodies in that far-off place. Then their nightmares began.

The prince was troubled by these dreams of his people. No one seemed able or willing to interpret them.

By now the prince was asking so many questions that he aroused the fears of the elders. They feared once again that he was going to undermine them and that he was going to destroy their institutions when he became king. They feared he would deprive them of power. He raised in their minds the spectre that he would be a dangerous king, with too many new ideas. They were afraid he would bring too many changes, that he would make women equal to men, that he would abolish the hierarchies.

Worse than that, they feared that he would change the nature of their ancestral religion, that he would alter the laws which made them the secret masters of the land.

They pressed forward with their schemes. They plotted ways of getting rid of the prince. Then one of them – Chief Okadu, the Crocodile – had the brilliant idea of somehow offering the prince to the white spirits, so that they might carry him off to the wide blue seas, leaving them, the elders, free to rule in secret, in the name of the king.

46

THERE WERE TIMES when the prince would stand in the centre of the village. The palace could be seen in the distance. He would breathe in the immemorial air of his people, their harvests, their traditions, births, deaths, wars, and festivities.

There were times he would watch the women on their way to the farms, the marketplaces, to the river, or on visits to their relations. And, unaccountably, he would weep.

There were times when he took in the ochre of the huts, the odour of the goats, the choruses of children's voices, the winding paths that led to evergreen forests, the piercing chants of the women, the blue quiver of the heavens, and the deep-throated songs of men gathered at dusk. Times when he would be struck by the sudden magenta cry of the women of the golden shrines, the moon white as the most perfect gap that leads to other worlds, the lonely call of the hunter in the hills, and the flight of the blue-headed sharp-eyed long-flying birds that precipitate auguries when they circle the palace three times before shooting upward into the silvery palm-wine coloured sky.

There were times when, overcome by all this, standing in the square, dreaming of his ancestors who had come from the land now forgotten under the sea, the prince found time had turned upside down, become scrambled; and the huts had turned to dust, the children had all fled or been captured, or only their spirits remained, that the forests had shrunk, the stream had thinned to a ribbon, that only the very old remained, and the elders had lost their memories, and aged mothers wandered the forests without voices, unrecognised by their children, that the white wind had wiped away the traditions, that only dreams and histories and bitterness, tinged with songs, lingered in the dry hot air where his tears of an exile turned into stones as they fell from his face and piled up, sparkling like diamonds, at his feet.

There were times, in the farms, as he worked with the men, carrying sheaves of corn, or cutting the long grass with a machete, or hauling yam from their mounds to the village, when time itself turned round and everything cleared and he found that the farms had gone and that he had fled from that distant land of slavery. He had escaped on a great ship and had found his way, after many years, back to the continent. He found himself on a remote shore and began his search for the homeland that he had been stolen from and which he hadn't seen for forty years. He was an old man, wise in sufferings, which illumination had taught him to endure. He searched for his homeland, travelling from one country to another. He went through nameless countries seeking for his nameless kingdom. It was a vast land that was simply called The Kingdom. He travelled through many countries with villages that looked like his and saw palaces that could have been his, but nowhere could he find the kingdom he had left behind. And as an old man, who knew slavery, who knew freedom, and who never ceased being a prince, who in spirit had never left, he sought for his homeland, in that brief time left, while he stood in the farm, dreaming. And he found his homeland everywhere and never found it at all. It was as if it had been broken into fragments and scattered all over the vast continent. The years passed in dust and dreams, and he never stopped seeking his kingdom. Then one day, by a narrow stream, he heard the laughter of the king in the wind and he fell down towards the beautiful brightness of the sun.

And when he got to his feet he found himself in the farm, surrounded by the women of the village. They loved him with all their hearts, as if he were their sons. They bore him in their arms, and carried him with songs to the edge of the farm, ignoring his protestations that he was fine and that he had only fallen into a strange spell of dreaming. And after they made him drink some water, which tasted strangely sweet, of earth and stone, and after they had prayed over him, and shared their food with him, they carried him to the palace, singing and cheering, as if he were a hero returning from the noble wars.

There were times when the prince stood in the square, in the middle of the village, and wondered about the kingdom. He wondered what the hands of destiny were weaving for those that walked the land of long shadows.

47

MEANWHILE THE MAIDEN was inflamed with a love that had no object. It was a love that gripped her like a fever. A love with no meaning and no purpose.

She went around with the feeling that she was being driven mad by a love that had come upon her invisibly. She felt under a peculiar spell.

Her parents noticed her madness. But they said nothing. They watched her mooning about the place, pining away like a gently fading rose. They watched her eyes grow hollow. They watched her staring at the moon and singing love songs. She wreathed her hair with hibiscus and flamingo flowers and skipped down the village paths, singing out loud.

Who am I in love with
Who has poisoned my soul?
Let me know, let me know.

Who has conquered my heart
Who has killed me with love?
Let me know, let me know.

Who am I a slave to
Who is now my destiny?
Let me know, let me know.

Someone has snatched my soul
Someone has captured me whole
Does it show, does it show?

Then while playing games with the little girls and boys, she would suddenly start laughing. Then she would burst into song, or start weeping.

She would trail behind her friends and would not dwell long by the river. She had lost her taste for the river and the sky and the forest. She didn't even think of art or look at the artworks that appeared in the square.

Often she walked round her father's workshop as if seeking the location of a hidden treasure. She would repeat the verses given her by the priestess of the shrine. The more she pondered them, the more obscure they grew.

48

ONCE SHE WAS sitting under a tree, listening to her friends in the remote constellation where she felt more at home, when a bird with yellow plumage landed in her lap and spoke to her. She could have sworn she heard it say:

The more you look
The less you see.
Let it be, let it be.

But she could not let it be and she seized the bird and took it to her father. The master was pondering how high a thing can be before human beings begin to grasp it; he was thinking how invisible a thing must be before human beings can see it; he was contemplating how light a thing must be before human beings cannot destroy it – when his daughter intruded on his thoughts with a bird that she claimed had spoken to her.

'What did it say?'

She told him.

'Then pay attention to it,' he said. 'First, let the bird go. Then return to your tree and see what happens.'

The maiden set the bird free. Then she went and sat under the tree again. With her back against the tree trunk, she fell asleep. When she woke, her head was clear. She felt a wonderful clarity within her. It was as though she had just had her first good sleep in a long time. She had a shining feeling within her, the feeling after a storm has broken, or the day after it has rained.

She still had the madness of her love, but it was a tranquil beautiful madness, like the face of the river on a clear moonless night.

49

THE NEW SERVANT returned from his visit home and resumed his life as a statue. No one had noticed his departure except the spirits and the spiders. On his return they began to weave webs about him again, layering the work they had previously done.

The new servant went deeper into the mood of his new life. He plunged into the silent mysteries of the tribe. In his deeper delving he found himself exploring the roots of legends, the source of myths, the dark secrets of creativity.

One day, or was it one night, he found himself falling into the abyss that was one of the strangest secrets of the tribe. It was a secret the tribe kept even from itself. He fell into the abyss and was falling a long time, in horror. He became dimly aware that the abyss, without form, dark beyond imagining, was the route through which the gods appeared in the minds of men and women.

He cried out in the abyss and no one heard him. He fell endlessly for days and nights without end. The fall into the abyss took him beyond nightmare, beyond chaos, beyond madness, and beyond death.

The fall took him to the placeless place where the gods dwelt, where all things were mixed into one, where the universe converged. It was the place where all beings merged and from which they emerged. They flowed into and out of one another as in one great unimaginable spirit that was neither darkness nor light. It was the place where all dreams were born, where all deaths died into, and where all life flowed from. It was a place of fire and darkness. In it there were seven great quivering columns, longer and deeper than it was possible to imagine.

He fell and still he went on falling. He fell through the dark secrets of the universe. He fell through all the versions of lives and dreams and deaths, of all beings. Even from unthinkable realms. Still he went on falling. There was no hope of ever stopping his fall, of ever emerging from the abyss, of ever getting to the end of his fall.

He might have gone on falling forever in that space that was not a space, a hole that was no longer a hole but a gap that led to the endless. He might have gone on in this bright dark infinity of a fall till he was no longer anywhere, till his body, woven in mysteries, would have turned finally into a statue of flesh, preserved by the spirits. He might have fallen into nothingness if it weren't for the master's hand on his head, raising him from this dying that was not a death.

50

So it was that on a certain day, now lost in time, the master laid his hand on the statue that was the new servant, and said:

'This is my new pupil. Get up! Arise!'

The prince rose in the dark, as from an immortal dream. He bowed gracefully to the master and to his daughter. He remained in the attitude of bowing till the master touched him on the shoulder. There was a flash of light from that touch which no one but the spirits saw.

The maiden drew breath sharply. Her amazement knew no bounds.

For the first time she had witnessed with her own eyes what she had only heard in rumours. She had seen her father bring a statue to life.

The rumours were true. Her father had spirits that worked for him, that did the carving, the shaping, the moulding for him. Her father's statues were brought to life by the power of his hands and they served him and did his will.

Her father was an artist-wizard and a creator of monsters. She had always revered her father. But now she was in awe of him. He no longer seemed human. He seemed something more. Something which she dared not specify in her mind.

She feared the new servant. She feared him because she knew that he wasn't real, was not truly flesh and blood. He had no heart. He was a thing made in the dark workshop of her powerful father and brought to life by the touch of his hand.

51

ON ANOTHER DAY, after his raising, the prince was instructed by the master to walk once round the workshop, in a circle, in an obscure symbolic ritual.

As the prince performed this rite, slowly and with dignity, he accidentally brushed against the maiden's dress, and she jumped back.

'Don't touch me!' she cried, in a confusion of feelings.

She felt the warmth of his body when he passed her.

'He feels almost human,' she said in wonder. 'Is he?'

She received no answer.

She avoided this new pupil and willed herself not to notice him. He aroused disquieting notions in her, awoke in her a warm incomprehensible aversion.

Then for a while he went back to being silent and still, and she did not notice him anymore in the period after his raising. She was therefore able to be truly herself. She was what she was, simply and purely, as he sat there in the workshop, among the images that would one day confound the minds of men and women.

52

THE NEW PUPIL, raised out of his immobility, began to participate in the life of the community. He ran errands and prepared wood for carving. He took part in the dawn installation of the master's lesser works in front of the shrine. He passed on secret code words from the master to other masters without knowing he was doing so. He performed many esoteric duties which seemed to him perfectly normal tasks. He became an active participant in the life of the tribe of artists.

There must have been a profound spell cast on him because whatever he did he was not noticed. He was never seen. Most especially, he was never seen by the maiden. He would trip and fall in her presence, he would spill water from a bucket on his head, he would speak to the air in front of her, but she simply did not lift her eyes to him. Even when she was the object of errands, even when the maiden must have seen the new pupil with her father near the shrine, taking measurements for a new work, still she did not register him.

He felt like an object in the world that light did not fall upon.

53

THEN ONE DAY the new pupil met the maiden's mother and without a word gave her a bunch of flowers he had picked in the moonlight. The mother for the first time noticed his gentle beauty, his slender body, and the peculiar radiance of his eyes, and fell into admiration of him.

That night mother and father talked about him.

'He's not normal.'

'No.'

'He is of unusual birth.'

'Yes.'

'A secret suitor?'

'Perhaps.'

'Or has he come to steal your secrets?'

'He has no interest in creating art. He wants to become art. I don't know what art he wants to become.'

'What other art is there?'

'There are many other arts greater than the art of making art out of wood or stone.'

'Like what?'

'Like the art of making life out of death, wisdom out of suffering, good out of evil.'

'You think your new servant is so exalted in mind?'

'Why not? He turned into a sculpture. He learnt to be a statue. He demands nothing, and gives everything. He does not listen, but hears. He does not appear to do anything, but does everything. Either his birth is noble, or it should be. Maybe his past beyond his memory is noble. He is like a master who cherishes lowliness.'

'Maybe you read too much into his insignificance,' his wife said, smiling.

'He allows his insignificance to be so much. Insignificant people don't have that tranquillity. They may have contentment, they may have innocence, they may have simplicity, but not tranquillity. Tranquillity in a person is an achievement. It is the result of great insight.'

'All this in one so young?'

'Some are young in body, but old in soul. You know that, my dear.'

'I do. Still we must watch him.'

'We will keep a stern eye on him.'

54

EVEN THE MASTERS of the tribe, in their irregular nocturnal meetings, commented on the new pupil.

After one of those long silences, during which, in the dark, many forms appeared, one of the masters said:

'A stranger can wake up a sleeping land.'

Another said:

'A stranger can raise men's minds towards the stars.'

'And he has passed the tests he did not know he was taking.'

'We might have to induct him into the darkness of the hidden tradition.'

'Without his knowing, of course.'

'In case we are showing disrespect to a god, or a king.'

THEN ON A night that seemed like any other the new pupil was given instructions to work in the secret forge deep in the forest. There he was initiated by the master, without his being aware of it, into the mysteries of fire and the esoteric art of turning ordinary metal into gold. It was an art known only to a few, brought from their old kingdom and nurtured as a secret tradition.

The new pupil also worked on the outer substance of things. He shaped, carved, polished, moulded, and did patina work on the sculptures, under the strict supervision of the master. He was forbidden to reveal all that he had obliquely learnt. He was made to swear a blood oath on this in the depths of the forest, in the initiation that he didn't know was one, conducted in complete darkness by figures whose voices were muffled by ancient masks.

There must have been a profound spell cast on him that night. For whatever he did he still was not noticed, not truly seen.

56

THE CLAMOUR OF the suitors got worse. They had lingered in the village, had created their art, and their art had been found wanting. They had made pilgrimages to spiritual centres. They had shown their piety, dignity, and seriousness. They had shown restraint. They had behaved well. They had made journeys back to their homes to conduct important affairs of state or business. And they had returned with gifts, both for the tribe and for the maiden's family.

They had made themselves a part of the village life. Some of them had become so much part of the artistic life of the tribe that they forgot why they were there and took other women as wives and dedicated themselves to new vocations in art which they had accidentally discovered.

But many of the suitors, feeling they were wasting time and expending their resources, became impatient and intractable. They ganged up together, finding common cause in the maiden's elusiveness. Presenting a united front, they stormed her house and demanded that she make up her mind about who she would marry.

They were angry. Being men of great importance in their realms – chiefs, aristocrats, famous warriors, sons of noble families – they felt they were being taken too lightly.

They laid down an ultimatum. The maiden must come to a decision within a fixed period or they would spread her name in infamy all over the world. Then no one would consider her in marriage ever again.

IN THE FOREST there are seeds of trees that lie in the earth for a long time and seem to be doing nothing. There are plants that are very small and over many years appear not to grow at all. The sages say that there are some prayers that take a thousand years to be answered. Some say such an interval is less than a moment in the mind of God.

There are people who take a long time to hear what is said to them, a long time to respond to provocation, a long time before they are roused to go to war.

There are people who take a long time before they acknowledge the greatness of one among them, a long time before mourning the death of a sage, a long time before they fall in love.

There are plants that never seem to flower and then one day to everyone's surprise they blossom with astonishing splendour. There are plants that never seem to grow or change and then one day, to the keen observer, they reveal a shining new leaf. Afterwards, they grow at a prodigious rate.

There are people who never smile, never play, and then one day they are like someone new, as if a beautiful sun has risen in their hearts. Different reasons for these things.

They say the gods delay the revelation of our destiny, till it is upon us and the revelation and the destiny are one.

They say that in the deep matters of life fools hurry, but the wise delay.

Sometimes delay is fear. Sometimes it is weakness. Sometimes it is uncertainty. But sometimes delay is prophecy. It is waiting for a sign, the right moment, an alignment, a harmony in the heart with the heart's star in heaven.

THE MAIDEN KEPT delaying her choice of suitor because deep in her heart she knew that the person she truly loved had not yet made himself known.

The more her suitors clamoured and threatened, the more she was possessed by the spirit of delay. She became fertile in the invention of new conditions, new trials and contests. She invented new doubts. She inclined one way, and then another. She said she could not see any single suitor among the many. She wanted them to give her breathing space.

She wanted to see not their actions, or their deeds, but their shadows. She asked each of the suitors to bring her their shadow, so she could see what their spirit was like.

The suitors were baffled. They did not know how to detach their shadows from their bodies. They consulted witch-doctors, herbalists, sages, wise old women, and witches, but no one could tell them how to do it. This kept them occupied for a long time.

All over the village, all along the great trading routes, among the masters of the tribe, and in the realm of spirits, this problem of how to give someone your shadow caused much discussion and amusement.

Everyone talked about it. But no one had an answer.

The conundrum soon reached the ears of the prince. He told his father, the king, about it. And his father roared with a laughter that made many seeds in the forest sprout, made many barren women pregnant, made many women who were pregnant suddenly give birth, made the rivers overflow their banks, and caused rain to fall in dry places. Then he said:

'My son, what an ingenious riddle. The answer is as simple as giving someone your love.'

59

NOT ALL THINGS glimpsed in a dream are clear. Dreams retain their mystery. Not all events glimpsed in the book of life among the stars are clear. Only while dreaming does the dream make sense.

When one awakes, that which made sense suddenly becomes strange and tinged with the unknown. When one dreams, one beholds a complete picture. When one wakes, one is left with a few fragments of what was a magical vision. With these fragments one tries to recreate a beauty that is lost when one returns from the book among the stars.

60

.THE OPENINGS IN the forest began to change. The prince at first did not understand how. On one of his visits home to the palace the prince saw an unusually blue dawn. The forest glimmered with silver. Mists gave off a roseate, golden hue. Dew sparkled on the cobwebs.

It was a dawn in which the trees and climbers and birds were stirring from a dream. Their dream was the bluish colour of the world. As he sought a clear opening that would take him home, the prince felt he was entering a world he had never seen before. Gods and spirits shone out from the haze of blue. Magic swords of heaven pierced the enchantment of the forest.

Pausing to retain the wonder of the moment, he found himself standing before a tree. It was a tree like any other, except that its bole was fresh like the face of a pretty young girl. Its leaves were like little green hands and its buds like the palms of children at prayer.

The prince sat under the tree, resting against the trunk, and was borne off to sleep. It was not a long sleep but many things happened to him that he would only remember in fragments in the years of suffering to come. He dreamt the beginning of all things and their end. He dreamt all the stories and the answers to the greatest questions. They were told him by an unlimited being in space. All that he was, all that he would be; all that was, all that would be; the solution to death; the answer of immortality; he dreamt them all in a moment of sleep. Then he awoke refreshed and found himself in a different space. The tree was in flower and birds were piping in the leaves. Nine maidens in white drifted past him smiling. Then the forest was gone.

The opening he sought stood before him like a ring of enchanted fire. He stepped into the fire and found himself near the river of his village. He was full of questions.

He made for the palace and summoned the elders. He knew his time was running out. He had little time left before his life would change forever. Everything he did or did not do would hasten time's swiftness.

He had to do what remained for him to do. He had to act swiftly and yet act as if he had all the time in the world.

61

AN INNOVATION OFTEN repeated becomes a tradition. This one took place in the presence of the king. Bards recorded it in future songs.

As if in the grip of a poetic vision, the prince demanded that all who were enslaved be freed and returned to their homes. He asked the chiefs and the rich to share their wealth with the poor. He offered to do the same with everything he had. He wanted to know how big the world was and what the people on the other side of the world looked like. Did they know things his people didn't know? Did they have different knowledge and wisdom? He wanted to link hands with them. Why hadn't the elders taken sufficient interest in the rest of the world?

He had visions, he said, that all people were children of the stars. He wanted to meet all his sisters and brothers of the earth. He wanted to know if there were better ways of living, of governing, of enriching the life of his people.

The elders were silent as the prince spoke. But when the king heard the avalanche of questions, he laughed as if there were nothing funnier than seeking knowledge about the wider world and its peoples. It was as if his son's quest for knowledge were a wonderful joke. The prince sensed a disquieting wisdom in his father's laughter. He was not deterred.

'Nothing is as it seems, my son,' said his father, between waves of laughter. 'What is up is down, what is down is up.'

The prince asked as many questions as the rising sun asks the sleeping earth. In legend, that day became known as the Day of Questions. It became a tradition. Every year there would be a day set aside in which people would ask one another the great questions of life and would attempt to answer them in meditation or in art.

The bards exaggerate when they say that the prince asked questions for seven days. They speak the truth when they say that after that day the prince never asked the elders another question again.

62

THE CHIEFS WERE concerned about the prince's new desire for knowledge about the people on the other side of the world. They feared that new knowledge would render them irrelevant.

'If he wants to know so much about the world,' one of them muttered, 'why doesn't someone give him to the white spirits? Then he will find out all the knowledge he wants.'

If they had not been so inward-looking all along, things might have been very different when the white wind came.

63

THE KING DECIDED to spend some time alone with his son to impart to him what he knew of the mystery of things. While the son slept he spoke to his sleeping form. He knew he was speaking into ears that would hear without resistance and into a mind that would remember nothing of what was said except its pure spirit. The prince would act in future from a wisdom that deep down he would have made his own.

In silence, the king said:

'There are barbarians of the high and barbarians of the low. There are barbarians of the intellect too, my son. Don't let the brilliance of people blind you to the fact that they can also be stupid. There are more intelligent people who are fools than fools who are wise. Intelligence can be a form of blindness; it can prevent people from seeing truth. People value their mental powers even as they increase their fundamental errors. Trust those who have simplicity of spirit, goodness of soul, and an inquiring mind. Beware of those who use the word "I" too much. Be wary of those who trust only their senses. They are limited people, easy to deceive and corrupt. Whatever they are is founded on the very limitations that they exalt. People of vision and good instincts are rare. People with sound intuitions and clarity of heart are rarer.'

The king laughed. His laughter spoke to the sleeping prince.

'People's opinions don't amount to much. Their plans work for a while then pass into nothing. Only convictions on the side of life really amount to anything. Do not fear sorcerers or those who conjure for the devil. As long as you do not believe in evil they cannot harm you. Fear is the most powerful form of belief. Do not fear anything. There is only one cure for fear, and that is wisdom. Knowledge of the tried and tested mysteries brought down from our ancestors. Keep to the ancient path that has led to your light and all else will follow.'

The king was silent a while. The son breathed gently on the bed.

'Notice the higher comedy in life. There is divine laughter everywhere in the universe. Human beings don't hear it because they are too confused by appearances. Find your own way, but keep a place in your heart for that divine humour.'

His voice became quieter.

'All power is a shadow of true power. There was a man who grieved because he thought he had conquered the world. He had nothing more to do. He could have conquered himself. Afterwards all that he conquered turned to dust. He could have found heaven in a single vision. His is one of the greatest comedies in the human story. There are kings who do not know what they are kings for. A human being ought to know what they are human for. It is a strange sickness to live a life, roaming the earth, without knowing why. There is no tragedy greater than a god that does not know itself. There is no comedy greater than a human being who looks at their reflection in a river and sees a stranger.'

The king traced a mystic sign over the sleeping prince and breathed an inaudible incantation over his spirit.

'We have three selves in one. Only one of them endures. But nothing perishes. All time is here. Don't trouble yourself about passing sufferings, fashions, ideas, disasters, failures, successes, or triumphs. All are illusions. Maintain a sublime detachment from all things and the greatest love will shine through you. Be silent. Be still. Sometimes our minds are our worst enemies. Do not hold preferences too strongly. Be guided by that still small voice within. Learn to listen to it. Drink the cup of suffering life gives you when it does. Pass through the narrow space. Do not cling to any fixed ideas of who or what you are. You are more than whatever you think you are. Being a prince is nothing compared to a man or woman who has discovered that deep down in them there are gods. Humility makes you great. Who can destroy the invisible thing that makes the universe real? Be as nothing. Be everything. Do not fear loss. Nothing is lost on the way that is not found among the stars. A way has been shown for you to reach me when you need to. The wisest ones of the universe are here for you in that still small voice within. All the guidance you will ever need is within you, as part of your mysterious nature. All human beings are princes and princesses. Only very few know their kingdom.'

NIGHT WAS DRAWING on. In three successive stages the king inscribed invisible magical symbols around the body of the prince. He cleansed the air above his head with the powerful breath of his spirit. He cleansed the air below his son's feet with a white powder. Into the heart of the recumbent form he sent the elixir of his spirit. On all planes the ritual operation for preparing the prince for his destiny was accomplished. It had taken great sorcerers to compress so much into so short a ritual. Then it was done.

The king went on speaking into his son's spirit.

'Throughout your life you will acquire a family of people from all over the world. Find them and help them to find you. We have many families. Some of them are not of this earth. Be responsive to them all. About the things of life, remember to stop when you have ripened. Call forth what you need only when you need it. The more you call forth, the more there will be. Live simply. Respect nature. Carry with you your shadow, and surrender it to the light. In spirit and in deeds, be light. Don't be above people. Lower yourself without being low. Have dignity without showing it. Be a prince without display-ing it. Let your wisdom be invisible to the eyes of men and women. Rule as if the people were ruling themselves. When power is needed, summon and use it. When war is needed, rise and go to war in the highest way. Win in the quickest way. Use your victory to create a better life for all. Especially for the poor. Many things are forgivable if you are truly extending the good in the world. Do not try to be perfect. Only be better. Dream higher. Don't carry any of what I say in your head. Forget it all. What you need to guide you is in you. Your light is your guide and your power. You have already awoken it. Whatever life brings you, keep the light alive. As you know, you are a child of the stars. All the universe is your home. But the centre of the circle is the home of your home. Dwell there always, in your heart, and you will transcend death. Then your life will not be a failure or a success, a comedy or a tragedy. It will be immeasurable.'

65

THE PRINCE SLEPT profoundly during the magic hour when his father gazed in silence over his sleeping form. The prince had dreams of great beauty, which he could not remember afterwards. He awoke a deeper and a lighter person. He dwelt more easily in the beautiful silences in the air. He smiled more and noticed that within him grew the mood of an everlasting laughter.

He also discovered afterwards that he could become invisible at will. Later, during his great suffering, which coincided with the years of his enlightenment, many techniques, many laws, and a clear elucidation of the way were whispered to him in half-dreams. He realised then that seeds of truth were being planted in his sleep. Sometimes they were planted in those moments when he dwelt in contemplation of wonderful silences.

Much later, during the worst years of his enslavement, he would perceive himself in the centre of a golden circle. He found that when he dwelt in the circle he transcended the agony of slavery. When they branded his flesh he felt simultaneously the burning pain and the spiritual liberation. Beyond the flesh burning in great suffering he knew the sublime fire and the illumination of the throne. He found himself then in the brilliant black centre of the golden circle of light.

66

Sometimes in the village of artists, running an errand or resting under an iroko tree in the forest, the prince would pass through a blue opening in the world and arrive at the torments of his enslavement in an alien land.

His bride was gone. His child was gone. He had survived the crossing of the sea of evil, in a ship where captives lay ankle chained to suppurating ankle, wrist to bleeding wrist, in the coffin that was the hold. The ship sailed on the waves of an empire's dream of power. He had arrived in a new land that was rich with blood and guilt and hope. He had survived the lash and the degradation. He had survived being less than a man, less than a beast, in the land of the long-named river. He had survived the loss of his love, his kingdom, his home, his earth. He had survived being forced into a marriage with a woman who was not his wife but the mistress of his owner. He found himself listening, in an odd calm, as his owner made love at night to his wife who was not his wife. He listened on many other nights too, gazing at the stars, dwelling in the black fire in the centre of the golden circle.

He knew then as now that it was a peculiar fate to live through such suffering while being blessed with such illumination.

In those moments in the forest, resting under a tree, passing into the blue openings, and seeing distant revelations, he often contemplated the paradox of his destiny. He would ask himself these questions. How do you survive the worst with the highest? What is the music of this paradox? What is its song? Can you show anyone its shadow, so they can see the conjunction of the horror and the sublime?

But in the present and future story, the prince always found within him the mood of an immeasurable laughter. It was unquenchable.

All this was born on the night when a father gazed with love on the form of his sleeping son.

67

ON HIS RETURN to the tribe of artists he found that the opening he sought had changed. It was now a hole of black fire.

The mood of the tribe had altered. A cloud of doom hung over everything. The air was bright, but the spirit over things was murky.

The maiden was withdrawn. Her delay in choosing a suitor was wearing down the tribe. A mood of restlessness and irritation and violence drifted among the buildings and floated past the men, women, and children.

The pupil resumed his service. There wasn't anything he didn't do. He carried, cleaned, washed, ran errands, and bore messages. He went to the market, made beds, aired rooms, and sat in stillness among the statues. He cleaned the latrines, drew water from the wells, and washed clothes at the river. He fetched wood from the forest, worked on the carvings and statues under precise instructions, and seldom spoke. All through this he lived within the being and the spirit of the maiden.

He studied her moods. He learnt to enter into her dreams. He listened in on her thoughts. He lived partly in her life and partly in his. He dwelt mostly in her being, as fragrance dwells in a wild rose. He was happiest there.

Sometimes he smiled. Sometimes he laughed. When he laughed he did so quietly, within himself. Moments later he would hear wonderful laughter circling the village. Not long after that the maiden would appear, with a smile on her face. The master would be hard at work. She would whisper a joke into her father's ear. Hours later, in the evening, in bed, with his wife, the master would find himself laughing as he shared the joke that he had only just understood.

68

THE MAIDEN'S DELAY began driving the suitors to the brink of desperation. Her father strove not to pressurise her. Her mother spoke to her obliquely, controlling her voice. They knew, in all fairness, that none of the suitors had solved the riddle of the shadow. So there was nothing to be done. But the tensions did not lessen.

Fights broke out between the suitors. They took to challenging one another to combat. They fought with weapons, with bare fists, and they wrestled. There were injuries and near-fatalities. It was in this way that the suitors decided among themselves to settle it through combat. The overall winner would be deemed the winner of the maiden's hand.

The contests would take place on the fields near the shrine and would last an allotted time.

Announcements were made, and a date of commencement was decided. This was how the tribe that was dedicated to art found itself a hostage to a contest of arms. They were about to witness, for the first time, battle among the suitors. Because of her unique gifts, her disdain, and her delay, the maiden had become priceless. To justify the time they had all spent wooing her, there must be a winner.

69

THE MAIDEN DISAPPROVED of the contest, and made her feelings clear. But events had passed out of her hands. The desire for an outcome took on its own momentum.

Never before had this happened in the tribe. The event was so fascinating that the people fell under its spell. The maiden withdrew and let it be known that she would not witness the barbarous contest.

What she said made no difference. It promised to be a moment of history. Everyone wanted it to happen. The brooding air, the quiet history of the tribe, the legend that was coming into being, they all seemed to call forth the spectacle. And so it had to be. Everyone looked forward to its commencement after the season of rain.

70

THE MAIDEN COULD have brought an end to all the conflict and rage simply by making her choice known, by making a decision. But she didn't.

She intended to delay long enough to know what was right for her. She would delay long enough to gain wisdom, to make the best decision.

She would delay till the person she loved appeared. The person who could also solve the riddle of the shadow.

71

THE NEW PUPIL quietly performed his duties in the master's workshop. The rains were late coming in from the sea. Before the time of the festivals, the shadow of a tragedy descended on the tribe that moved the people considerably.

The new pupil learnt about it first from the maiden. She came into her father's workshop one evening and fell on his shoulders crying and couldn't seem to stop. At that moment the sound of wailing was heard from the streets and workshops. Loud weeping was heard from the marketplaces and the priestesses of the shrine. It was some time before the people made any sense of this phenomenon of sadness that was sweeping the community.

The maiden couldn't seem to get her words out as she sobbed. At last her father led her to the main house.

The lamentation spread. When anyone was told the reason why there was so much weeping, they fell into weeping themselves. The sorrow gathered over the tribe like thick rainclouds and broke over them all. Whenever someone heard the news they stood still and couldn't speak. They just stared. Then they would have that blank look on their faces people get when they hear that someone very dear to them has died.

As no one noticed the new pupil, no one told him the reason for the sadness. But he picked up the mood and felt sadness for an event he did not know about. Something truly terrible must have happened for the people to feel it so badly, he thought. He brooded on this mood of sorrow for days.

There was a subdued air in the village. The suitors were silent. The marketplace was muted. The workshops were quiet. The women were hushed. A wind blew through the village, whispering of death and change.

At night the moon was unusually large and white in the dark sky. At dawn strange footfalls could be heard on the dust. Birds kept circling the village. Dogs barked unaccountably. Cats padded about warily with shining silver eyes.

Everyone was touched by the sadness. But the children seemed to feel it most.

72

SUDDENLY, NEW WORKS of art began to sprout from the tribe, while they waited for the rains. They made sculptures and masks unlike anything they had made before.

The sorrow brought forth this new burst of creativity. These strange works were the only way they could express their sorrow's depth. It seemed to them that the sorrow they felt included the unexpressed sorrow of the centuries, the tragic moods they had borne in them through the long shadows of history.

Like a land rich with the flower-seeds of suffering, the tribe exploded into bloom during this time. It was a brief golden age of fruitfulness. Sorrow was converted instantly into beauty. It was as if sorrow were beauty's secret, beauty's mother.

73

ONLY A FEW times before had the tribe known such intense fertility. This was the last time they would enjoy such a blessing. As with all such miraculous moments in the life of a people, they were not aware of it at the time. They did not know how fleeting or how mysterious the phase was, in the fugitive dream of life.

Later the world would wonder at such a prodigious concentration of art. The works created were so beautiful and so elusive, so unprecedented, that many in the future could not accept that the tribe of artists had made them. They were ascribed to the hands of another civilisation across the seas. Some detected the influence of a faraway people famous for their tragedies and their gods. Some hinted at aliens from fabled planets who had descended briefly on a backward land and inspired a gasp of brilliance.

Some would whisper about a divine spark that had animated, for a time, the hands of a forgotten people.

IT WAS FROM these works that the new pupil discovered the cause of the sadness. The works had been created by anonymous hands, members of the tribe. They had been displayed around the shrine and dotted the village square. They stood among the trees in the forest. They sprouted in the fields and the marketplaces. They quivered in front of the cracked mud huts. They bristled along the shores of the river.

Then the artworks began to vanish. They began to leave, taken away, most of them, by travellers and merchants on the great trade routes. They were spread and disseminated. And it was only after these works of amazing variety and richness had left the village, to circulate in the kingdom through invisible routes, that the tribe of artists could speak of that which had brought them such sadness.

Only when they had expressed it first in art, and had time to contemplate that which they had expressed, did they know how to speak of it.

75

WHEN THE NEW pupil heard the news he too was saddened. He joined the men and women and children in their vigils by the shrine. They went there to pray for the prince who was a good soul and who they had heard was dying. They were there to express their sorrow at his fate.

Everyone spoke well of this prince they did not know. They said he was a prince in a faraway kingdom. He cared for the poor and the simple and the lonely. They said the evil in the world had broken his heart and now he was dying. He would die unless the people put enough sweetness into the air to make it possible for him to live.

No one knew who the prince was but everyone was moved by his fate. The new pupil was moved too and often thought of the prince with a sigh.

'How lucky he is to be so loved,' he thought.

Because his story took so long to reach the tribe of artists, he did not know that he was the prince everyone was talking about.

ON ONE OF those days he overheard the maiden talking to a friend.

'I would like to make a journey to this prince and make an offering,' she said.

'But no one knows where he is,' the friend replied.

'That shouldn't stop us.'

'But how will you do it?'

'I will find a way.'

'What will your offering be?'

He never heard the answer because the two friends wandered off into the forest, towards the river.

NOW THE MAIDEN was being quietly hailed as a seer. People began to understand the enigmatic sculpture which had baffled the tribe, her sculpture of a dying prince. They marvelled at how she had executed the work so far in advance of the news itself.

The maiden was the only one who did not know that she was considered a seer. She had forgotten the sculpture. She saw no connection between her work and the news that had saddened the tribe.

THOUGH IT PASSED slowly, the prince knew there was little time left.

79

THE TRIBE KEPT vigil for the prince. The masters lit special fires in the forest to keep alive the light of his soul.

They worked for healing in dreams. They worked in the many ways the spirit works to heal things in the unknowing world.

It was a subdued time when the rains came. They waited to hear if he who was dying was dead or would live again.

The rains were fierce. In the heavens thunder battled with lightning. In the legend of the tribe good battled with evil for the soul of the prince. Dire judgement hung over the whole land. It was said that if the prince should die the land would die and the white wind would conquer it forever. Then death would grow in the farms and bestride the hills like a colossus.

The rains were frightening. Those with unusual sensitivity saw the battles between the monsters of the deep and the creatures of the lightning flash. The rains were merciless and lashed the farms and over-swelled the river and carried off huts and abodes and became a racing stream that rushed through the forests uprooting trees and creating gaps. The stream carried off goats and farm animals and young children who had not heeded their parents' warning.

While they awaited news of the prince's fate, the rains seemed to go on forever. It was crueller than it had ever been. It tore down totems and disintegrated homes and wrecked farms and marketplaces and works of art. The rains made the people forget their concern for the prince, drowning their sadness in more immediate tragedies.

The community battled as one to hold their lives together, to rescue their homes and sculptures, and protect their village from being washed away by the angry deluge. The river broke its banks and swept through the village. A few perished in the floods. There were miraculous survivors.

People forgot their other troubles. Some masters wondered if they were not being punished for their neglect of the gods. Other masters hinted that the flood might not be as negative, or as terrible, as it seemed; that it might be an inexplicable form of cleansing.

80

THEN JUST AS suddenly as they appeared, the rains ended, the flood subsided, and the land bloomed as never before. It was its last bloom.

The shrine had been unaffected. If anything, its pale yellow walls shone with a brighter light. The paths and roads were all new and clean. The marketplace faced a different direction. Many thought the village was better than before. The fields were fertilised with death and river-silt that made crops sprout and grow as if transformed. The alignment of huts and houses was more auspicious. A new harmony appeared among the devastation.

Most of the artworks which were lost turned out to be the ones which were quite useless. But some quite invaluable works were lost too. This had the effect of reminding the tribe about what they lived for, their true purpose, which they had partially forgotten.

The masters and the priestesses of the shrine staged a grand ritual, in which the whole tribe participated. It was for the re-dedication of their lives to the highest dreams of art, a new covenant with their deity and their destiny. It was a ceremony of great inspiration.

When they learnt of the recovery of the prince, they all rejoiced in a double jubilation. Good omens and good events, at last.

81

THE NEW PUPIL performed many feats, which nobody noticed, during the flooding. He rescued women who were drowning. He helped strangers save their possessions and carried vital supplies to dry places in the hills. He built impromptu huts on high ground. Families that had to move found him invaluable. He kept up the spirits of those who had lost their homes and brought food for the homeless in the hills. Children huddled miserably in the high places were soon laughing at the faces he pulled and the stories he told. He helped the men of the community lift the shrine to the dry mouth of a cave. They bore the gods up to the stone terraces.

It was at this point that the pupil began to teach. He spoke to them of one God, one father-mother, one source as the source of all. They heard him, but they didn't listen. It was at this point he began to speak of the unreality of death. Life is stronger than death, he said. Death is only a shadow, a brief darkness, a fearful mask that frightens those who only use their eyes. Life is a light that shines forever. They listened, but did not hear him.

He performed miraculous healing on the sick and the diseased and on those traumatised by the floods and those who had died for a long moment while drowning and those with broken legs and broken hearts. He performed miraculous transformations on the spirit of the community, but he didn't know it.

All this he managed in innocence, while still looking after the workshop of the master. He moved statues and carvings to safe ground and made sure nothing was lost or carried away by the raging of the storms during that time of confusion.

And through all that time the maiden avoided him. As if she were still under a spell, she did not notice his existence. Nor did anyone else in the village. Except those he helped and the masters, who saw, but kept silent.

Except also some young women who were touched by his spirit and fell in love with him for the rest of their lives. They passed on the legend of their adoration, in oblique songs, to their children.

82

THE FIERCE RAINS journeyed on to drier destinations. Normality began to return to the tribe. The people began to sort out their lives and make the best of the devastation. Girls sang and laughter was heard among the flowers. This was when the new pupil, unnoticed by the maiden, decided it was time to reveal his love.

One day he began to speak to her in his mind. He spoke to her dreams. He had learnt from the statues, through stillness and unnoticed oddness, how to appear in people's dreams. Then, within her dreams, he spoke as himself.

At first she did not notice because she did not pay much attention to her dreams. A backlog of unread messages accumulated in her. Then one night, after sitting in silence in the moonlight, listening to inaudible whispers in the wind, she fell asleep and all the messages and dreams came through all at once. They came in a rush and tumble. This alarmed her.

He went on speaking to her tenderly, taking many forms. Once he was a rose that she was twirling in her hands in a dream. His face appeared on the petals of the rose and he spoke to her. Sometimes he spoke to her as the moon. When she was in a canoe on the river, he was the canoe, or he was the river. When she was riding a lion in a dream, or an antelope, or she was playing with a gazelle, he was the lion, the antelope, or the gazelle.

He was a white bird that she dreamt of which returned often and lay still in her lap. Then circling her head three times, it flew away to a distant star, leaving her quite alone. Sometimes he was just a person she knew in her dreams, a familiar person whom she could not quite place, but one for whom she had a great affection.

Through these forms he spoke to her of their ancient love that went back centuries, born on another planet. He spoke of the brevity of time given them here in which to meet and love and be happy. Brief was the time allotted them, he said. It was less than the time between one moon and another. Then they would be separated till the next time they would meet again, in another realm. And they would have to start all over again learning to recognise their ancient and future love, their great love.

He spoke love verses into her dreams.

When the moon is full
It spreads a light
That is round and cool
All over the land that is you.
That moon is like my love.
Even the air knows this is true.
But my love never wanes like the moon –
My love is not there only at night
That like a ghost is gone before noon.
My love has the power of seven.
My love is the light
And the promise of heaven.

SOMETIMES, IN HER dreams, he took her hand and journeyed with her through all the happiest places in the universe. He took her to the stars of ecstasy and the planets of delight and to some of their homelands in faraway galaxies. He showed her their palaces of pleasure, their castles of love, their cities of happiness.

84

WHEN HE WAS not speaking to her in dreams, he arranged anonymous surprises for her when she was awake. Children brought her a bouquet of rare feathers. Strange girls brought her rich brocaded cloth.

When she was musing by the river an old man gave her a single flower that no one had ever seen before, or ever saw again, in the same way. He said the flower came from the stars and that he was a messenger of one who could not be named. The maiden accepted the flower hesitantly and inhaled its fragrance. At that moment something happened in her heart. She was not sure what it was. But suddenly she felt things more clearly.

The fragrance altered the wind. She heard the faintest echo of a melody. The river was calm. She looked and saw that the old man had turned into a mild mist of gold fading in the green cloud of the forest.

The flower would never wilt, never die. Sometimes it became invisible and was lost. But it would reappear again, depending on how she was feeling. That flower, along with her only child, was the legacy she passed on to the next generation.

Every now and again, for a decade, or for twenty years, the flower would be invisible. Then on an auspicious day it would appear in the hands of one of her descendants. When it did it always clarified the heart.

THERE WERE OTHER gifts that the new pupil caused to come her way. One morning a beautiful young woman brought the maiden a rare ruby. She claimed it came from the heavens and that she was a messenger from one who could not be named. Another lovely girl, with a dazzling smile and a bright countenance, brought her a pure white stone, not of this earth, and repeated the magic words of the other messengers.

A child dressed in gold brought her a white bowl. When the maiden later ate from the bowl she noticed how well she felt, how contented in body and soul. The bowl somehow enriched her food. She ate little and was not only more quickly satisfied but she also had a sense of unusual spiritual nourishment.

These gifts puzzled and frightened her a little. But she kept her puzzlement and fear to herself. She kept her silence. Not even her curiosity diverted her from her chosen course of delay. She awaited the wisdom of the revealed hour.

THEN TIME QUICKENED for the new pupil. Time was hurrying towards the great gaps, pulling him towards martyrdom.

In dreams he spoke of love to the maiden. He spoke of how love saves. But time spoke to him as he sat among the raw wood or rough stone changing into art, changing with the ambiguities of the air. Time and an invisible sheen, vital elements in the atmosphere, pressed into the surfaces of the new carved works.

As they changed from wood into wonder-bearing forms, from stone into enchantment, he changed too. He changed from the new pupil into one who, through gaps in time, would find himself in the hold of a ship. He was bleeding, starving, raw with beatings, and crushed with a thousand others. His ankles and wrists were in metal chains.

He was unable to connect one moment with the other: a life in his own land, a pupil, a prince, free, and then less than an animal, in chains, in a ship bound for hell.

He was snatched more frequently in spirit to that terrible condition. Was it the future or the past? He couldn't say which it was.

More and more it encroached on him, this martyrdom, the final suffering before his everlasting freedom from the mighty wheel of mortality. More and more he felt the great suffering drawing closer, till he could smell his blood on the chains, smell the stench and the deaths and the agony of the others and their disintegrating flesh all around him in the dark hold of the ship, in a torment that cannot be lived while being lived, and yet cannot be forgotten. Sometimes he wondered if it wouldn't have been better to have died beforehand, considering what came later.

Among the statues he sent out to the world a message of the heart: 'Make the most of the happiness in your life; it may be a prelude to something strange.'

In his vision he saw something worse than death, and he lived it. He saw a suffering beyond endurance, but which was endured; the suffering of a people so great that some of its excess had to be endured before and afterwards, in the form of irrepressible happiness.

Then he saw why some peoples had such an extraordinary gift for joy and ecstasies of the spirit: it was the excess left over from the suffering to come and the suffering that has gone. It was the conversion of suffering into moments in paradise while alive, a divine compensation for enduring the unendurable.

87

AMONG THE SHADOWS, the new pupil foresaw the songs in the air and the stones turning into art through time's alchemy. He foresaw his suffering to come. It was another life; a martyrdom and a crucifixion in time. In that future it occurred to him that man enchained and enslaved and gagged with metal ought to be the symbol of a new religion. Its sacred text ought to reveal how human life was sacrificed to create wealth for others, to the building of civilisations. Its crowning gift the liberation of human beings from all forms of bondage, the exaltation of freedom.

The new pupil found this so, in the dim hold of the ship, with his flesh broken, his bones eaten by the chains, his skin flayed with the lash. The only thing that saved him then, in extreme agony, was the vision that a human being is a vast spirit and a body, a miraculous light surrounding a living mould of flesh and bone.

Enlightenment does not reduce suffering.

88

THE RAINS CAME and went. Time sped on with epic grace; and the contests began. The maiden, in love with one unknown to her, went on delaying. She kept a charming distance from the contests between suitors.

During the rains most of the suitors returned to their homes for the replenishment of their resources and for spiritual fortification. They came back with magic potions and spells and praise-singers and witch-doctors to help them with their campaigns.

The contests were violent and full of wonderful events which the bards elaborated in songs and legends. All over the kingdom these marvels were the stuff of moonlit stories around which children weaved improvisations.

The contests drew great crowds. People came from distant places to witness them. Many forms of fighting and skills of self-defence were displayed. The crowds gazed in awe at the jump-kicks of the Northern suitor, the anaconda wrestling style, sinuous and oily, of the Eastern suitor, the leg-hooking techniques of the suitors from the Southern creeks, and the gyrating swirling style of the Western free-form suitor, who fought to the wild elliptical beat of a sinister and mesmerising talking drum.

There was a suitor who used a curious crab-like stalking technique. There was a thick-set suitor, with a devilishly low centre of gravity, who was as impossible to shift in the wrestling contests as the squat hills around. There was a suitor with legs so baked and dry, master of the art of kick-fighting, that he proved a nightmare to his opponents, whom he kept at a safe distance with the repeated tattoo of peppery kicks to the knees and face. And there was one who crouched like a cougar, who fought like a whirlwind, and moved with the hypnotic rhythm of drumbeats administered by his austere-looking witch-doctor.

The fights were unpredictable, engrossing, and passionate. No one was killed, but many were wounded and bent out of shape and some were disfigured for life.

The contests became legendary, and the Mamba proved the eventual winner.

THERE ARE ANCIENT tales where a man is faced with an obstacle that blocks his destiny. He goes into the forest to sleep with the demons of the deep. He wrestles with wild animals and does battle with death. He lives a wild life, alone in the depths of a cave, and then he returns to the world transformed. Sometimes he brings with him fragments of a new religion. Sometimes he returns with a vision. Sometimes he comes back as a witch-doctor, herbalist, or sage.

Something like this had happened to the Mamba.

The Mamba was spooked by the uniqueness of the maiden and the awkward kink in her spirit. He saw that he was being progressively undone as a man. He saw that he was doing it to himself because he was all askew. Finding life impossible in the village, one night he disappeared without a word.

He simply vanished from the life of the tribe. No one knew where he went. No one heard about him for a while. No one speculated about his disappearance either. When he was there he had too much presence. When he wasn't there he had too much absence. It was a sort of curse. He was not a man that anyone missed.

Then things happened which ought to have been strange but were not seen as such by the wise ones. His father died suddenly one night, after screaming that his heart had been loaned to a shadow.

Not long afterwards his mother died, after wailing that her spirit had been stolen by a shadow. The Mamba did not reappear to bury his parents. He sent no word; he sent no emissaries. His absence at the burial of his parents was not remarked on.

Then his parents' compound began to be haunted by dark forms that whispered like bats, shadows that stood up straight and walked like real beings and danced in the moonlight.

The rains came and the Mamba's abode was completely unaffected, but no one remarked on this as strange either. The rains passed and one day, in the middle of the contests, people saw that the Mamba was one of the contestants.

He had returned. It was then that people began to speculate. It was said that he had gone hunting a rare animal with which to amaze the woman who would be his bride, that he had gone seeking unusual powers in the deep dark places of the world. It was whispered that he had traded the lives of his loved ones for invincibility against known and unknown forces, power over the innocence that had spooked him, and that he had gone to acquire magic that would bend the hearts and minds of all people to his will. It was rumoured that he sought mastery over women, and power over that which mysteriously perplexed his desires. It was also said he had gone mad with love and lust and guilt, and had been taken to a deformed herbalist in the hinterland to restore his sanity.

WHEN HE REAPPEARED he was darker, fiercer, and more menacing than ever. He was also more silent. He wore black. His eyes had changed. They saw deep things. He had stared into the depths of his own madness and had seen things and was initiated into the new art of the deep and the dark.

Upon his return he was feared more than ever before. The very mention of his name sowed dread and made grown men quake. His very presence made some tremble, made some flee. When they didn't flee they were rooted to the spot, mesmerised by a terror they couldn't explain.

When he spoke, people's minds went blank. He had become truly fearsome, like those spirits who, when they show themselves in war, make armies abandon their weapons and scatter across the plains.

The Mamba reappeared, dressed in black, in the middle of a fight. Before anyone could register the profound change that had come over him, he had beaten up all the contestants in a manner so cruel that the crowds were appalled and fascinated in equal measure.

He had broken the neck of one suitor, cracked the spine of another, and dumped the swirling dervish suitor on his head so roughly that the crowd was stunned by the sound of his head crunching into his body. The Mamba was simply the most brutal contestant among all the suitors.

Oddly enough, many women gasped in admiration whenever he appeared. They secretly wanted him to win. When he did win husbands were dismayed, but some of the women rejoiced. It was said that he had mastered the secret of women's hearts, their deepest desires.

When he won the contest people wondered what would happen next. They wondered what the maiden would do.

91

It was simple. She refused to recognise the validity of the contests. She decreed that whoever told her the best story and the finest dream and solved the riddle of the shadow would win her hand.

Time was quickening for some but slowing down for others. Time was running out in the land.

The new pupil continued speaking to the maiden in her dreams. The dreams made her happy. She looked forward to sleep and its fragrance of wild roses. She lingered by the river, turning over in her mind the delightful elusiveness of her dreams. If only she could grasp them clearly and understand them, she thought, she would know what she needed to know and would be happy.

She spent her keenest hours by the river, gazing into the blue of sky and the gold of heaven. Puzzling out those fragments of verse, those images, gave her a strange sense of contentment.

In all this self-absorption she still didn't notice the new pupil. Sometimes an invisible hand would deliver a sign to her, in the form of a carving. It prompted odd thoughts in her mind. Sometimes she would catch the glimpse of a face – familiar, frail, and beautiful, a gladdening image in a dream. She would blink and the face would be lost in a crowd. Sometimes a voice would reach her heart and she'd jump. Then she would wonder whether she was awake or whether she was by the river, where a god had once spoken to her. Then she would ponder the injustice she had done by forgetting.

Sometimes, in a reverie, a voice tender with great understanding, and light as a feather, would whisper odd words into her soul. The words pierced her with sweet fire.

Time is not with youth;
Time is with truth.

And she would fall headlong into a waking dream, where carvings spoke and statues danced and a white horse, of dazzling beauty, beckoned her with mischievous eyes to take a ride to paradise.

92

MAYBE SHE WAS too young to notice what she saw. She only noticed much later, in another land, in the burning heat of the difficult years. Then, looking back, she saw what she should have seen, what was obvious to see, but which she hadn't seen.

93

SHE WAS TOO young to realise how fortunate she was. She was loved and lucky and blessed and watched over. She didn't know that brief was her hour of glory, her blessedness, living in beauty in the land of art.

She was too young to notice things. She saw only dreams and ideals and hopes. She lived in a vapour of time. She didn't see evils looming. She didn't see the contests. She didn't notice the Mamba. She loved her parents more than she noticed them. She loved her land more than she noticed it. She loved its skies, its hills, the women, the mass of faces, the smells. She loved her father's workshop, the shrine, the forest, the farms. She loved the river where she dreamt and played. She loved them more than she noticed them.

It was only later that they became so real. It was only later when she had irredeemably lost them all. Only later did she learn to see that which she had loved in the blur of her being.

94

SHE WAS TOO young to notice that when the new pupil smiled the sun lingered in his smile long after he had left the person he was greeting. She was too young to notice how quickly the smile vacated the faces of most people who had just left off talking to her.

She was too young to notice many things about him.

But he saw her more clearly than anything in the world. He studied her hidden nature every moment of his being, as if she were his secret soul.

Often when he pondered her and entered her dreams he saw her in strange images and in peculiar notions. Sometimes a lamb-like creature would be left in the wilds of life and years later in its place would be a lioness. How to see the power that would later emerge in the youth that was there now. How to remember the lamb that was the lioness.

Riddles of the shadows.

THE MAMBA WAS infuriated at the shift in the rules for winning the maiden's hand. Convinced that he had won, and that there was a conspiracy against him, his paranoia grew deeper. But it was an unfocused paranoia, without an object.

Then one night he saw the maiden's silhouette in a spell of moonlight. His head went slightly crazy with the beauty and mystery of her. All the powers that he had acquired from the deep did not protect him against her profile in the moonlight. In fact, all his powers worked against him. For they too, like the tides, fell under the sway of an invisible force that captivated his heart. Suddenly he felt like a broken colossus. Hallucinations passed before his eyes. Odd voices sounded in his head, whispering of insanity.

> Beware of the moon
> Too soon, too soon
> It shines on the hair
> Of the girl who is fair.
> Madness and hell
> Ring their bell
> From the silk
> And the milk
> Of the moon
> Too soon
> In her hair.
> Beware.

The Mamba, in his hiding place among the baobab trees, gazed at her and was lost to the voices and the hallucinations.

Then suddenly he saw the slender form of a man. Maybe it was squat and round. Maybe it was tall and strong. It kept changing. He wasn't sure.

He suddenly felt a laceration of heart and a fear and suspicion and dryness of mouth all at once. Then he knew that this changing form of a man was his real enemy and rival, though he had never seen him before. But then maybe he had.

This other man stood under the eaves of the master's workshop. The moonlight did not fall on him. Behind his head was the shape of a lamp. He was in deep shadow, but the Mamba could make out something of his presence.

The Mamba sensed that he was seeing the reality of a vision he once had, the vision of one who would spell the destruction of the tribe, their ways, their art.

The other man gazed at the maiden, as if he were the moon.

96

I<small>T WASN'T LONG</small> before the Mamba noticed the new pupil. He was the first to publicly notice him. The new pupil lost his protective invisibility when the Mamba drew attention to him.

The Mamba disliked him on sight. Without provocation, he began a campaign against the new pupil, to get him evicted from the village as a spy. At first no one paid the Mamba any attention. But he became obsessed, and his obsession, fed by the bitterness of having won the contests but not the maiden's hand, gave him a powerful clarity, a prophetic authority.

Not for the first time, the Mamba was losing his mind. But this time it appeared he had never been in greater control of himself. He had won the fights with skill, brutality, and a display of mastery. This, coupled with the dark mystery he drew to himself with his disappearance, meant that the Mamba was now seen as a potential figure of power and leadership.

People felt inclined to follow his lead. They felt, for the first time, that here was the leader they had never had, a man who could take them to a new destiny.

Sometimes a sense of doom makes a people susceptible to that which in normal times would horrify them. Maybe that is why in history a people sometimes chose the very leader who would lead them over the very precipice they feared in the first place. They chose the one who would deliver them to the doom which they dreaded.

Inexplicably, the Mamba became the voice of the tribe. Inexplicably, the tribe ceased to heed the warnings of the oracle. They ceased to listen to the masters who, for centuries, had brought them to various stations of their promised land.

445

THE MAMBA SPOKE out with a new voice of the destruction of the tribe by strangers from beyond. He spoke of the stranger among them who was invading their lives, insinuating himself into their secret ways.

He made a powerful and terrifying speech at the gates of the village, where he conjured visions of the end of their history, of hordes descending on them on white steeds. He sang passionately a song called 'Destruction is coming' and another called 'Beware of the stranger'. He had the women in tears and hysterics and the men quaking with fear and foreboding.

Then later that day, under the unpredictable spell of his obsession, and to the complete astonishment of the tribe, the Mamba challenged the new pupil to the ultimate contest.

The tribe was amazed at this act because they had never noticed the new pupil before. Nor did they know that he was considered a suitor.

THAT SAME EVENING the Mamba turned up at the maiden's house. He brought out of his leopard-skin bag a gigantic skull in beautiful ebony that he had carved. With a sinister and charming smile on his face, he slammed the skull down on the table and said:

'This is my shadow. My transformation is my story. Your love is my dream.'

Then he strode out of the house. No one had ever done that before.

After a long silence, the maiden's mother said:

'Trouble has come to our house.'

After another silence, the master said:

'Only the deep can speak to the deep.'

THE NEW PUPIL did not know what to do. He had been challenged. He was no longer invisible. He did not believe in fighting. But there was no way out of it.

For many days he pondered what to do. He knew that he could not withstand the power of the Mamba. He knew that by himself he did not stand a chance. He was in the forest one day when it occurred to him to ask the animals and the birds to teach him how to prevail.

He asked them to teach him how to win without fighting. The spider taught him to catch people in the web of their own confusion. He learnt the cunning of the small from the ant. Intimidating with stillness he learnt from the lion. Oblique motion was the mosquito's lesson. Disorientation was the mantra of the fly. The elephant's insight was that weight can be a hindrance. Awkwardness was the instruction of the crab, the art of the unthinkable was that of the snake. The unpredictable leap was the trick of the frog. The craft of surprise was the idea of the eagle, and ferocity that of the lioness. The art of the fall was the education of the cat, speed that of the antelope. Patience was the wisdom of the tortoise. Inducing sleep in a campaign was the strategy of the tse-tse fly. The heron showed him the invincibility of the higher way. Fighting with beauty of spirit was the intuition of flowers. That a good fight is a form of devotion was the offering of the praying mantis. Trees hinted at economy of movement. Seeds whispered their secret of being reborn when dying. Dew initiated him into the meeting of heaven and earth. Sunlight made him aware that all things come from an eternal source. And the laughter echoing faintly in the air reminded him of his noble origin.

100

To those who looked with ordinary eyes it seemed a disaster for the frail new pupil. But to those who looked with intelligent eyes the unexpected was the most natural outcome.

The fight was won and lost even before it began.

It happened, it was quick, and it was a mystery that was never unravelled.

How the new pupil vanquished the Mamba is still talked about all over the world. All that the people saw was not the fight itself, but its shadow, its aftermath. They were there, but they missed it. Sometimes the eyes are not enough to see the mystery of things.

On the day, the Mamba appeared in all his mythic and physical glory. His muscles glistened like polished bronze. He stood in the centre of the ring like a giant. When the new pupil appeared he seemed small and slight. He stood in a corner of the ring. He was smiling. The women's hearts went out to him. He seemed so vulnerable and alone, like an orphan.

The Mamba pounced, and caught a shadow. He wrestled with that which had no form. He lashed out and in his fury struck the face of the wind. He chased after that which flapped. He heard buzzing in his ears and an unnatural roar in his head. The Mamba couldn't find the cat which sped beneath his hulking shape. He was perplexed by the stillness of that which wasn't there when he charged it. Then he found it was behind him. The Mamba heard whispers of falling leaves. Then a light flashed in his brain. The Mamba charged the thousand forms of the same thing all over the ring and out into the crowd. He cried out for the new pupil to stay still. The next moment he begged the new pupil to move and to fight. Then the Mamba saw the glory of the sun shining above the head of a crowned prince. The Mamba, bleeding from so many self-inflicted wounds, heard a sublime laughter in the clouds. He sank to his knees, and fell in prostration. With a howl of terror and a cry of joy, the Mamba fell over on his back, and didn't move again for three days.

The new pupil hadn't struck him once. The masters declared the fight to be one of the greatest works of art they had seen in a generation.

THE MAIDEN FELL completely, lucidly, and shyly in love with this new revelation of man. She fell in love with one whom she had not noticed, but who instantly healed her of all her sicknesses.

And at last she recognised the one. She recognised him for what he was. Anonymous. In disguise. A part of all the delays. There and not there. In the contests, indirectly. In secret, humbly, winning them all, without entering them and without knowing.

That which she had been seeking for, she had found – lowly and humble though it seemed. To everyone's astonishment she declared him to be the one she loved, the one she would marry.

HER FATHER'S RESPONSE to all this was hard to read. He unveiled what he had been working on in secret. He had created one final sculpture to heal the horrors the last one had unleashed. Then he would sculpt no more.

His tone of tragic sublimity vanished from the land, echoing now and then in the lesser works of those who came much later.

His last sculpture was a work of pure beauty. It had the same effect as the last one, but in the opposite sense. The masters said it was his spiritual offering to the mystic wedding of his daughter, a wedding that took place among the stars.

People came on pilgrimages to see the sculpture, even as the suitors and their entourage left the village. Their rowdy presence was replaced by pilgrims to a new art.

The sculpture was beautiful and its beauty was strange in the way it affected people. It induced sleep, graciousness, and good manners. It provoked profound and vivid dreams in which guides appeared. It also induced an odd vacancy in all those who saw it. The young wanted to die in its presence and had to be restrained. The old who were dying wanted it to be the last thing they saw before they passed away into the long walk of the spirits.

What was this valedictory sculpture?

It was the figure of a being. It could have been a man or woman or god or goddess or dream. The figure stood with both arms stretched out unnaturally wide, embracing the universe in a mighty act of acceptance.

Creating a shimmer of illumination around itself, from the spirit-charged nature of the stone from which it was made, it concentrated the magic of the heavens into the illusion of space.

Arms outstretched and legs spread wide, it doubly embraced all of life, all suffering, all joys, the beginning, the end, life, death, and beyond.

103

THE KING WAS wandering in the kingdom, watching over the sleeping forms of his people. He was marvelling at the beauty of the darkness and the stars when he came upon a maiden. She was kneeling in white in front of the village shrine. Turning a smiling face towards him, she genuflected without speaking.

'What are you doing here at this hour when the world sleeps?' the king said.

'I found myself here not knowing how.'

'Then you must have a reason.'

'This evening, wandering and thinking and trying not to think, I found myself here.'

He didn't say anything. He watched her fondly.

She listened to the music of the constellations. She did not expect a response from this august person. She had the wisdom to listen to his silence. It was the silence of a river at night, when all is still and all the stars are out.

'Here's an offering,' she said.

She revealed the piece of sculpture she had placed before the shrinehouse. It was of a seated king on a throne wearing a ten-pointed crown. In his right hand he held a staff around which two serpents were coiled. At its summit was a globe-like structure. His left hand held a book that was also a six-pointed star.

The sculpture pleased the king immensely. He laughed warmly and the young lady, touched by the humour of this majestic being, found herself laughing too. It was a beautiful night and they laughed under the clear stars of the sleeping world.

104

SHE WOKE EARLIER in the morning than she had ever woken before. She woke with a strange joy in her head and an irrational hunger between her legs and a hollow happy feeling in the pit of her stomach.

She could not seem to breathe properly. Whenever she drew breath she felt her heart go light. Her head swam. She had the queerest sensation that something was going to jump out of her body and leap out into the air, towards the sun.

Her head was clear but she could not think clearly. She got out of bed and bathed and dried her body. Then she anointed herself as if she were going to be presented to a king. Everything was done dreamily. For she didn't know if she was dreaming or not. Didn't know if she were alive or if she had become a spirit. Didn't seem to be in her body. She was in a bliss that was like a beautiful death.

When she got dressed, feeling so happy and lovely that she lost all sense of herself, she left the house and went to her father's workshop. Her father was not there. The new pupil was not there either. She was so surprised that she went among the statues and touched them one by one. She stared into their faces, into their eyes, expecting one of them to move and come alive, revealing the one and only love she would ever have in her life, in this life and the next.

But not one of the statues moved or stirred or became the one who could not be named, who lived in her, and for whom she yearned.

Then a sort of terror came over her at the thought that she would never see him again. She felt how ironic a fate it was that she had not seen him when he was there, and now that she could see him he was not there.

As she stood among the statues of stone and wood, she felt that there was nothing left for her anymore on earth or in life. She stood there a long time in silent lamentation for one she had loved without knowing it and for one who loved her as the sun loves the earth. Death seemed the only answer to her loss.

She locked the workshop and wandered to the forest. She sang a lullaby. All those who passed her that morning thought she looked both happy and mad.

105

SHE WANDERED THROUGH the forest in a daze. She picked wild roses and white lilies and blue flowers with suggestive calyxes and yellow flowers and marigolds and drooping hibiscuses. She held them to her face and wandered to the river, gently singing a song of happy death.

She did not notice anything. She did not hear the birds, nor the wind in the trees. She did not see the quivering yellow of sunrise, nor did she feel the dew or the sand beneath her feet. She thought only of love. The angel of love had blanked out her mind to all awareness. She thought of the happiness to be found with her love in the depths of the river.

She began to sing farewell to all things. Then she fell silent. Holding the flowers in her hand as an offering to the goddess, she began to walk towards the river, away from life. She was gone from life now, gone from her body, gone from the earth. She was going to the only legend that was true, the legend of love and death, beneath the river.

But then she heard the voice on the wind that she had heard long ago. It was the voice that had first woken her from the sleep of her existence.

All about her everything sprang to life. All at once she saw the swollen and mighty river and she feared that it would suddenly engulf her and sweep her under to its unknown kingdom.

The sky was vast and clear. Its blue was so pure she felt it might snatch her soul away. The sunrise shimmered on the rim of the river. It was so beautiful that she felt if she breathed she would be borne away to some homeland beyond the stars.

Then she heard his voice again. All the clamour in her heart, the agitation in her belly, and the irrational hunger between her legs came awake in her. She stood rooted to the sand, not hearing what was said.

A darkness passed over her eyes. When it cleared she found herself staring into the adoration of his gaze. She did not see the sky or the river or the sunrise. She saw just his eyes. His eyes were all the world. She was lost to everything else on earth and in heaven. Maybe she found everything that she sought on earth and in heaven.

Before she knew it they were lying side by side on the shore, near a bank of wild roses. They mutely gazed into one another's faces, almost without breathing.

106

THEY SAY THAT it is not just things of this world that are seen. Sometimes one does not know what one is seeing.

As the prince and the maiden gazed into the white and gold of one another's eyes, they caught glimpses of what they had been to one another in time past, beyond memory. They glimpsed what they would be to one another in the time to come, beyond death, in another life, where their true story of love would begin.

They gazed into one another's hearts and were mesmerised and a little frightened by the depth of love each saw deep within the other. It was a love too strong for mortal life, a love that would make itself the sole purpose of living. It was a love like eternity gazing into the mirror of eternity, a love that wanted nothing but simply to exist in the blissful light of the other. Like the light of the sun after the darkest night.

In their silence they exchanged all the signs of mutual recognition, so that if they were to meet again in some future life, it would take only a glance to know that this was the one love they were seeking. With one look into the other's eyes, from among the millions of people on earth, they would know.

And so they planted the certainty of finding one another again in the next life to come. They planted it by the depth of speech in their mutual gazing.

As they gazed they journeyed through time, through many planes of happiness where they already lived the life they were meant to live. They touched those other lives and returned fresh and assured.

Then the prince changed the nature of their enchantment.

107

WITHOUT SEEMING TO breathe, trembling in the warmth of the world at dawn, the prince peeled off her wrapper and her white blouse and beheld the beauty of her skin. It shone like the face of the river in the tenderness of sunrise.

Then without touching her he passed his palms along her skin. Not touching her and yet touching her more deeply than a passionate embrace.

He passed his hands over her face. He lingered over her eyes, her cheeks, her ears, her forehead, and her chin. He hovered over her throat. She was still. Her eyes were shut. She breathed gently.

Then something happened to her. She felt a fire in her heart. It burned right through in a golden pain and then she was gone. Every breath she drew was a sweet agony. As he passed his hand slowly over her body the more piercing was the fire in her heart and the hunger in her belly.

She began to cry out an unknown name and was not aware of it. Her cry and her love, her fire and her joy, were one. It was so unbearable that she opened her eyes in a wild abandon, full of an inexplicable yearning.

Then he lay down next to her. He lay so close they were not touching and yet not close enough that they were almost one. He brought his lips to her soft lips.

There was something forbidden in the way they kissed. It was their discovery. They had kissed in this way in times past and times to come. It was unique to them. It was the way angels kissed. They did it with their souls. It was the only way their souls could speak to one another and be understood.

After this secret kiss, their lips touched. Then they moved

into the second chamber of their forbidden kiss. The maiden was now the prince and the prince was now the maiden. Each to the other was an eternity.

There is a kind of love-bliss that borders on blasphemy. It breaks the unwritten law of life in the body: thou shalt not feel too much.

Lost in the labyrinths of their kiss, they had somehow gone back to a forbidden moment under the sun. Their lips came together fully and they did not move. The laws of time and space were torn asunder. What was going to happen to them pressed closer. It was as if the power of coming together, the dissolving of one soul into another, provoked the evil that was to befall them.

Is it possible that too much love can awaken an evil destiny? Why else are love and tragedy so twinned on earth?

108

IN THEIR KISSING they plunged past the tree of good and evil and lived its consequences. They came to the tree of knowledge and waited under its dangerous fruits. Not moving, their hearts still, they glimpsed the angel of ecstasy and went past the tree of knowledge in their kissing. They came to a golden place and dwelt there, like two swans in the lake of paradise.

Then seized by a sudden violence, she began to touch him all over. She moulded every part of him, mapping him in her pleasure, singing to him in her mind. She never knew that there could be a pleasure on earth greater than feeling the wood or stone out of which a statue emerges. She never guessed that flesh and the body of a man could be more beautiful than dreams. She had such inexplicable feelings as she lavished her senses on the smoothness of his skin and muscles and trembling limbs.

When she felt him all over she found her fingertips tingling, and her palms shimmering inwardly, as if possessed by a radiant energy. She had never known such a miraculous sensation before. His skin shone all over as if she had polished a lamp of gold.

The light around him, full of many colours, resolved itself for a second into an aureole. She was so overcome that she fell on him in tears of adoration. They held one another as if they wanted to become spirit again and enter each other's being, right to the core.

Tight in their embrace, they did not know where one ended and the other began. They lay still, merged in love, and drifted away together.

They could hear the wind on the river. They could hear the call of a sunbird far in the sky. They could hear the cry of a baby in the depths of the kingdom. They could hear footfalls drawing closer to them. They heard murmurs and rumours and roots clasping the black earth and flowers opening to the sun and the dew forming in the calyxes and the wings of a butterfly and music in space. They could hear all manner of thoughts and dreams, but they could not hear one another breathing or weeping in silence.

109

HAVING BEEN TAUGHT by her what to do, and how deeply it was possible to feel, he began to touch her too, mapping in his soul the memory of her body. It was as if he knew that this was the only time in this life that he would be able to love and enjoy her beyond the limit of what was possible.

He prayed for the art to be able to love her beyond the limits of the body, during the moments of being alive, having her before him in all the glory of her youth.

When she felt him entering her the fire between her legs made sense at last. After the first sharp pain, she let herself slip into the warm waters of the river and sink into the realm of the goddess. She was all liquid and fire and senselessness.

They moved together, sometimes as one, often in odd wild rhythms of waves crashing on the shore or lapping gently on the rim of the land. They were both the river and the land, the sun and the earth.

And then she was falling not into an abyss, but deeper to the bottom of the river. She was falling without end and she was happy in her fall. She became aware that she could not breathe and she loved it. The more she gasped for air, the more bliss she felt. This got worse and better and worse and reached a point beyond which it was dangerous to go. She knew she would surely die, and she wanted to, and she let herself go. He went on moving and kissing and clutching at her in an irregular way and then she went over and panicked, for she saw something dark and inviting. It was a thing dark and bright in her bliss. She had come to the end of her inability to breathe and was getting lost and cried:

'Save me, I'm drowning!'

He didn't hear her at all. He had caught a dangerous fire. He was on the crest. Every movement he made touched a spark that could not be put out. It got unbearable till the core of his being was burning. He went past a point and rushed over.

Neither of them could stop moving now. Neither could stop racing towards their doom and their redemption. She gasped and her mouth opened wide and she cried out long and silently. His mouth was also open wide, uttering no sound, but a noiseless high pitch.

Then out of them came a long-sustained, much-delayed, much-desired cry of creation.

Then stillness, as if they had been momentarily transformed into statues of pleasure.

BOOK FOUR

The Secret Alchemy of All Things

1

THERE WAS REJOICING in high places. They had made love once, but that once was enough. Each changed the other's world and the story of the earth changed too.

Nothing could undo what was going to happen, what would continue to happen, because of their coming together. After centuries of missed opportunities, their love had at last found its great moment. Their love in a future time would last a lifetime for having finally conjoined on this earth, where such a possibility is all too rare.

There was rejoicing in high places.

2

As NIGHT FELL, the maiden said:

'I always thought you weren't real.'

'Did you?'

'Yes. I always thought you were something strange, like a dream.'

'A dream?'

'A white horse in a dream. I always thought you were something brought to life by a miraculous touch. Not entirely human.'

The prince laughed.

'I thought you were created by my father's magic art.'

'Your father's art is magical.'

'Now I have to see you as a human being and love you as a man.'

'Is that so bad?'

'To me you will always be something more than a human being.'

'What?'

'Maybe you are just my dream.'

'I'm a dream and not a dream, real and not real.'

'There is one thing left.'

'What?'

'How do you give me your shadow?'

'I have already given you my shadow.'

'How?'

'I have given you my death and my love.'

'But you haven't told me a story.'

'We're living it.'

'The best dream?'

'You've dreamt it.'

3

AFTERWARDS CAME THE changes. Everything happened so fast. Their lives passed from happiness to despair in a lightning flash of unreal time.

But the moments in which they were happy were themselves a lifetime. These moments were deep enough to last in the memory that never fades, till they were to meet again. Then they would live the lives of two lovers whose time to be happy and be together at last arrives on earth. Or somewhere else.

There would be no need to tell that story. Their happiness would be too complete.

4

BUT THAT NIGHT by the river, as they stared naked at one another in the afterglow of their shattering pleasure, they sensed that their magic moment was over. They sensed that such joy was not meant to last. In the calm of their passion maybe they knew that their consummation was a brief gift, a consolation for what was to come.

They had been followed. As they lingered in the rapture of their love-making, they were set upon by the Mamba and his followers, bearing flaming torches, leaping out from the undergrowth, with kaoline on their faces.

5

In confusion and horror the two lovers fled into the forest. The maiden ran till she was exhausted. Unable to keep up the fury of the pace, she asked the prince to make his own escape.

'Come back for me when times are right,' she said.

In the chaos of the moment, the prince told her about the openings in the forest.

'If I am successful in my escape or if you don't hear from me, you must know the right opening to choose when you come seeking for me.'

'But how will I know?'

'You will know. The opening you take will be your destiny.'

The cries and noises of the Mamba and his followers drew nearer. They held one another in a last embrace. She was calm.

'One way or another, we will meet again,' he said.

Then he ran off into the darkness of the forest.

6

IN HIS HASTE, in the trap sprung by fate, the new pupil chose the wrong opening between trees. He chose a fiery opening with a dark light.

He appeared in his village when the plans were hatched and ready to be sprung. Chief Okadu and the usurping elders had decided, should he return, to have the prince delivered up to the white spirits and borne off into oblivion.

7

THE PRINCE DECIDED not to go to the palace when he found his way back to the village. He hung around in his nakedness in the dark, waiting near the village shrine for anyone who might go past.

A woman with a bundle on her head, returning late from the market, heeded his call. She saw him crouching and at first was suspicious. His voice reassured her. Stripping off a layer of her wrapper, she covered his nakedness. From her he learnt about the changes that had happened in his absence.

Under the protection of darkness, she led him to her humble family abode. The prince collected his thoughts and fortified himself with food. Then he prayed and went into a deep meditation.

What he had found out was momentous. The world had spun off its axis. Celestial night had fallen over the land.

8

WHEN HE ARRIVED back home, his father was no longer there. Only his laughter now ruled as an echo in the kingdom. It was said that his father had simply vanished on a white wind, and had left all his laws and his legacy in his laughter.

No one witnessed the disappearance of the king.

Even the laughter could no longer be heard in the growing wastes of the land.

The elders were now rulers of the kingdom.

When they heard of the return of the prince they immediately denounced him as a fraud and decreed that if caught he should be killed.

There was a dead new silence in the kingdom without the laughter of the king.

Some say that it was with this silence that the real fall of the kingdom began.

9

THE SPIES OF the new dispensation got wind of the prince's hiding place in the abode of the market woman. They learnt of his presence not long after his return. Fortunately the prince was informed that they were coming for him. He cut short his prayers and began his final sojourn away from the land. His exile from his kingdom began in his prayers.

For the second time that fateful day the prince had to flee. He fled, in the dark, on the margins of the forest, right into the trap of the white spirits.

He was caught and chained and gagged with a metallic contraption. Then he was hauled off on a long trek across the savannah to a waiting ship. In its hold he found the others. Their blazing eyes regarded him as he was chained to a metal clasp in the wall of the hold.

Those who were caught and chained together in the stench of the hold were from different tribes and nations and spoke different languages and could not communicate with one another except through gestures.

Thus began the great trial and the unimaginable suffering of the race. Those who did not perish under the lash, who were not thrown overboard, who did not die in the crush and torture of the hold, those who made the crossing, men and women and children, were sold as slaves and worked the fields and the earth of their alien enslavers.

They took with them a new destiny. They took with them the spirit of freedom, the colour of justice, the fire of a new humanity, the mystery of music and art to a new world.

The prince was sustained only by the laughter of the king. It sounded all over the universe, beyond the power and the evils of men.

THAT IS ONLY one side of the story.

On the fateful day when the Mamba pursued the two lovers, the maiden managed to escape. She knew the forest well. She made it back home, in a state of near-deranged nakedness.

What followed is unclear. In the book among the stars one reads with the spirit and interprets through memory. There is much that is vague when the spirit is not perfect.

The masters decreed that the tribe commence one of its migrations, to escape the cycle of doom that had been hovering like a thundercloud over them.

Too late, they declared the Mamba an outlaw and banished him from their midst.

The maiden bore her child. Having waited many moons for the return of her loved one, she left home one day and went looking for him. She too went through the dark opening of destiny, was captured by the white spirits, and suffered the sea crossing which should never be forgotten in the forgetfulness of men and women.

11

W HEN SHE DISAPPEARED, the tribe of artists lost its soul.

Then one night, through the same fated opening in the forest, which had widened enough for history to come through, the white spirits descended on the unsuspecting tribe. It would never have happened but for the activities of the Mamba and his followers.

They had become marauders in the forest. The Mamba's chief obsession was to find and kill the new pupil who had humiliated him.

Often the Mamba and his followers raided villages. They plundered and pillaged the surrounding countryside. Often they would return to the edge of their old village and look on at the preparations the tribe made for their migration. They looked on and wept at their banishment...

But it was the Mamba and his followers who attracted the attention of the spies of the white spirits. The spies followed them one night and saw a village without fortifications. That night the white spirits fell on the tribe and carried away its strong and its young ones. They destroyed the village and scattered its inhabitants among the seven hills.

Those that were caught were gagged and bound and sent across the seas. Many of them perished in the crossing. Those that made it over, in their suffering, spread an unconquerable spirit, a new vision, in the new land, because their spirit, from ancient times, had always been strong.

WHAT WAS LEFT of the tribe of artists regrouped. Guided by their dwindling masters, they changed location. They moved on. They grieved.

After the destruction there was a scattering of the tribe, its dream, its people, its art. They became etiolated and slowly vanished in the mists of time. Then there was silence...

... and it was only after a century, in different forms, on several continents, that their fire was kindled again...

But in the old land, after the silence of their ways, only standing stones and mysterious sculptures endured the wrath of time's decay. The works lingered in sacred places in the forest, among wild plants and mahogany trees that had grown over the tribe's old habitation.

Their shrine had turned to dust and returned to the air.

Their gods returned to the deepest realms of dreams.

13

THE ELDERS RULED for a while in the kingdom, in the absence of the king. They ruled without wisdom. Dissension broke out among them. The people distrusted and undermined them. One by one they fell to each other's blades at night or to secretly administered poisons by day.

Their children were lost to a terrible lassitude. Some of them fell into a madness that took the form of incurable fits of laughter. They laughed themselves into early graves.

The gaps began to devour the kingdom.

Then the full force of the white wind descended on them and wiped out great swathes of the past and obliterated memory and dissolved many traditions.

The white spirits came and the land lost the spring of its ways. Forgetfulness followed and new ways grew over the oblivion of the old.

And because of the great gaps and the onslaught of the white wind that almost created a desert out of a flowering land, those that came after were not heirs to those that went before.

14

FOR A LONG time it seemed that all was lost. But after a century a myth sprang up in the minds of historians and artists. They sought an explanation for how such a rich artistic heritage came to be. They wondered why the community that created such wonderful works had so suddenly and completely disappeared.

Their legacy spread throughout the world. Their art enriched the hearts of strangers and the children of the tribe all over the globe.

The masters maintain that nothing is ever lost. They maintain that all things abide in the dreams of humanity and in the eternal book among the stars.

But time passed in the land. Children played in the dreamtime of their innocent years, when spirits are as real to them as birds. Such children would one day stumble on the statues and monoliths, the enigmas in stone, of the vanished people. They would release ancient spells into new centuries.

It seemed that only their dreams given form remained. When these works were discovered it would be surmised that they were created by masters from a distant planet, a more advanced civilisation.

They were thought of as artists creating in solitude and homesickness for their magic constellation.

Creating there in the forests.

15

THE PRINCE HAD undergone his final test. As a slave he endured his last crucifixion. Among slaves he spread dreams of freedom, dreams of illumination. Those dreams never perished.

By all accounts he was a secret master who saw it all, suffered it all.

That was his last time on the wheel, in the dust of living.

After the years of slavery, spreading a new message in the undergrowth of those who suffered, he returned to the realm of the laughing king. It is said he served the kingdom in the highest way, among the stars, in the whispers of the soul.

16

THE MAIDEN'S PARENTS and their grandchild survived. The tribe gathered itself together from among those who scattered in the forests and the hills. Then leaving everything behind, they quickly began their migration. They never stayed anywhere long enough to be noticed.

Time passed and one day a deputation of wise men and women from a diminished kingdom appeared among them claiming the grandchild as their future king. They brought wonderful gifts.

The masters of the tribe recognised this act of destiny and the maiden's parents acceded to this extraordinary claim. In ceremonial splendour the grandchild was led back to the palace of his paternal ancestors. He was led to his rightful inheritance of the throne. His coronation was legendary.

But the kingdom forever awaited the return of the prince. The laughter of the original father, in faint harmonies, growing in clarity, was heard again throughout the kingdom.

THOUGH THEY REGROUPED, the tribe of artists only partially recovered. Their strength was no longer able to hold out against the dissolution brought on by the destruction of their old ways.

But the tribe survived long enough to have one last flowering in the last golden days of the old dispensation before vanishing into the dust of time.

They must have felt acutely this swansong. An elegiac mood pervades their works. They created with the intensity of a people who know they are dying and want to fertilise the universe with the potent seeds of their creativity.

These last years, before they succumbed to oblivion, were their most poignant.

Everyone created in stone and wood and non-durable materials. Everyone dreamt on cloth and in songs. It was as if they were turning their lives into forms that must endure the passing of their bodies and their hearts.

Children created as intensely in their youth as the aged shaped passionately in their dying.

They began to create their testimonies, their whimsies, fantasies, and prophecies. They made pure forms that had no other purpose than to salute the joys of living.

THE MAIDEN'S PARENTS were now very old. Most of the masters had gone to join the ancestors.

The Mamba and his followers raged in the forest for a time. They terrified the surrounding peoples. Some of them had been caught and dragged off to slavery across the seas. Others had also grown old and were heard from no more.

No one knew what really became of the Mamba. Tradition has it that one day, following the legend of the gaps that led to fabulous kingdoms of gold and happiness, he had stumbled into one of the worst gaps of all. While passing through the gap he was seen spontaneously combusting into wild green flames from which he could not be rescued.

Such was the nature of his fiery consummation that those who were left of his followers were terrified by the sign. They fled from the forest to the open plains and sought ways to redeem themselves among the living.

19

How DID THIS tale come down to my mother, this tale that she began to tell me when I was a child?

Somebody creates a myth. Someone turns a life into a legend. Someone projects a story into the future.

This is how a fragment of that legend came down to me.

AROUND THE TIME of the swan-song of the tribe, the maiden's father, in great secrecy, invented a new kind of drama. The tribe was in its elegiac phase. The master was on the verge of death.

He had long abandoned the art of sculpture and had been silent as an artist since his daughter disappeared one night and was never found again.

Out of his great silence, his great age, and the profound nature of his myth, he created a new form to magnify the memory and the rituals of the race.

ONE DAY ACTORS appeared near the shrine and performed a new kind of play. The first act went like this.

A storyteller stands in the centre of a circle.

   Storyteller:

   Memory is better than gold.
   Listen to this legend as it is told.
   Now there is little left of time
   Tell it quickly, tell it in rhyme.
   Listen deeply and listen whole;
   Listen wisely with your soul.
   Enter this tale, become this play
   Which these actors are about to say.
   Listen to the masters not dead
   Who are a light in your head...

Then silence. Then in the darkness there are different voices, interspersed with bells, drums, flutes, and stringed instruments.
The voices recite these lines.
First Voice:

   If you enter through the magic gate...

...YOU WILL FIND them carving wooden sculptures in the open workshop of the world, hammering at bronze, singing poignant songs in groups, in lovely harmonies.

You will see children making art out of rejected things, broken combs, calabash shards, and disused chairs. Or drawing pictures on the ground.

You will see women painting myths on cloth, in vivid colours, creating new forms with jewels and cowries, carving giant totems, practising new dances in the square.

You will find the old at work, directing great projects, carving ancestral doors patterned with legends, telling stories to the young, listening to the dreams of maidens.

You will see sculptures everywhere, in wood, in bronze, copper, and stone. You will see the sculpted shapes of animals dreamt or imagined, of visitants from the sky, of gods, ancestors, the unborn, spirits, the noble busts of sages. You will see images of harvests and beautiful men and strong women, images of the future, shapes drawn on walls.

You will find a place alive with art in every corner, art in the square, art around the shrines, a world humming with constant creativity.

This is the place the prince entered as a humble man, in quest of love.

From tales of gods who turn into gentle animals to gain the love of women, he understood that to win a good woman's heart he had to be as simple as a swan. To be low was the only way to gain her trust. The highest became the lowest to do its work. The seduction of maidens by the gods he took to be a metaphor of enlightenment, the penetration of the soul by the ecstasy of the godhead. The soul is a beautiful virgin. These thoughts he toyed with in the forest as he set out on his quest.

When he came to the tribe of artists he was overcome by the beauty of their way. He felt at home here.

He offered to be the master's servant, for nothing. But the master saw the spirit of the prince in the guise of a beggar, and set him seven tasks of love and art.

When that evening the prince caught a glimpse of the maiden crowned in moonlight, he could not breathe for his concealed joy...

That was how a fragment of this story came down to me.

THAT WAS HOW it seemed before that cycle ended, before their golden age perished, before they passed away into the sands.

That was the high point of their culture. It had no name then.

Not long afterwards the maiden's father joined the ancestors. Her mother followed him a short time later. Then the tribe disintegrated from loss of vision and guidance.

Why was it that only minor works followed their fall?

Afterwards, during its descending ages, the works displayed were of rumours, abominations, incest, men making love to animals, animals making love to women, images of helmeted colonisers and big-bellied children.

Tragic nobility left their art because when the art spoke clearest, the people did not listen. When it spoke with the greatest beauty, the people did not see.

They did not interpret clearly. They did not prepare. They did not heed the warnings in the golden light

And so their golden age passed away, their true way died, and their world lost its axis. They got set on a new course, at the low ebb of a new cycle, that may never again know the simple grandeur of its past.

24

BUT ALL WAS not lost. It only seemed that way for a century or so. In their disintegration the tribe of artists all but disappeared from the known spaces. They finally learnt their lesson.

Their works continued to materialise on the trade routes, in marketplaces, in palaces, and in the new centres of the changing world. They became the world's tradition and future. They followed the fragmented guidance of the masters. They moved often, till they dwelt in a place called no-place. They thrived in quietness, responding to the unknown needs of the world in art.

The decades passed. As the world settled round the ideas of the new centuries, the tribe lost its taste for migration, and became visible again.

But they were not the same as they had been. Their art had much diminished. Their golden age was now a whisper. They didn't have a connection with the magical art that was all over the kingdom, mysteries in the forests and in caves.

Their artistic creation was good enough to inspire fleeting delight among the uninitiated, but not astonishment among themselves. They are now a small and celebrated community in the land. People from all over the world make long journeys to see their latest creations. If you walk into the village, down its streets, you will see paintings and sculptures on display but you will not see what was once a...

They were not heirs to themselves.

25

AND YET SOMEWHERE, as yet undiscovered, among images of prophecy and vision, in the vast storehouse of the tribe's hidden trove of artworks going back to its earliest times, among these works that foretold world wars and genocide and the destruction of great cities and the assassination of world leaders and the death of whole peoples by unnamed diseases and the vehicles that can fly and the first acknowledged encounter with alien beings from distant constellations and hints of the end of the world which is really the beginning of illumination, among these undiscovered works that hide underground, in deep forests, there is a sculpture of haunting beauty and simplicity, made of pure lines, a heavenly light, and an unaccountable pathos – the image of a dying prince.

But among those works which have been found was the bronze bust of the maiden becoming a princess. These works were taken away from their home in Africa. They now live on the other side of the sea, in museums, behind glass. They are displayed as the works of a primitive people. They stare mutely at the incurious eyes of generations who do not know the serenity and the wisdom of their origins.

26

THE WAYS OF time are indeed strange. Events are not what we think they are. Time and oblivion alchemise all things, even the greatest suffering.

27

ALL IS NOT lost. Greater times are yet to be born. In the low tide of things, when all seems bleak, a gentle voice in the air whispers that spirits of creativity wander the land, awaiting an invocation and the commanding force of masters to harness their powers again to noble tasks and unimagined luminous art.

They wonder at the unseeing hearts of men and women, who dwell in splendour and darkness, in an unseen world.

28

WHAT MORE IS there to tell? Just fragments seen in the book of life.

All stories lead to infinity. There is no end to them and no beginning. Just an epic sensed in the unheard laughter of things. Just fragments seen in the murky mirror of mortality, when bright beings shine momentarily in the brief dream of living.

London
2-2-22

XML 1 FF